'But the Society put Jazz and me together in the first place! We never would have met if—'

'My beloved, you're not that stupid. They put you together for a reason. Now they want to take you apart for a reason. You're just tools to them. And given our similar histories, I'm surprised that you didn't consider that from the beginning.'

She was silent, staring at him. Aware of a lot of things, suddenly—of the fever still burning inside of her, a heavy feeling in her lungs, the carefully hidden trail behind the FedEx that had delivered something deadly to her offices.

It could have been Eidolon, trying to throw suspicion on the Cross Society. It could just as easily have been the Cross Society using a double-blind. *They hadn't sent it through Borden.* Maybe Borden was still too valuable to them. Maybe James Borden, with his heart lost to Jazz Callender, wasn't going to play their game any more, especially if it turned deadly for his friends.

Any of it could be true.

Or none of it.

Welcome to the shadowy psychic underworld of Jazz and Lucia from *New York Times* bestselling author Rachel Caine

'Rachel Caine gives us a major kick-butt, savvy, swift and smart heroine in a tense, fast-paced story that demands to be read in one sitting!'
—P.N. Elrod, author of *The Vampire Files*

Available from **Rachel Caine**

DEVIL'S BARGAIN
DEVIL'S DUE

devil's due

RACHEL CAINE

...is to use papers that are natural, renewable and
...cts and made from wood grown in sustainable forests.
... manufacturing processes conform to the legal
...regulations of the country of origin.

...nd by
...) Ltd, Croydon, CR0 4YY

H HARLEQUIN®MIRA®

Published in Great Britain 2013
Harlequin MIRA Books, an imprint of Harlequin (UK) Limited,
Eton House, 18-24 Paradise Road,
Richmond, Surrey, TW9 1SR

© Roxanne Longstreet Conrad 2006

ISBN 978 1 848 45187 2

60-0213

Harlequin's p
recyclable pro
The logging a
environmental

Printed and bo
CPI Group (U

Rachel Caine was born at the ultra-secure White Sands Missile Range—site of the first atomic bomb tests—and has kept that non-traditional attitude ever since. She's been a professional musician, accountant, accident investigator, web designer and graphic artist…all at the same time.

She is the international bestselling author of the Morganville Vampires series. Visit her website at www.rachel caine.com.

It's an unusual thing to do, dedicating a book to a couple of bestselling authors, but here goes:

Thank you to Charlaine Harris and Carole Nelson Douglas for being such amazing people and writing such amazing work.

I'm privileged to know you. Not deserving, but extraordinarily, overwhelmingly privileged.

Prologue

CASE NOTES
LUCIA GARZA
FILE #20050228-1
PRIVILEGED AND CONFIDENTIAL

INVESTIGATION SUBJECT: BENJAMIN McCAR-
THY, 44-year-old white male
BACKGROUND: Exemplary Kansas City police detective. Decorated multiple times and given awards
for meritorious service. Served with the KCPD his entire career, from 1985 until his suspension and subse-
quent conviction for murder in 2003. Incarcerated in
the Ellsworth correctional facility. Appeals continue.
PERSONAL: McCarthy was born and raised in Kansas
City to a middle-class family. Background prior to
joining the police department is relatively unexcep-

tional. Scholastic history indicates high aptitude for problem solving. Parents reside in a retirement community in Arkansas. One brother, a commercial fisherman living in Florida. No evidence of close ties with other, more distant relatives. Never married, although he has been involved in two documented serious relationships, both prior to becoming a detective. (Neither with *Jazz Callender,* see separate file.)

FACTS OF THE CASE: At 2:34 a.m. on October 4, 2002, three bodies were discovered, bound hand and foot, shot in the back of the head execution-style. Victims were identified as Joseph Lozano, 23, a convicted drug dealer; Katherine "Kat" Vargas, 18, Lozano's girlfriend; and Navio Veracruz, 19, also a known drug dealer. No drugs or money found on the bodies. Forensic investigation yielded several key pieces of circumstantial evidence, including tire tracks taken at the scene and footprints preserved in mud. However, the ballistics tests came back with a startling result: the bullets matched another case on file that had recently been entered in the computer system, an officer-involved shooting.

The bullets came from the service weapon of Detective Ben McCarthy.

McCarthy was unable or unwilling to provide a reliable alibi for the time in question, including any corroboration from his partner, Detective Jasmine "Jazz" Callender. Convicted on the basis of ballistic and forensic evidence, he was sent to Ellsworth for thirty years. Callender insisted on his innocence, but no supporting evidence was found. It does not appear, even on detailed examination of the facts, that Det. Callender was party to his criminal acts. Her dedication to clearing her partner's name has been noteworthy during the period of his trial and incarceration, and likely resulted in the state in which she first came to my attention: broke and verging on a serious drinking problem.

ADDITIONAL NOTE: Files regarding Det. McCarthy's case and Callender's investigations were stolen from her apartment recently, during an apparently unrelated breaking and entering. We have turned up no information about the whereabouts of the files.

NEW EVIDENCE: Last month, Callender received a set of photographs, via former FBI agent Manny Glickman, that show McCarthy at a separate location during the time period of the murders. (*Manny Glickman* has been investigated. His background is clear and, in many ways, more convincingly above reproach than Callender's. See separate file for details.) Photographs show McCarthy accepting envelopes from two known members of an organized crime family and are evidence of corruption. This explains why McCarthy chose not to use the alibi at trial, relying instead on the hope that he would be acquitted. Separate investigation has thoroughly authenticated the provenance of these photographs.

I accordingly submitted the photographs and supporting materials to the district attorney and McCarthy's defense team as exculpatory evidence. The district attorney, moving a great deal more quickly than is typically the case in these matters, has moved to vacate McCarthy's conviction.

On a personal note, I wonder at the speed with which this has been accomplished. In my professional experience, the right thing rarely happens quickly in the judicial system.

Lucia Garza

Partner

Callender & Garza Investigations

Chapter 1

The gavel fell, and Ben McCarthy was free. *Mira,* that was fast, Lucia thought, stunned. She'd been expecting…something else. A bit more theater, perhaps; at the very least a token few questions or some fussiness from one attorney or the other.

The prosecutor looked pale and drawn in the early morning hour, squinting against the harsh overhead lights. She was a hard-looking woman, with dark hair and a fashion sense that tended toward square-cut shoulders and block skirts with sensible shoes. No doubt she won a lot of cases, but it wasn't on style points.

Lucia didn't begrudge her the lemon-sucking expression, considering how humiliating it was to have to publicly acknowledge a prosecutorial mistake of this magnitude. This had been a gigantic miss for the cops and the district attorney's office. A murderer had gone free, and a cop—not a good cop, granted—had been wrongly accused and convicted. McCarthy's life was over, professionally speaking; he was damn lucky that it wasn't over in every sense. The time he'd spent behind bars had been hazardous. He had the mended bones to prove it.

As soon as the gavel hit wood, McCarthy turned to look over the sparse crowd in the courtroom. Looking for Jazz Callender, Lucia knew, because he and Jazz had always been close, and it was reasonable to expect her to be present for his exoneration.

As Jazz would have been, if not for a conspiracy between Lucia and Jazz's beau, James Borden, to keep her safe at home.

The judge rose in a flutter of black robes and escaped back to his chambers. Apart from the usual complement of guards and court stenographers, there was the sour-faced prosecutor, the cheery defense attorney, Ben McCarthy— somehow still neat and striking even in a prison-issue jacket—three bleary-eyed reporters...and a man sitting two rows ahead of Lucia, hunched forward.

McCarthy's eyes gave up the search for Jazz and fastened on her, and Lucia felt an undeniable surge of...something. Not a handsome man, McCarthy, not in any sense she could name, but there was something about him that was compelling. Clear blue eyes in an expressive face, a force of personality that could freeze you solid or melt you to syrup, depending on his mood—she'd learned that quickly, during their prison interviews. He wasn't tall—in fact, in heels she probably topped him by an inch—but he was strong, and there was something graceful about him. The way he moved. The deft, neat hands.

She saw the flash of disappointment. But the flash was only that, and then he smiled at her—a warm smile—and nodded his head. This wasn't unusual; men smiled at Lucia Garza a lot. She was beautiful, and she was a careful steward of the gift; she took pains with her hair, her makeup and her clothing, and she stayed in shape. She was used to male attention.

And still that smile made her go entirely too warm in secret places. They'd gotten to know each other well these last few weeks, while Jazz was recovering from being shot, and Lucia assumed the primary investigator spot for McCarthy's case. It had started cautiously, but Lucia, much to her surprise, hadn't found McCarthy the typical closed-off cop nor the equally typical closed-off prison burnout. He'd been… interesting. Literate and smart and cool.

She had, in fact, interviewed him more than was strictly necessary, professionally speaking. Fifteen visits in all, two with Jazz, the rest without. He had remarked, the last time, that it had been the best interrogation of his life.

She'd subsequently spent more than a few hours wondering why Jazz had never succumbed to temptation with McCarthy. But Jazz had assured her—the third time loudly and profanely—that she'd never slept with him, and never really been tempted. They just hadn't clicked.

Whereas Lucia seemed to be clicking with him like a castanet.

She stood up and willed herself to keep it cool and professional. She edged down the row to the central aisle. McCarthy stopped to exchange some words and a back-slap and handshake with his attorney, then a not-very-cordial look with the prosecutor as she snapped her briefcase closed. No handshakes necessary on that one.

He turned toward Lucia, and took two steps in her direction.

Someone came between them. A man, tan suit, rounded shoulders, wire-tight body language. Lucia scanned him instantly with the unerring instincts of someone who'd spent sweaty months in counterterrorism training; the man spelled trouble, even from the back. He wore a cheap summer-weight suit coat with a grubby look, as if he'd worn it for months at a time. Even from ten steps back, Lucia had the unmistakable impression that he needed a shower. He wasn't much taller than McCarthy, and a great deal more nervous; from behind him, Lucia could see the jangles and twitches in his arms and legs. Emotion, possibly, or drugs.

"McCarthy," she heard him rasp, in a voice like silk ripping on wire. "You son of a bitch."

Ben McCarthy's face went still, the blue eyes opaque. He shot one fast glance at her over the man's shoulder and then focused on his opponent's face. McCarthy stayed still, a total contrast to the man facing him, who had tension vibrating through every muscle. Lucia could feel it like an electrical field as she moved steadily forward. She had her weight poised, in case she needed to move fast, and she focused in on the balance points that were her targets.

She didn't have a gun—a wholly unusual circumstance

for her—but that wasn't an issue. Neither did the man facing down McCarthy.

"Stewart," McCarthy said. "Hey. Thanks for coming."

Ken Stewart. Kansas City Police Department, Detective First Class. Lucia let the adrenaline course a little faster, let her heart rev up another couple of beats per minute. Stewart was, at best, unpredictable. At worst…Jazz's bitter assessment came back vividly: *He's got the winning personality of a rottweiler raised by wolves.* He'd always struck her as volatile, but now she was convinced he was a Molotov cocktail in search of a lit match.

"You think I'm here to smile and kiss your feet like these other assholes?" Stewart asked, and took another step into McCarthy's space. McCarthy didn't back away. He tilted his head a few degrees to continue to stare into the other man's eyes. "You hear me? I'm not letting you just walk away from a mass murder, you bastard. If it's the last thing I do, I'm going to make you pay."

McCarthy said nothing for a few seconds, then glanced at Lucia. "Detective Ken Stewart," he said, calmly and steadily, "meet Lucia Garza. Since she's a witness to you threatening me, you should probably be formally introduced."

"Oh, we've met," Lucia said crisply, as Stewart turned around to look at her. He had blue eyes, too. Crazy ones, shallow as glass. His skin looked pasty, unpleasantly shiny, and his hair stuck up in greasy spikes. Very unattractive indeed.

He tried the crazy-eye with her. She stared back, a faint smile on her lips, until he whipped back around to McCarthy and muttered something under his breath, then pushed past to talk to the prosecutor.

It was comforting to see that the prosecutor didn't look any happier to see him, especially when she entered ground zero of his body odor.

McCarthy took a deep breath, let the coldness fade from his face, and said, "Sorry about that." He came the last few steps to join her, but his attention was still on the other man, who was haranguing the prosecutor in a low, furious voice.

"No problem. It isn't the first time Detective Stewart and I have locked horns."

"No?" That got his attention, with a vengeance. He was wearing a blue sport coat that was too large for him, blue jeans that were perfectly acceptable, and a plain, open-collar shirt. No tie. Relaxed for a court appearance, but then he'd been there to get out of jail, not to try to avoid going in. He smelled of a particularly cheap aftershave and an underlying astringent scent that was probably prison-issue, as well.

"He's made a run at Jazz a few times," Lucia murmured.

Ben started walking toward the courthouse doors. She kept pace. "Bet she handed him his nuts on a platter," he chuckled.

Lucia grinned. "I don't think she bothered with the platter."

"Yeah, she's not much in the kitchen. So…where is she? I admit, I kind of expected to see her…." McCarthy opened one of the doors and stepped aside to let Lucia pass. She glanced at him, but there wasn't any calculation in his eyes. It was automatic gentility. He wasn't even aware of doing it.

She suppressed another smile as she thought of how little gestures like that would have chafed on Jazz. She liked her independence and saw every common courtesy as an infringement upon it. Jazz should have been born in the Old West, where she could have made a living on the frontier, riding rough, drinking hard and swearing at the top of her lungs. Calamity Jazz.

McCarthy was fishing for an answer to a question he hadn't asked. Lucia obliged. "Truthfully? Borden and I kept her away. We didn't want her presenting a clear target." James Borden had volunteered to keep her distracted—not exactly a sacrifice; the man had been madly in love with her for almost a year—and the significant lack of Jazz's presence this morning might mean that they'd finally tipped over from flirting to…something more.

Or alternatively, knowing Jazz, it could mean she'd had a massive fight with Borden, gotten drunk, belligerent, taken on a motorcycle gang in a fistfight, and was celebrating her victory with a hospital visit.

McCarthy looked somber. "She okay?"

"She's fine."

"You're sure?"

"I'm sure." Again, a little white lie. Jazz was all right in one sense, in that the past few months had made a huge change in her life. Since the day Jazz had been given her first red envelope—the same day that Lucia, halfway across the country, had received one—her life had begun an uphill climb, after the downhill express she'd taken following McCarthy's arrest. But the offer Lucia and Jazz had

jointly received—to open a new detective agency with fund-
ing from a rich but highly secretive donor organization—
had come with trip wires attached, and Jazz had been a
casualty. When they'd followed the last lead, from instructions in one of those damn red letters from the Cross
Society, she'd nearly died.

Lucia had no idea how much of that Jazz had shared with
her former partner. Knowing her, probably little.

No new envelopes had arrived recently. Lucia allowed
herself to think that perhaps, just perhaps, the insanity was
over. A faint hope, but she refused to abandon it just yet.
All of this unexplainable conspiracy-theory stuff was just
too odd to live with for long, if you expected to have a firm
grip on reality.

McCarthy had noted her brief mental detour. "Somebody's
still gunning for her, right?"

"Why do you say that?"

He grinned, a flash of humor that lit his eyes like sunlight. "Hell, you tell me. You're the one who kept her out
of the courtroom."

"Well, somebody *was* gunning for her. Are they still?"
Lucia shrugged. "I don't know. But I prefer to be careful."

"Good plan."

They moved out into the hall, and he suddenly stopped
walking. She looked back at him with eyebrows raised. He
surveyed the corridor, the people coming and going as the
day began to come alive. The glow of dawn outside the
courthouse windows.

His eyes had a wet shine to them. Tears.

"McCarthy?" she asked gently.

He took in a breath. "Yeah. Freedom. Kind of took me by surprise," he said. "Give me a second."

"Take your time," she murmured. She knew how it felt. There had been a dark time in her life—pitch-black, in fact—when she hadn't been sure she'd ever see daylight again. The emotional impact of realizing that the trauma was over, that you were free…it could be overwhelming. It wasn't relief. It was terror.

When you get used to the dark, the light can burn you.

He blinked, and smiled slightly. "Sorry," he said, and cleared his throat. "So. Want to have breakfast with an ex-con? I mean, it's not like we're not acquainted already. Fifteen hours of interviews has to count for something."

First, second and third dates, most likely. She cleared her own throat, banishing the thought. "I'd love to."

"Got to confess, I'm low on funds."

"They confiscated your ill-gotten gains?" She made it an ironic question, not quite accusatory. He met her eyes without shame.

"I asked them to," he said. "Wanted to start out fresh."

"Ah. My treat, then."

He offered her the crook of his elbow. She put a hand in it, and they resumed their walk down the long paneled hallway, to the free world.

Chapter 2

Over breakfast at the restaurant in the Raphael Hotel, which was a good deal fancier than his suit jacket warranted, McCarthy wolfed down a Hangover Omelet stuffed with chili, chorizo and potatoes; Lucia stuck to a large fruit cup and dry toast. She enjoyed watching him eat. He seemed enchanted with everything he tasted, but then, she supposed nearly two years of prison chow would do that. She suspected he was always a bit of a sensualist. Something about his eyes, his smile, the clever exact movements of his hands…

She pulled herself back from the dizzy edge of that thought, and said, "Do you have any idea who could have used your gun to commit the murders?" Because the circumstantial evidence had been convincing. McCarthy's gun had been matched to the bullets in the bodies. There had been footprint evidence at the scene, too, and an eyewitness who'd seen McCarthy with the victims half an hour before their murders, although Lucia doubted the authenticity of that. Eyewitnesses were often wrong.

"Oh, I know who did it," McCarthy mumbled around a mouthful of eggs and cheese. "Stewart."

"He didn't."

"Crazy enough."

"Jazz checked it out. Stewart had an alibi."

"So did I. Funny how that is."

"Stewart was booking a carjacker downtown at the time of the killings, in front of twenty other cops."

McCarthy studied her with those intense blue eyes as he chewed and swallowed, wiped salsa from his lips, and for a second she thought he was going to argue the point. Instead he said, "So what's your story?"

"Excuse me?"

"Fifteen hours of talking, and I don't think you said boo about yourself. Name, rank and serial number, but you didn't exactly meet me halfway. So tell me how you got mixed up in all this—and why the hell you care about a guy like me."

Lucia was, for an instant, thrown. She disliked talking about herself, especially when faced with someone like McCarthy, who was certainly a damn good investigator. She chose her words carefully. "Did Jazz tell you how we came to be partners?"

"Yeah. A letter to each of you, offering to put up the money to open a detective agency. Some kind of nonprofit agency. I get why Jazz took the deal. Why did you?"

"I didn't," she said, and speared a slice of electric-green

honeydew. "I turned it down." She enjoyed the look on his face as he assimilated that. "I was leaving when Jazz got shot in a drive-by attack—you know about that?"

He nodded shortly, face set.

"I had my doubts about her as a partner," Lucia continued. "But I don't like people shooting at me, and I don't like people shooting my friends. Even new ones. So I decided that it might be a good idea to stick around. One thing led to another, cases came up, we solved them. And here we are."

She nibbled the fruit. He watched her, concentrating on her mouth, and she felt a surge of self-consciousness that surprised her. Something about McCarthy threw her off stride. He made her hyperaware of how her clothes fit, of the tiny imperfections in the way the sleeves hugged her arms, the way the lapels didn't quite lay straight.

The way her skin shivered into gooseflesh when he stared at her.

McCarthy tilted his head. "Jazz is a walking disaster, but somehow, she does okay. She's also a pretty good judge of character. Me notwithstanding." He continued to watch as Lucia chewed and swallowed. "I know what you mean about sticking around her, though. I wasn't going to be her partner—I was just saddled with her for a week. But she grows on you. You want to protect her from herself. Doesn't generally work, though. She ends up saving your ass more than you save hers, and before too long you're joined at the hip. And then you realize that's not a bad thing."

"Regarding ass-saving, I believe the score's just about even between us now," Lucia replied.

"That tells me something about *you*."

"What?"

He surprised her with a wicked grin. "You're damn good at what you do. Whatever it is."

"Obviously, I'm a private investigator."

"And I'm your maiden aunt Sally," he snorted. "I've known a lot of P.I.s over the years, and none of them ever came looking or sounding like you. You avoided the question. What's your story?"

"I'm avoiding the question because I don't want to answer it."

"Because…?"

"Because it's none of your business, Mr. McCarthy," she said evenly, and took another bite. Pineapple, fresh and sweet and pulpy. She savored the juice on her tongue and the look of surprise on his face. "I helped Jazz get you out of prison, that's all. I don't owe you any information, any conversation, or anything else."

"Yeah? So what's this?"

"I said I don't *owe* it. I can still give it of my own free will."

He'd demolished the omelet, and now he set his fork on the plate with a clink and took a drag of coffee from the heavy white cup. Around them, the well-groomed breakfast crowd in their expensive suits and trendy casual wear chatted and smiled. We're both out of place here, Lucia thought, even though she seemed to fit seamlessly into the crowd. There was something different about McCarthy that spoke to the wildness at her core. It wasn't his prison-roughened image.

McCarthy smiled at her. "Okay, so you don't owe me. I was hoping you liked me enough to want to answer, anyway."

"I don't like anybody that well."

"Harsh."

"Pragmatic," she countered. "I hardly know you, except that you might not be guilty of murder, but you're surely guilty of other things. Add that to the fact that your friends and relatives were hardly crowding the gallery today—"

His face shut down even further, hiding emotion. Lids drifted lower to hood his expressive eyes. "Let's leave them out of it," he said. "I was a cop, and my buddies were all cops. Cops stay away, times like these, until they feel better about the facts. Stewart's not the only one who still, deep down, thinks I pulled the trigger on those people." McCarthy stared at his coffee and took another deep swallow. "My brother would have been here, but he's on a tuna boat this season. My parents—" He shook his head.

She took pity on him. "I doubt they could have made the trip," she said. "Your mother is ill, isn't she?"

"Old," he said. "Your folks still alive?"

She smiled noncommittally. "So I'll forgive you the low turnout among your admirers. Still, it does say something, doesn't it? To have more reporters than supporters?"

She got a thin slice of a smile. "Careful when you cut me like that. You'll have to buy me a new shirt. I'll bleed all over this one."

"I'm tempted to buy you a new one whether you bleed all over it or not."

"That's kindhearted of you."

"Call it fashion charity."

He was studying her again, with lazy interest. "I just can't picture you and Jazz as friends."

"Why?"

"She's just—one of the guys, you know? Not so…" He gestured vaguely, letting her finish the sentence with whatever adjective seemed best. Wise of him. "I was surprised how good she looked, last time I saw her. Your influence, or the counselor's?"

He knew about Borden, then. Yes, of course he did. Lucia shrugged. "Maybe both."

"She's not drinking so much."

"No."

"Not getting into fights."

"Well, we're working on that part."

"Good luck with that." He grinned, and caught the attention of a passing waiter to get a refill on his coffee. He drank it black as the devil's heart. "So, if you're not going to tell me anything, I'll just have to tell you three things about yourself, Miss Garza."

"Is this popular at parties?"

"A riot on cell block six."

"Then please, enlighten me."

"One, you manipulate people. Sometimes for their own good, but always to your advantage." He sopped a piece of toast in a remaining bit of peach jam and ate it, watching her reaction. She kept her face bland, but felt the barb sink unpleasantly deep. "Two, you use your looks as deception. You look warm and girlie and elegant, but I'll bet you can hand most guys their asses in a fight."

He was right again, of course. She didn't allow herself to blink. "And three?"

"How am I doing so far?"

"We'll see. And three?"

He shrugged. "You're lonely."

She laughed out loud. "Excuse me?"

"You heard."

"Hardly!"

"I didn't say you don't get attention. Every guy in here has checked you out at least once, and half the women, too. I said you were *lonely*. A woman as beautiful as you is nothing *but* lonely. Even when you're with somebody, you're wondering if they're into you or the glossy package, and sweetheart, just from the fifteen—no, make that sixteen—hours that we've been talking, I can tell you that you're high on the paranoid scale, anyway. So the point is, you don't let anybody close these days."

It hit hard, under the armor, right in a soft place she didn't know she had. Years of dealing with a string of men who'd professed love and delivered obsession. Years of mistrusting and holding back and staying cool.

For a second, she hated those blue-diamond eyes and their ability to see everything.

"You're wrong. I'm not lonely. Far from it."

He gave her a slow smile. "That tells me something else

about you. You think you're a good liar. And hey, for most people, you are."

"Do you make a habit of insulting people who do you good turns?"

"Usually they want something. Speaking of that, what is it *you* want?"

Once again, he caught her off guard. "Me? I'm only here out of courtesy."

"Courtesy?"

"It has something to do with manners. Perhaps you've heard of those."

"Sorry, not exactly popular where I've been." She'd struck a nerve; she could see it in the subtle reactions of his face. "You just came in Jazz's place, is that it? Second string?"

Lucia took the insult without reaction. "I want her to be safe, yes."

"What about you? Aren't you in just as much danger, if the two of you are supposed to be partners?"

It was an excellent question, and one to which she didn't have an answer. They were working for the Cross Society, but she had only the vaguest hints as to who those people were and how they operated; for all she knew, the danger that Jazz had run into head-on had come from someone inside the Cross organization.

She'd seen cutthroat competition in nonprofit groups, but if true, that might be a new low.

In any case, whether it was the Cross Society or—as their mysterious benefactors insisted—the rival Eidolon Corporation, they hadn't sent soldiers after Lucia specifically; she'd only been in the vicinity. Jazz was the target. Then again, the enemy didn't seem prone to doing gentlemanly things like firing warning shots.

Lucia wondered if McCarthy had deduced why she'd taken a table in a protected corner that had no direct view from the windows.

She'd also stayed vigilant for any hint of trouble. The only problem she'd identified so far was an overdose of cholesterol that was surely going to spell trouble for McCarthy's arteries in the future.

She let him see her confidence, embodied in a slow smile. "I think I'm safe enough," she said. "Why? Are you volunteering as a bodyguard?"

"Well," McCarthy said, "I do need a job. Prospects coming out of the big house aren't good, unless you're into loading trucks, making French fries or beating up people for a living." It was said lightly, but she heard the ring of truth. There was a certain grimness in his eyes, the set of his mouth, as he finished his coffee in a long sip. "Okay, the truth. I've got a hundred dollars in my pocket right now, my apartment's long gone and the KCPD wouldn't have me back even as a janitor. So yeah, I wouldn't kick a little work to the curb. Bodyguard, investigator, whatever. If you need it."

"Your job prospects aren't any worse than for anyone else walking out of jail."

"Since my job used to be a police officer, yeah, I think they kind of are. Look, I never deserved to be there in the first place. I lost two years of my life to this crap." He'd gone intense again, head inclined toward her, voice urgent.

"I don't even know where I'm going after breakfast. You know how that feels?"

She did, but it didn't seem the time to tell him so. "You begin your life again. That's what people do, Mr. McCarthy. Start over. Reinvent themselves. Become someone new and, hopefully, better."

"Nothing wrong with who I am right now."

"Isn't there?" She raised her eyebrows slowly. "Are you sure?"

She accepted the leather folio containing the check from the waiter. McCarthy gestured for her to hand it over.

"I already said I was paying," she said. "Remember?"

"That was before you pissed me off. Now I'm paying."

"Don't be ridiculous," she retorted, and pulled her wallet from her black leather purse. It was specially reinforced to hold her containers of Mace, clips for her gun, a six-inch collapsible truncheon, handcuffs, and—sometimes, but not today—a Taser. "You'll have a hard enough time without worrying about picking up the check for me."

"Then I'll owe you. And pay you back."

"Without a doubt. This isn't a date. And I'm not some prison groupie." *Ouch*. She really hadn't meant it to be so harsh.

He was staring at her, hands on the clean white tablecloth. Just…watching. As if he knew that last part had been, in some small measure, a lie. She had found him attractive. And yes, this had been a date, hadn't it? Unorthodox as that might be…

She handed the folio to the waiter, who whisked it off

so quickly his apron fluttered. Probably afraid that Ben McCarthy, who was looking more than a little feral in his cheap coat and ragged haircut, might come after him and wrestle him to the ground for it.

As she watched the waiter go, she said, "Allow me to make some insightful comments about *you,* Mr. McCarthy—"

"Just Ben," he interrupted. "This mister-miss crap is getting old."

"Fine. Ben. You are tough, clever, and you're probably the single best liar I've ever met in all of my life. And I've met almost as many as you have."

Her turn to score a hit; she saw him blink, saw the prison-hard Ben McCarthy waver for a second to reveal someone far less armored.

"Why do you say that?" he asked.

"Because Jazz never believed you were guilty of anything," she said, "and you were a dirty cop. She's incredibly sharp, and you had her completely snowed for years. Do you have any idea how much that hurt her, by the way?"

He stared at Lucia for so long that she felt uncomfortable. Whatever was going on in his head, none of it was showing in his face.

"Yeah," he finally said. "I know. And you're right. I'm a son of a bitch."

"Have you changed? Has prison reformed you?"

He gave her a small, cynical smile. "Doesn't it reform everybody?"

Outside, the day was cool and clear, the sky a pale, sun-bleached blue. Lucia took in a deep breath to catch the scent of damp earth and green growing things. She missed that, living in the city. Hadn't been out to hike and climb for too long now, other than on gritty training ranges. She had the credentials to visit Quantico if she wanted to do so; the woods there would help her get her center again, and she could visit the gun range for an excuse…and God knew, the marines would be more than happy to drive her to the edge of endurance in heavy, sweaty field exercises.

The valet arrived in her silver Lexus, parked and stepped out as she came around to the driver's side. She was watching McCarthy over the top of the car, but something caught her eye, something…

Something about the valet. Not right. Something…

McCarthy was talking to her. It was noise. Her world had narrowed to the out-of-focus blur of the valet standing there, holding the door for her.

She started to turn her head toward him, and as she did, she saw his hand emerge from his pocket.

A brilliant glint of silver in the morning light.

Fear bolted through her, there and gone, replaced by a deadly smooth calm. *Too late. I'm too late.* She brought her elbow in, drove her left forearm out in a stiff arc. It hit squarely against his extended arm, and knocked his hand into the door frame.

"Ow!" The valet stepped back, surprised, and what he'd been holding thumped to the ground. A small metal clipboard, with a receipt stuck under its holder. "Jeez, lady. Chill. I was just getting a signature. New policy."

She felt herself blush as the adrenaline chased out of

her system, leaving a thick aftertaste of embarrassment. She apologized as she retrieved the clipboard and signed on the line next to her tag number. She slid a twenty dollar bill under the clip holder. The valet's attitude improved considerably.

In the silence of the car, McCarthy kept studiously quiet about it. She put the car in gear and pulled out, around the circular drive and back onto the street.

"So," he said slowly. "About that bodyguard job."

She glanced at him. At the ill-fitting sport coat, the prison-styled hair, the shirt and shoes so cheap they were the next thing to disposable.

"I've already got a bodyguard," she said. "However, I could use another good investigator. Under one condition. You let me make you look presentable. I wouldn't want you giving a bad impression to our clients."

"Deducted from my wages. Like a uniform."

"If you insist."

"I do."

"Then yes, deducted from your wages."

"Yeah. Okay." He eyed her mistrustfully. "When?"

"Now." She thought for a few seconds, mentally measuring him. "Thirty-two regular, I think," she murmured. "Italian cut. French collar and cuffs. How do you feel about Magnanni?"

"Am I supposed to know what that is?"

"No. Shoe size?"

"Ten."

"Fine. One other thing."

"I knew you were getting to it."

"I'm taking you for a haircut."

"Do I get to pick the barber?"

"No. It will be a stylist, and there will be a manicure, and, if you're not polite, skin treatments."

He sighed and said, "Pull over. I'm getting out."

"I don't think so. We've made a deal. Believe me, this works better if you just let it happen."

"Great," McCarthy said grimly. "Just like prison, with product."

His reaction to being marched into Lenora Ellen's Day Spa was, she thought, gratifyingly furious, but she'd left them with strict instructions, and him with enough promises and threats to ensure his cooperation. Besides, she could see that he secretly craved a little relaxation and pampering. So long as he never had to admit it to, say, Jazz.

Ben's fate sealed, Lucia turned to practicalities. Her over-reaction with the valet was out of character for her, to say the least, but it told her something of what her subconscious was doing: worrying excessively.

It was time to set up some insurance. As she pulled her car into a parking spot outside one of the most exclusive men's stores in the city, she hit a speed-dial number on her cell phone that she'd once promised never to dial again.

She'd never been good at keeping promises when it came to Omar.

He picked up on the second ring. "Tell me you're not in trouble," he said, and she laughed, because it was just like

Rachel Caine

Omar. "Okay, then tell me you hit the wrong number in your speed dial."

"No, *querido,* I'm calling you. And maybe I'm not in trouble—have you ever thought of that?"

"No," he said. "I heard you'd moved. Kansas City, right?"

"Right."

"Would it surprise you to know that I'm in the neighborhood?"

"Tremendously." It didn't. Stranger things had happened, every day before breakfast.

"Just finished up a job in Saint Louis. So. I'm sure you didn't call just to hear my voice, lovely as it may be…" And it was lovely, low and full of warmth. Just now, he was using his native accent, which was cultured and British, but he was equally at home with French, Spanish, American, German and a wide variety of Arab inflections. She'd even once—hilariously—heard him do a fabulously broad Scots.

"I adore your voice, which you very well know," she said, "but no. I was checking to see if you were available."

"Well, I'm not currently seeing anyone—"

"Professionally."

He became quickly serious. "Long term or short?"

"I don't know. We'd best say at minimum a month."

"Huh. Usual rates?"

"Have they gone up?"

"Cost of living, my love, cost of living. Or, at least, the cost of not getting killed."

She sighed. Omar did not, of course, come cheap. "Fine. Your usual rates, plus expenses."

"Starting when?"

"How soon can you get here?"

He was silent for a few seconds. "Lucia, this sounds a bit more serious than your usual tangle. It's not—"

"Our mutual uncle?" Meaning Uncle Sam, of course. "No. Strictly private. And it's not serious…exactly. Just—uncertain."

"I'm peace of mind, then."

"I can think of no one better."

"But of course!" She could imagine his wide, charming grin. "I am reliably informed by the wonder of the Internet that there is a morning commuter flight leaving in forty minutes. Where do I go?"

She gave him the office address. "There's a parking garage, we're on the second level. I need you positioned there today."

"Hmm. Watching for what, exactly?"

"I don't know. Call me when you're in position."

"Two hours," he said. After a beat, he said, "Lucia? It's nice to hear from you."

"Likewise," she said. "Don't get arrested in the airport."

He laughed. It was something of a standing joke, but not a very funny one, all things considered. Before she could say anything else, he was gone.

She sighed, ordered her thoughts and got on with her part of the bargain with Ben McCarthy: shopping.

One of the first things she'd taken the trouble to do, when she'd moved her operations to Kansas City, was to find the premier clothiers in town, for both men and women. She had a personal interest, of course, but there were always professional considerations. Clients to dress. Undercover agents to outfit for special assignments...

And she always did like to buy quality.

She was choosing the right suit to flatter McCarthy's coloring and body type when she realized that she was being followed, and had been for some time.

She kept her movements slow and natural as she placed the suit back on the rack and turned to a display of French-cuffed shirts. White would make his prison-pale skin look even more translucent. She held up one the color of cream, studying it, and readjusted the focus of her eyes to the mirror a few feet away.

There was someone outside the store, looking in. He was in shadow, backlit by the morning sun, but she recognized the ill-cut suit. Detective Ken Stewart was dogging her. *Why me? Why not McCarthy?* Although the thought of Stewart infiltrating a day spa made her smile.

Stewart backed up and moved along, an easy stroll, as if he'd just been idly browsing. He was good at this. That was disturbing. She much preferred dealing with amateurs, and professionals who had inflated ideas of their skill levels. If she hadn't spotted him before... *You weren't looking for a tail,* she reminded herself. *You had no reason to suspect anyone would follow you on something as mundane as this.* Maybe not, but she'd been hyperaware with the valet. It bothered her that she'd missed Stewart.

After a few more seconds another man passed the glass, this one short, fat and dressed in a dirty blue jean jacket.

Shaved head. He hesitated at the door, then opened it and came in. He looked nervous, but that might have been the natural tentativeness of a man ill-used to high-end suits coming in to browse.

No. It wasn't.

In the mirror, his eyes focused on her. Not in the way that a man normally examined her either—this was a pattern-recognition way, as if he'd been given her description. Or a photo.

She carefully put the shirt back on the table and positioned her hand close to her hip, a split second from going for the gun concealed by the tailored jacket she was wearing. She automatically swept the store for collateral victims. The clerk was positioned safely behind a counter; he'd surely duck if gunplay started. Odds were good he'd survive, unless her newcomer was carrying an Uzi, or was an incredibly poor shot. No other customers, unless they were in the dressing rooms. Nothing she could do to minimize the risks.

She balanced her weight lightly around her center, ready to shift at a moment's notice, ready for anything, as the man made his way closer. One hand in his jacket pocket...

She'd humiliated herself with the valet. She wouldn't make the same mistake twice. That meant waiting until a weapon was actually visible and identified, which would put her at a disadvantage, but...

She turned, and time slowed to a crawl. *Tick,* and his eyes were rounding in surprise. *Tick,* and her hand moved the small distance inside her own coat, her fingers touching the cool grip of her gun.

Tick, and his right hand emerged with nightmare slowness from his pocket…

…carrying a red envelope.

Time fell back into a normal rush of color and noise, and Lucia felt her heart hammering, knew there was heat flooding her cheeks. Adrenaline was an earthquake in her veins for the second time in an hour.

The courier held out the red envelope to her. "Here you go, lady. No signature required." He sounded spooked. She wondered how she had looked to him, in that instant when she was making the decision whether to kill him.

"Thank you," she said, and took it. Automatic courtesy; she certainly wasn't feeling grateful. He backed up and hurried out of the store fast enough to make the bell hung over the door clatter like a fire alarm.

She turned the envelope over in her hands, frowning down at it. The size and shape of a greeting card envelope. It felt like one sheet of paper inside. Her name was block printed on the outside; the courier had, no doubt, been told exactly when and where to find her, even though her choice of this store had been an impulse.

No point in delaying the inevitable. She reached in her purse and took out a slender little pocketknife, flipped it open and slit the side of the envelope, very carefully. Preserving what evidence there might be. She slid the paper out with a pair of tweezers from her purse and moved shirts to lay it flat on the table.

It didn't require much scrutiny. It read, ONE OF YOU HAS MADE A MISTAKE, and the letterhead said Eidolon

Corporation—easy enough to fake, if someone went to the trouble of doing it. No signature. She held it up to the light. No watermark. No secret messages. No hints as to its meaning. "One of you"? Meaning her? Jazz? McCarthy? A member of the Cross Society? Impossible to tell. It was a meaningless taunt, a message designed to unnerve; showy, like the delivery by courier. Designed to prove that they could literally find her anywhere.

Just like the Cross Society. Presuming that someone in the Cross Society hadn't sent it in the first place.

Stewart had been following her. Was it possible he was Eidolon? Eminently, she decided. Cross Society? She hadn't exactly been provided with a full and forthright disclosure of their membership, but somehow she couldn't see Ken Stewart believing in the things that the Cross Society took for granted: things like premonitions, and psychics, and the ability to alter the future.

Then again, maybe that explained the erosion she sensed in him, the jittery nervousness. The world was fraying around him, and he was unraveling with it.

She could completely sympathize.

Jazz would probably have ditched the note and pelted down the street, collared Stewart and pummeled him until she got what she wanted to know....

Jazz.

Lucia's smile faded as she flipped open her cell phone and speed-dialed Borden's number. He picked up on the second ring, sounding lazy and sleep-soaked. He sobered up fast when she identified herself.

"Hey. Um, good morning. What time—crap. It's late. I overslept."

"Is Jazz with you?" she asked.

There was a short pause and then the tenor of the call changed; she heard the rustle of sheets, a sleepy murmur, the quiet closing of a door. He'd stepped into the bathroom, or the hall. "She's asleep," he said. "I don't want to wake her up if I don't have to. Do I? Have to wake her up?"

"Soon," Lucia said. "A courier just delivered a note to me in a red envelope. Did she get one?"

"No deliveries—shit. Hang on." The phone rattled, set down on a counter, she guessed. He was back in less than ten seconds. "Yeah. Somebody slid it under the door. Is it a job?"

"Don't you usually compose the messages?"

"Sometimes," he said cautiously. Borden was Cross Society, in it up to his neck; Lucia liked him a great deal, but at times like these, she was bitterly aware that trust might be a separate issue. "Look, I can't go into the way it works, not on the phone."

"Yes, I get your point. Open it."

"You're sure?"

"Yes."

There was a rattle, a pause…. "It says, 'One of you has made a mistake.' On Eidolon Corporation letterhead. Holy shit." She heard his breathing go faster. "They know where we are. I have to get Jazz up, right now."

"Wait. Have you ever seen one from Eidolon before?" Lucia realized that she was pacing, a habit when she was nervous. The store clerk was watching her. Not, she was relieved to see, in any way that implied he was a conspirator; no, this was the plain, unvarnished interest she was used to attracting. She gave him a small smile and he found something to be busy with that took him out of her line of sight.

"Lucia, *they know where we are.* She's not safe here. Hell, I'm not safe—"

"Have they ever sent you a message before?" she asked again, with strained patience.

His composure broke completely. "Look, *I* don't get messages from anybody. I'm not a goddamn Lead!"

She felt a hot flare of irritation. *Leads.* According to the Cross Society, she and Jazz were Leads, carrying major roles in the chaotic, enormous play of life and death on Planet Earth. "Actors" influenced certain events at crucial moments, but—again, according to the Cross Society's rather esoteric theory—Leads operated at a kind of nexus point. Jazz had told her, in a quiet voice that meant she had come to believe it, that the Cross Society psychic, Max Simms, had summed it up: Everything you do matters.

It was a frightening thought. It didn't get any less frightening the longer it stuck around.

She kept doggedly on the subject. "Have you ever heard of Eidolon contacting anyone in the Cross Society directly?"

He sucked in an angry breath. "No. If you're done—"

"Almost. Who knew where you were taking her?"

"Nobody."

"You didn't make the call from—"

"I booked the reservations at an Internet kiosk using a

one-time-only card. Fake name. Believe me, nobody knew we were coming here."

There were ways, nevertheless, if the opposition was strong enough. And if Eidolon Corporation was what Max Simms had claimed, a major technological entity with ties to the federal government, then retasking a satellite and painting Borden's car with a laser tag wouldn't have been very difficult.

If, if, if.

Borden suddenly said, "It's us. Me and Jazz—maybe it has to do with us."

"You think being in love with her is the mistake they're referring to?"

"I never said—" He gave up on the reflexive male denial, to his credit. "No, I don't."

"Then it's entirely possible it might be referring to the events of this morning. To my helping McCarthy get released."

"Then why not just send it to you? Why send it to you *and* Jazz?"

"McCarthy's connected to both of us now. I think the better question is, why would Eidolon warn us? Wouldn't they *want* us to be making mistakes?"

"I have no idea what Eidolon wants," Borden growled. "Look, I barely know what my boss wants half the time. So as far as figuring out motives, good luck. Screw this, I'm waking her up and getting her out of here. Now."

"Yes, you'd better get her back to Manny's." If there was any such thing as a safe place, given what they'd learned about the world and the Cross Society and Eidolon, it would be in Manny's Fortress of Solitude. Wherever it currently resided, since he moved house as often as banks took holidays.

"You're talking like a cop," Borden said. "If Eidolon wants us, they can find us. Well, they can find me, anyway. You and Jazz, it's tougher, since you're Leads. They can only predict you through the effects you have, not your exact location."

"Then how did they just deliver me a note? How did the Cross Society deliver one to Jazz that first night?"

He gave a rattling sigh. "It's too freaking early for philosophy and physics, Lucia. But Leads blip on and off the radar. You're a blur most of the time, but sometimes they can see you clearly. It's like somebody who usually drives really fast having car trouble. But on the more mundane level, have you considered that somebody could have been following you?"

Stewart, again. And if she accepted the idea that the note was legitimately from Eidolon, the Cross Society's adversary in this war of premonitions, then…it changed things. Not for the better. "All right. We'll need to have a strategy meeting later at the office—one o'clock? Bring Jazz in through the garage entrance—it's the most defensible. I'll have someone meet you."

"Someone who? You're not giving Manny a gun, are you?"

She laughed. "Not that Manny would need one of mine. But no. I've hired a friend to help us out. His name is Omar. He'll meet you in the garage."

"We'll be there."

There was hope for Borden yet, Lucia thought as she folded the phone and slipped it back in her purse; he had said *we* without a trace of self-consciousness.

If only they could get Jazz to do the same, a relationship might truly be on the horizon.

"Madam?" The clerk was watching her again, this time with a trace of a frown. "Is everything all right?"

"Fine," she said, and retrieved the blue suit she'd been studying. Much as she hated off-the-rack on men, no doubt McCarthy would resist the idea of tailoring even more than day-spa grooming. She added the ivory shirt and handed the items to the clerk, who blinked at the price tags, then smiled.

By the time she'd added the glossy, sleek Magnanni shoes, he was very happy.

She asked him to help her carry her packages to the car, tipped him and slid behind the wheel. As she slammed the door and clicked the lock shut, Ken Stewart rounded the far corner, his hands in his pants pockets, doing his best to look jaunty.

She cruised slowly past him, watching.

He pulled an empty hand from his pocket, pointed it at her windshield and cocked back a thumb. *Bang,* he mouthed, as he let the imaginary hammer fall. *You're dead.*

She braked the car, rolled down the driver's side window and leaned over. Her smile must have been disingenuous enough to lure in even a bitter, cynical specimen like Stewart, because he shuffled a few feet toward her.

"One of us would be," she said softly, and let him see

that her hand was on the gun in the passenger seat beside her. "And before you ask, yes, I do have a permit to carry it, Detective."

He bared his teeth at her in a crazy grin. *A rottweiler raised by wolves.* She felt a cold touch at the back of her neck, but allowed only an ironic tilt of her eyebrows as he leveled both hands at her—two imaginary guns, like a kid playing cowboys and Indians—and peppered her with imaginary rounds.

Then he mimed blowing smoke from his fingertips, and those fiercely cold, slightly insane eyes bored into hers. He said, "You be careful, Ms. Garza. It's a dangerous town if you make the wrong enemies."

"Are there ever any right enemies?" she asked, and drove away at a calm and leisurely pace, showing no signs of temper or nerves.

Four blocks later, she stopped at a red light and wiped her damp, shaking hands on her pants.

Chapter 3

At five minutes to one, Lucia's desk phone rang in her office. She picked it up and said, "Omar?"

"Yo, girl," he said. Omar had a sly, amused tone, as usual. He found everything a source of humor, from *The Simpsons* to the evening news. He claimed it had something to do with Buddhism, and seeing the world for the illusion it was. That might have been true. Omar was famous—infamous, really—for having done a seven-year stretch in Folsom as part of one of the most grueling covers in the history of law enforcement. After the takedown of one of the most vicious criminal enterprises on the East Coast, he'd declared himself out of the cop business.

But he did favors from time to time, and Lucia was on his list. Omar was about the most reliable, calm and effective man she'd ever worked with.

He was also one hell of a friend, and once upon a time,

he'd been more. Not much more, though. Omar's Zen out-look precluded more serious entanglements.

"Good morning," she said. "Having a fabulous time down there?"

"Unbelievable. Your friends are here. I'm sending them up. Don't shoot 'em."

"Thanks. Keep sharp." Not that she needed to remind him. Omar, for all of his built-in serenity, was rarely caught off guard.

As she hung up, she focused on McCarthy, who was sit-ting on the sofa at the far end of the room, looking out the tinted windows. The view warped a little; the glass was bullet-resistant, replaced after Jazz's office had been tar-geted by a sniper. All of their security procedures were considerably upgraded these days. But the offices them-selves remained elegantly appointed—not that she and Jazz had put much effort into it. In some ways, the region's eco-nomic downturns had favored start-up businesses. They'd inherited this space fully equipped, including desks, lamps, chairs and decor. She'd added touches of her own, but it hadn't taken much.

"What are you thinking?" she asked him.

McCarthy looked up and smiled. "I'm thinking it feels like I've been here before." He shrugged. "That's weird, right? Maybe I was here when the building was under con-struction."

"Maybe it's just nerves."

"Why would I be nervous?"

She smiled and looked down at the paperwork on her

desk. Always plenty of that to keep up with. McCarthy got off the couch and paced the office, hands behind his back; she tried not to watch him, but for some reason she couldn't seem to concentrate on the report she was reading. Her eyes kept straying.

He came to a stop as the office door swung open, and Jazz and Borden entered the room.

The look on Jazz's face when she spotted McCarthy was, quite literally, priceless.

"Ben?" she asked, as if she really couldn't believe it. Lucia glanced over at him and felt a pleasant aftershock as well, even though she'd gotten over the initial impact. Lenora Ellen's had done an astonishing job. His gray-salted hair was trimmed just enough to give him style. Whatever skin treatments they'd done, he looked healthier than he had three hours before. Freshly shaved, too. The suit seemed thoughtlessly elegant, and she'd chosen the colors well— the midnight-blue set off his eyes like foil to a diamond. He looked...gorgeous, she admitted, and promptly dismissed the thought, because it was inappropriate.

McCarthy was giving Jazz a wide smile, stepping forward, arms open. And she was rushing into them like a delighted child.

Jazz looked good, too. Fresh-faced, glowing, ever so slightly tousled. She never failed to look as if she'd forgotten to brush her short-cut blond hair, but on her, it worked. She'd made an effort with wardrobe today, too—a well-fitted black pantsuit and blue shirt, medium-heeled shoes.

She was taller than McCarthy, but somehow she managed to make it look as if he towered over her, even in the hug.

Lucia met James Borden's eyes as he took a seat on the leather couch in the corner of the office. He was casual today—blue jeans and a gray T-shirt. His brown hair was gel-free, and it made him look unexpectedly vulnerable. As did the glance he darted at McCarthy and Jazz, locked in their hug.

"Counselor," Lucia said in greeting, and went to sit next to him. "So, I presume you had a good evening?"

That woke an entirely satisfied, private smile. "We did all right."

"So I see. She looks very happy."

"Happy to see McCarthy."

Ah, already the jealousy. Men. They were, if possible, even worse at relationships than women. "She's been waiting years for this. You might let her enjoy it."

He had the grace to look ashamed of himself. "I am. I will." He passed over a red envelope. "Same as you got?"

Lucia unfolded it, studied it and nodded. "Mine was hand-delivered."

"Get anything out of the courier?"

She had to grin at the thought of interrogating the round little man in one of the dressing rooms, while the clerk sweated in terror and phoned the police. "Not a good time. But it doesn't matter. He was simply doing a job."

McCarthy and Jazz had finally pulled apart. He was holding her by the upper arms, giving her the once-over. Lucia glanced over at Borden, whose face had gone very bland,

and wondered what he was thinking. No, she knew. She'd been there before, sitting as the spectator.

"Hate to break up the happy moment," she said, raising her voice, "but we should talk. All of us."

"About what?" Ah, McCarthy still hadn't forgiven her for the day spa; the wall went up the second he turned toward her.

"Lucia's right," Jazz said, and pulled up a chair—a straight-backed one that she could straddle, resting her crossed arms on the top. "They're on to us again. I sure as hell don't want to go back to hiding out and worrying who's gunning for me for the rest of my life. We need to figure this thing out, guys. And now that Ben's on board, we have a lot more of a chance to do that."

"Don't," Borden warned, and shot Jazz one of those serious looks. "Don't do this."

"Don't do what?" McCarthy asked.

"Jazz, I mean it. He's not—"

Jazz, of course, ignored him. She had the look. Lucia was frankly surprised that Borden hadn't learned to recognize it yet. "He has to know. If he's here, he has to know everything. See, the people who funded us, the ones who gave us the money—"

McCarthy held up a hand. The spa had done a good job on his manicure, Lucia noted. "You work for the Cross Society, and they can predict the future," he said. "They're asking you to do things. Weird things. Telling you it's all to prevent more people from dying, right? Am I close?"

Silence. Even Borden looked stunned. Lucia deliberately

got to her feet, drew all of their stares and said, "I'll get coffee. We clearly have a lot to talk about."

Jazz wasn't taking it well. For that matter, neither was Borden, but for entirely different reasons.

"Seriously," Jazz said. She was pacing the room, hands behind her back. From time to time, she gnawed on the cuticle of her thumbnail, a habit that Lucia had hoped she'd lost. "You worked for Simms."

"Yes," Ben stated, for about the fourth time. Lucia kept her silence, watching the two of them; tension was growing like a storm in the room. "I worked for Max Simms. Freelance, at first. One or two jobs, no big deal. Didn't seem like a big deal, anyway, at least at first—"

Jazz interrupted him. Her face had gone from white to flushed, and her eyes glittered. Lucia inwardly winced, watching her; she knew that look. It normally was followed by a hard right cross, or a well-placed kick.

"Didn't seem like a big deal?" Jazz snapped. "Are you telling me that you knew about all of this crap *while we were still partners?* And what, you just kept that to yourself? Oh, but then, I guess you would, wouldn't you? Secrets were your thing!"

Well, it hadn't been a physical blow, but the words connected; Lucia saw him flinch. "Jazz—"

"You know what, Ben? Fuck you and your damn *secrets!*"

"Jazz!" It came out as a deep-throated roar, full of pent-up fury. "Dammit, will you shut up and listen to me?" He strode over to her and stood there, right in her space.

Lucia tensed, ready to lunge in as referee, but painfully aware that these two would get in plenty of damaging shots before she could put an end to things. *If* she could put an end to things.

"I was just like you, Jazz!" he continued. "Idealistic! Thinking these guys knew the score, were doing good work. But it's not like that, and you need to clearly understand, doing good is a sideline for them. It's all about winning, and let's face it, to win, sometimes you have to play dirty. And they did." He laughed wildly, bitterly. "Oh, they did."

Lucia had a sudden flash of insight. "Don't tell me they were the reason—"

"The reason I landed in jail?" McCarthy swung away from Jazz and locked gazes with Lucia instead. His hot blue eyes were full of pain and anger. "If I'd known either one of you was into this thing, don't you think I'd have spoken up? But no, you had to play it cagey, keep it all to yourselves—"

"Wait a minute." Jazz interrupted again, still with that hot-metal edge. "How did the Cross Society land you in jail?"

"You don't think they've got ways? Listen, I—" He checked himself, a hesitation so brief Lucia wasn't sure she'd actually seen it. "If I could prove it, I'd tell you, but the way everything clicked together and lined up like little tin soldiers? *Cross Society.* They're chess players. They don't get their own hands dirty. Their sacrifice pawns are the ones who bleed and suffer and die. And pay."

"Pay for what?"

Lucia was surprised to hear Borden ask the question,

because he'd said nothing at all for a long while. He was studying McCarthy with half-closed eyes, looking bland. A damn fine poker face. She felt a prickle along her spine, and thought about reminding Jazz that Borden, regardless of how true his love, was also a card-carrying member of the Cross Society. But Jazz knew that. She never forgot it.

"Disappointments," McCarthy said. "They wanted me to stand by and let somebody get killed. I couldn't do it."

Shades of Jazz; she'd been asked to do the same thing, Lucia remembered. Asked to stand by and see an innocent man die. As had Borden. It had been a crisis of faith for him, knowing that his friend was marked for death by Eidolon, and the Cross Society had elected to do nothing about it. He'd turned to Jazz for help and almost gotten her killed for it, but together they'd managed to prevent the murder.

And what's to stop Eidolon from trying again? Lucia had wondered that for a while. Maybe things had changed. She didn't understand how it worked. She suspected nobody outside of the inner circles really did.

She hated the idea that all of this happened somewhere in secret, behind a curtain. *Playing God.* It reminded her why she'd left the government.

"Yeah?" Jazz challenged. She was still looking wounded and furious and betrayed, and in no mood to believe McCarthy. "Who did they want to kill?" She was demanding proof. Names and dates. Facts and figures she could check. Jazz was nothing if not thorough.

McCarthy hesitated for so long that Lucia thought he wouldn't answer. He was studiously examining the carpeting, hands in his pockets, shoulders hunched. His hesitation seemed odd, considering the passion he'd already displayed. And then he said, slowly and in a much quieter tone, "Remember that hallway, three years ago? When the guy came out from under the stairs?"

Jazz went pale. Lucia watched her knuckles tighten on the back of the chair, her blue eyes narrow. Her mouth attempted two tries before she was able to ask the question. "Me?"

"Yeah. You." He risked a look at his ex-partner, a startling flash of eyes. Lucia shivered at the expression in them. Pain and resignation.

If Jazz saw it, it didn't make any impression. She was staring past him, stunned, seeing something miles away. "You knew? You knew that guy was there?"

"No. I knew something was going to happen, because they wanted me to wait in the car."

"You *did* wait in the car."

"For a while," McCarthy said, his voice low and furious. "And then I came in and I shot the son of a bitch who was trying to kill you. Shot him in the back. Twice, if you remember."

Silence. Lucia didn't think even Borden was breathing. Jazz and McCarthy were staring each other down.

Links and circles. That officer-involved shooting had been McCarthy's first and only. That put his service revolver's ballistics information into the database, which had later linked him to murder.

Lucia turned on Borden. "Did you know this?" He mutely

shook his head. "*Borden*. Did you know McCarthy worked for the Cross Society?"

"No!" he snarled, and got up off the couch to stalk to the far corner of the room. "Don't you think I'd have told you if I'd known? Look, it's not—it's not like it's an open book. I don't think even Laskins knows everything. Some of it—maybe a lot of it—happens between Simms and his agents, and we're just—"

"Just what?" Lucia asked. "Protective coloration? What is it the rest of you do for him that he can't do for himself?"

"Maintain the network," Borden said. "Deliver his messages when he needs it. Attend to the money and the business."

Jazz had turned away from McCarthy, and now she was staring at Borden. "Did you know they'd put him in jail?" she asked. Whatever logical path Jazz had followed inside her head, there seemed to be no doubt in her now that McCarthy was telling the truth.

"No," Borden said. He sounded suddenly weary. "I'd have told you."

"We can talk about that later," Lucia said, after a few seconds of painful silence. "McCarthy. The money you were taking, the payoffs. Were they payments from the Cross Society to you?"

He didn't answer. Maybe that was answer enough.

"What were you, *stupid?*" Jazz yelled. "Didn't you see how easily they could turn you? How deep they had their claws in you?"

"Not until I killed that guy," McCarthy said. "And then it

was too late. Simms already had me. The payments used to come through a bank, then they came through some friend of his, then they started making the drops at the Velvet. Then pretty soon it was handovers from Big Sal and his crew, and there was no point in fighting it anymore."

"You could have walked away."

He looked grim. "I tried."

"Oh, so taking that last payoff on camera, that was, what—for the widows and orphans fund?" Jazz demanded. "Don't bullshit me, Ben. Don't you dare."

He shook his head tiredly. "No point in doing that, either," he said. "Look, you believe me or not. This is why I never even tried to explain any of it to you. How do you think this would have gone before you'd seen how it works for yourself?"

She wasn't done yet, Lucia saw. "So what were they paying you to do, Ben? Compromise evidence? Get cases thrown out?"

"*Fuck!* Come on, Jazz! You can't believe—"

"I *don't* believe!"

"I wouldn't do that. I was a cop!"

"Yeah? You thought about letting me die, didn't you?"

He swallowed, and some of the anger drained out of his expression. "No. I just thought—look, I didn't know they were talking about killing you."

"So it was okay if they just messed me up a little? Crippled me? Where's the line, Ben? It's okay for them to put a scare into me, not to touch me? Or okay to throw me a beating, so long as it doesn't scar?"

They settled into mutual glaring, jaws tight, teeth set. Lucia let a few seconds of silence go by, and then cleared her throat. "If I may continue," she said carefully. "Evidently, the Cross Society decided you weren't of use to them any longer. Was that because you moved to save Jazz when you did?"

"Doesn't matter. I'm out. I'm not taking orders from those creepy sons of bitches anymore, and neither should you. Either of you." McCarthy turned a glare toward Borden, who was slumped against the wall by the broad windows. "And you should get rid of him. You're sleeping with the enemy, Jazz. Watch what you say around him."

"Hey!" Borden said sharply, and straightened up. "Watch your mouth."

"Why? You're not sleeping with my partner?" McCarthy showed teeth. "Or do you just not want to admit to it? Ashamed?"

Borden's eyes turned dark and cold. "I mean it, man. Shut up."

"Jazz wants me to shut up, she can say something about it."

Jazz didn't seem inclined to say much about it either way, Lucia noticed. Her mouth was closed, her jawline tight. Her hands were fisted on her thighs, knuckles white.

Borden towered over McCarthy when McCarthy walked toward him, but it seemed obvious to Lucia that it wouldn't matter. McCarthy was the dangerous one here. Borden was tall and rangy and could probably hold his own in most situations, but McCarthy had done two years of hard time, and he'd gone in hard to start with.

And Lucia didn't like the flat look in his eyes.

"Gentlemen," she said, her voice pitched low and calm. Standing up with deliberate grace, she moved to form the third point of a triangle—not between them, but pulling their focus away from each other. Jazz, still seated behind her, would have done it differently; she would have waded in, shoving and shouting. That would work, but it would take time to sort out.

This worked instantly.

McCarthy stepped back. "Sorry," he said. "You're right. Your house. You want to have amoral bastards in it, that's not my business."

"Borden stays," Lucia said. "He's proved himself to us. You haven't, Ben."

"Hey, wait a second!" Jazz snapped.

"Jazz, shut up." Lucia gave her voice an edge of steel.

Jazz pressed her lips together, eyes blazing.

"I'm talking to you, Ben," Lucia continued. "The three of us, we've been through a lot together. You're new to this agency. You don't just walk in here and throw doubt on Borden, do you understand? And you don't try to pull me and Jazz apart by playing on old loyalties. If you do, you can walk out the door and find your own way."

Jazz badly wanted to speak, but somehow she controlled herself; Lucia watched the battle on her face. The outcome was a lowering of her blond head, deep breaths and silence.

Lucia transferred her attention back to Ben.

"I'm not working for the Cross Society again," he said. "Get that straight right now."

"Fine. If you want to work for us, you do straight-up work," she agreed. "Straightforward investigation. You don't deal with Cross at all."

He thrust a thumb over his shoulder toward Borden. "Do I have to deal with *him?*"

"You have to deal with *me* if you disrespect him," she said. "Are we clear?"

He nodded—one sharp movement, nothing more. After a few seconds, he said, "Thanks for the suit."

He meant it to be embarrassing, as if he'd conned her out of something. She gave him a cool smile. "You're representing us now. Can't have you looking like a lowlife ex-con."

Borden glanced from one to the other. "Did I miss something? You *hired* him?"

"Over breakfast," Lucia said. "Jazz? Will that be a problem?"

Jazz didn't answer. She was watching McCarthy, waiting for something.

He walked over to her, took her fists in his hands and slowly smoothed her fingers out. He wasn't looking at her face. Borden had stiffened at the touch, Lucia noticed in her peripheral vision.

"Jazz," Ben said quietly. "I couldn't tell you any of it. Don't you think that was hell for me? I was almost glad they set me up. At least then I didn't have to face you every morning and lie to you. Look, I know you can't forgive me for it, but—"

"I forgave you a long time ago," she said. "I forgave you when there wasn't a reason to do it. That's why I'm angry."

"Ah," he said, and nodded. "Thanks."

"Don't thank me. If you work here, I'm your boss. You think I won't make you pay?"

He smiled. It was one of those warm, sweet smiles that had such devastating effect, and Lucia saw it had the same impact on Jazz that it did on her. "I'm counting on it. I owe you."

"Damn straight. And I'm going to get every nickel." Jazz flicked her gaze over to Lucia and deliberately nodded. "Yeah. It's okay with me."

Borden let out a sigh. It wasn't quite loud enough for Jazz or McCarthy to hear, but Lucia shot him an amused glance.

"Then if that's all the thunderbolts we have to impart," she said, "let's get back to work."

Chapter 4

An hour later, Lucia was knee-deep in files at the conference table. Borden had gone back to change into his business
suit for a client meeting across town, so just she, Jazz and
McCarthy were seated there. Hot, bright sunlight stream-
ing through the blinds striped the long table, making Lucia
squint, but she could tell that McCarthy was enjoying it; she
refrained from pulling the shades.

"Okay," she said to him. "That stack is bread and but-
ter—background checks for corporations, individuals worried about their daughter's fiancé, et cetera. We charge an
average of two hundred for a public records and Internet
search, the basic package, for individuals. For corporations,
we do the whole due diligence, and that costs them an average of two thousand, in time and fees. We have sixteen
corporations as clients for that sort of thing, so we always
have backlogs to move through. You can start with that."

McCarthy nodded and pulled over a half-dozen folders, flipping through them, reading with quick little flicks of his eyes.

Lucia nudged the next, smaller stack. "These are ongoing investigations. Mostly corporate, of course, because that seems to be what we gravitate toward."

"And you don't end up freezing your ass off in a parking lot at 2:00 a.m., videotaping a cheating husband with a hooker," Jazz added, then considered what she'd said. "Not that it can't be fun."

Lucia rolled her eyes. "Jazz is currently restricted from anything that involves undercover or stakeout work—"

"Because of the death threats," McCarthy said.

Jazz snorted. "And I keep telling you, that's over. There hasn't been a peep out of them since—"

"Since they tried to shoot you through your office window?" Lucia said dryly. "Yes, well. Forgive me for wanting to come down on the side of caution. Give it another month, and then we'll see about stepping down protection."

Except for an expressive roll of her eyes, Jazz remained businesslike. "Yeah. So, you see the problem—my investigations mostly consist of talking on the phone. So I could use your assistance on some of these when there's legwork to be done."

He nodded again. "I'll read the files. What's the third stack?"

The shortest of all, in red folders. She glanced at Jazz, who looked back. "Cross Society," she said. "You'll have nothing to do with those."

He didn't like that, she saw, but he wasn't going to come out with it, not in his first few hours of gainful employment.

"Now, to details," she said. "We need to get you a carry permit, which shouldn't present a difficulty, as your conviction has been vacated. But the sheriff's department may decide to drag their feet. By law, they have to make a decision within forty-five days of application, and issue within three days of approval, so we'll hold them to it. Here's the application." She pulled one from a folder and slid it across the table to him. "You know how it works. I'll give you cash, and you can drop it off yourself at the sheriff's office. Until we go through the process, you won't be able to legally carry a weapon in Missouri."

"The key word," Jazz said, "being *legally*." She reached into a case she'd set by her chair, clicked it open and pulled out a weapon. She cleared and checked it with professional ease, then handed the gun to McCarthy. "Manny says hello, by the way."

"For as long as you are illegally carrying, should you choose to do so, you won't officially have any connection to this firm," Lucia continued. "No employment paperwork to tie you back here. No paychecks. You'll be paid in cash, from my own pocket. Got it? As far as the state of Missouri knows, you're pending employment based on approval of your carry permit."

McCarthy examined the gun, even though Jazz had already done so; he removed the clip, checked the chamber, then snapped it all back together. Smooth, artistic motions. "I understand," he said. "Good plan. How is Manny?"

"Better," Jazz said. "He's working with us now."

"What, in the *office?*"

"No, he's got his own lab. You know how he is. He doesn't get out that much, but he does get out." Jazz grinned. "He's dating Pansy. Our assistant."

"You're kidding me. Manny dates?" McCarthy took the holster that Jazz handed over, slid the gun inside and removed his jacket to don the harness. He took his time adjusting it, making sure it was comfortable. When he put the jacket on again, he left it open.

"I didn't know the guy ever had a girl in his life," Ben added. "What do they do? Compare forensic swabs?"

Lucia couldn't resist a smile; Jazz outright laughed. "I try not to think about it," Lucia said. "So look those folders over. Let me know what you want to tackle first and we'll figure out the next step."

McCarthy looked from one of them to the other. "And you two? What are you doing?"

Lucia silently picked up the top red folder. Jazz sighed and took another half-dozen folders from the largest stack, the background checks. "I frickin' hate this," she said, and ran a hand through her hair. "I'm going to die of paper cut poisoning. See if I don't. Maybe Simms will see *that* coming!"

Lucia smiled and met McCarthy's eyes.

McCarthy was, Lucia found, a good investment: thorough, efficient and effective. He knew his way around a computer, which was a relief, and his reports were composed, like Jazz's, in a brisk, no-nonsense style that laid out facts and conclusions in a logical fashion.

The only problem was that he was actually *too* good at background checks, Lucia discovered when reviewing his first six assignments. They were seated in what was unofficially his office—bare except for a desk, computer, chair and stack of folders. Oh, and the ever-present coffee cup. He couldn't seem to function without one in sight.

"This one?" Lucia held up a folder. "This one should have been passed."

"Why? The guy has a criminal background."

"It was an arrest twenty years ago for drunk and disorderly, and he was in college. Not really relevant to whether he's a risk for a major corporation now."

McCarthy leaned back in his chair with a creak of metal, aiming a stare directly at her eyes. "You want me to pass him even though he fails the standards."

"I want to give our client a viable candidate. We can write a note putting his prior history into context. As someone who might fail the test yourself just now, you might consider being a little less...harsh."

That put a spark in his eyes, but nothing else. "You're the boss, boss. Say, this one, the one with the cocaine habit—you want me to pass him, too? Call it a treatable medical condition?"

"Just keep it in mind. Our clients want us to be cautious, but let's face it, there's something in everyone's background that could disqualify them, if you dig deep enough."

She knew as soon as she said it that it begged a question, which he obligingly provided. "Yeah? What's in your background?"

She was silent for a few long seconds. He'd probably intended it to be a softball, but it was something of a grenade, really. "Mine?" She smiled. "Deep, dark secrets. The kind that get you killed."

Why in the world had she said that? She hadn't meant to. Her past wasn't a seduction. The last thing she wanted was for him to learn more about Lucia Garza, and what she'd done in the name of causes and country.

"Intriguing." He pushed back his chair and tilted his head, returning the smile. "Come on, I gave you mine earlier. Just tell me one."

She had no business even thinking about it. The silence stretched, and she knew it seemed odd; she was taking it beyond simple idle conversation into a much more serious realm.

"I worked overseas," she said. "For the government."

He raised his eyebrows. "Spy stuff?"

"I'd tell you, but—"

"—you'd have to kill me, yeah, I know the drill." He held out his hand. She gave the file back. "I'll amend the report. Mr. Student Protester gets a free pass."

She nodded. "Do you have a place to stay yet?"

"Figured I'd find a cheap motel. Just temporarily, until I can close on that penthouse with a city view. And please, don't tell me you've got recommendations for a cheap motel. I like to keep my illusions."

"I'll find you a place," she said, refusing to be baited. She was familiar with the process; she'd been through it with cocky, aggressive men in every job she'd ever had. They all felt they had something to prove.

"I didn't think you wanted a paper trail back to the company," he said.

"I don't. It won't trace back to us."

"Aren't you the clever one."

"Allegedly." She paused in the doorway, looking back at him. He'd pulled his tie askew, and his collar was unbuttoned. Sexy. Very sexy. "Are you having dinner with Jazz?"

"Yeah. Indoors, since you don't let her out without body armor and the Popemobile. Want to join us?"

"No, thank you. Somebody's got to catch up on the work."

On her way back to her office, she felt a flash of guilt. That had been a passive-aggressive thing to do, a cheap shot; she'd implied that Jazz wasn't pulling her weight. And it wasn't true. Jazz was more than fulfilling her half of the agreement, even handicapped by the death sentence that they had to assume was still in effect for her. It was hell for Jazz, no question; she was the active one, the one more suited to running over rooftops and wrestling suspects to the ground than having polite conversations over the phone.

Lucia sat down at her desk and picked up the phone. "Omar? Hey, man. Need a favor. Can you book a room for McCarthy? Nothing too cheap, nothing too expensive. Very bland. Safe house quality. You know what to look for."

"For how long?"

She considered that carefully. The spy in her hated to leave him in one place for long; she was unconsciously considering him a compromised source, she realized. If anyone—say, Detective Ken Stewart—had a grudge against him, leaving him booked at just one location under his own name would be asking for trouble.

"Listen, could you book him at four places, a week each? Four names, none of them his? I'll give you cash."

"Some things never change," Omar said, amused. "Yeah. I'll come up."

She counted out bills from a lockbox and wrote out a receipt, put them in a plain white envelope and had it on the corner of her desk when Omar knocked on the open door and strolled in. He was a big man, well-muscled but not bulky. He was also of Arabian descent, and had found himself out of his chosen work in fairly short order after 9-11. Nobody wanted to hire Arabs as freelance security, and Omar stubbornly had refused to give up. He was proud. It was his principal characteristic, and it was something Lucia loved about him. That, and his liquid dark eyes and wicked smile.

He came in and pocketed the envelope. "You know I'm going to get the looks when I do this. The I'm-calling-the-FBI looks. Hell, I'll be lucky if they don't shoot me."

"Try to, you mean," she said. "But I can't hand McCarthy a pile of money. He'd take it personally."

"Yeah, you'd never do that yourself—take anything personally," he said. "Apart from acting like the new guy's travel agent, is there anything I can do other than hang around in your dungeon, guarding cars?"

"It's important work, guarding cars," she said. "You're all that stands between me and an oil leak."

He kissed his fingers at her and left. She shook her head, smiling. Omar was a good friend, and he'd once been a good lover, but that was long past. It wouldn't happen again. She'd seen him at his very lowest point, and a man like Omar didn't forget.

Better to keep it light and loose, these days.

She picked up the phone and began the first of the day's phone calls. By the time she was done with the second conference call, Omar was back at her office door, holding out a series of small key folders marked with the stamp of four popular, ubiquitous, utterly anonymous motel chains.

"He does anything, I'm going to be very unhappy," Omar said. "I had to use my own cherished fake ID. And I have no doubt that the clerks are probably alerting the FBI right now. When you hear about a Waco-style raid on a cheap motel, they're shooting it out with your ex-con."

"You're enjoying this."

"Damn right I am. At last I get to act furtive and guilty, as befits my race. The dream comes true." His words were clever and light, the bitter twist of his mouth was not.

"I'm sorry," she said, and meant it. Perhaps she hadn't been wise to use him, but the truth was, she hadn't had a surfeit of choices. "Back to work, Omar."

"Harsh mistress."

"You haven't *seen* me harsh."

It was the wrong thing to say, because he had, actually,

and it was one subject they didn't talk about. Omar looked at her for a few seconds, and then nodded and walked away.

It always surprised her how quickly the hours could pass when there was a full slate of things to do. Jazz stuck her head in at some point and announced that she was heading home, with Omar as an unwanted passenger, riding shotgun. Lucia checked the clock and found it already after office hours. She gathered up the motel cards that Omar had secured, and went down to McCarthy's office.

"Here," she said. He was standing up, putting files in a cabinet, and he looked at the keys over the top of some little half-glasses he'd put on for reading. They made him look leonine and oddly daft.

"Home sweet home," he said, and reached for them. "Which one's first?"

"Motel 6, on top. They're in order. Omar booked you for a different place every week."

He nodded, as if that was the most reasonable thing in the world. "Omar?"

"You'll meet him later. He's a friend of mine."

Her eyes touched his, then moved on. *Not that close a friend,* she wanted to say, but there didn't seem to be any way to do so that wouldn't sound…ridiculous. "Sorry for the cloak-and-dagger, but Detective Stewart seemed quite— intent. I thought it was better to give you some breathing space for a while."

"Thanks. Sure you won't join us for dinner?"

"You've already had a meal with me today. This should

be Jazz's evening with you. Besides, I'm boring dinner company."

"Somehow, I doubt that." He looked at her over the top of those glasses, and the blue eyes came as a shock. Again. "Come. I hear that Manny likes you well enough to allow you into the Inner Sanctum."

She didn't need much persuading, and that was a traitorous thing, a thing that disappointed her. "Fine," she said. "Jazz is on her way there. I'll stop off at home to change clothes."

Which drew his eyes involuntarily down her body, and she felt it like a physical touch. He caught himself, and focused back on the files.

"Do you want a drink?"

"Sorry?"

"A drink?" She had no idea where that blurted offer had come from, but once it was out, she couldn't back away from it.

His hands paused. He leaned on the desk, looking down. "Yes," he said. "Got any Scotch?"

"Blended or single malt?"

"You're kidding, right?"

"Single malt."

"There is no other kind."

"Follow me."

She was acutely aware of him in the hallway, his warmth at her back as they passed the empty spaces. Jazz's door was closed. Pansy Taylor, their assistant, was still there, sorting mail, her glossy dark head bent toward her desk. She glanced up, and Lucia caught a fast smile before she turned her attention back to her work.

Lucia shut the office door behind McCarthy and motioned him to the couch in the corner, near the window. He settled. She opened the cabinet in the back and took out chunky crystal tumblers and a sealed bottle of Glenmorangie, then walked back over to sit in the chair next to the couch. She filled glasses, set the bottle aside and contemplated the russet-amber liquor for a few seconds before sipping. The taste was as warm as the color—a harsh bite that faded to a mellow, smoky glow in her mouth, then woke an answering fire in her stomach.

Neither of them had said a word, she realized, and it wasn't an uncomfortable silence. More as if they were in perfect agreement about what a lovely moment it was, sipping single malt.

When his glass was dry, McCarthy said, "I can't get used to the quiet. It's never quiet in prison. Always some sound— footsteps, talking, things moving. Crying, sometimes. You can't sleep deeply. Always waiting." He held out his glass, and she mutely refilled it. "They thought they'd kill me, putting me in general population."

"You survived."

"Yeah." His smile was weary and bitter and just a touch sad. "You do that, if you can. No matter what it takes."

"Do you want me to ask what it took?"

"Just saying." He rested his head against the leather back of the couch, watching her through contemplative, half-closed eyes. "You understand how I feel about the Cross Society, right?"

"I understand that you think they betrayed you."

"No, it wasn't that personal. They just stopped having a use for me, that was all. Look, you and Jazz, you got caught up with them. I understand that. So did I. I think you need to get out now, while you can. You get embedded too deeply..." He shrugged. "Consequences can be harsh."

"I appreciate the warning, Ben."

"Yeah, I'll bet. So, you and Jazz. Good friends?"

"I like to think so."

"This Borden guy, he good enough for her? Apart from being a Cross Society asshole?"

Lucia fought back a smile. "Oh, I think he's very good for her. Good *enough?* That would depend on your point of view. What's yours?"

"Older brother. I'd say father, but that's just depressing."

"And untrue. You're only, what? Forty-four?"

"Just like the gun. And I get to say that two years in a row. Ain't I lucky?"

She laughed and tossed back the rest of her drink. "I like you, Ben." She meant it lightly, but his eyes flashed, and she felt something bloom hot inside. Insanely hot. Ridiculously so. One glass of whiskey wasn't enough to make her feel like this. Not even one glass of Glenmorangie.

"Careful," Ben murmured, and drank the last of his as well. "Men like me, fresh out of prison...only got three things on our minds."

"Such as?"

"Food."

"We had breakfast."

He leaned forward and put the glass on the side table, next to the bottle of whiskey. "Finding a place to stay."

"Lucky you, you have four of them."

"You really want me to go on?" he asked. "Because the third one on the list wouldn't be gentlemanly."

"Can't have that," she agreed. "You've been a perfect gentleman so far."

"You have no idea how hard that is."

Lucia had a sudden, vivid image. No, not an image, really—a full sensory mirage. McCarthy moving her back to her desk, sweeping the top of it clean. Her legs wrapping around him, their lips meeting and devouring. His hands...

She cleared her throat and stood up, aware that she was flushed, and not sure whether it was a product of the whiskey or her imagination. She reached for the glasses, and he was there ahead of her, handing them over.

Their fingers brushed, and it was like an electric current. The slow drag of his skin on hers made her pull in an involuntary breath, and she saw the answering response in the pupils of those blue eyes.

No, she told herself sternly. *This is not you. You are not reckless and foolish. You hardly know a thing about this man, and for God's sake, he just came out of prison....*

Which wasn't necessarily a downside; ungovernable passions were terrifying and compelling at the same time. She wished she hadn't thought of that. Gasoline on a brush fire, that thought.

She transferred the glasses to her other hand and reached past him for the bottle. Close enough that their chests touched, brushed. It would be easy to kiss, from that intimate distance. Easy to do a lot of things.

He didn't move.

He didn't move away, either.

"Excuse me," she murmured, and looked into his eyes. Just for a second, and then her nerve failed and she turned and walked to the cabinet, where she put the Glenmorangie away and placed the crystal tumblers in the small bar sink. Her hands were shaking, ridiculous as that was; she'd been through firefights with less emotional reaction.

Lucia stayed with her back to him, facing the cabinet, head down, fighting against an unexpected tidal wave of longing that was threatening to drag her under.

"You okay?" His voice came from close behind her. She felt herself flinch.

"Fine," she said. Her voice was, as always, calm and controlled. "I need to make a couple of calls. Would you mind…?"

"No. I'll be in my office, going over my important work," he said, with dry amusement in his voice. He knew. He damn well *knew* what kind of effect he was having on her, and he knew how much it was angering her to lose control.

She didn't turn around. McCarthy walked away—she was acutely aware of the sound of his shoes on the carpet—and opened and closed the door. The deep breath she took in smelled faintly of him—the hair products they'd used on him at Lenora Ellen's, an elegant cologne, an underlying crisp male scent that she was starting to understand was uniquely his own.

She went back to her desk and sat down, hands flat on the surface. The couch at the far end of the room was a nice tan leather, a match for the one in Jazz's office. The walls were a cool, clean cream. Black-and-white, oversize photographs hung there, plus a selection of color photos that showed her in air force dress uniform, and receiving a civilian commendation from a former president. As much of her history as she wanted to officially remember these days.

She was contemplating the couch, and possibilities, when a knock came at the door and Pansy opened it wide enough to look in. She was a cute, efficient woman whom Jazz had hired—partly out of spite—away from James Borden's law firm of Gabriel, Pike & Laskins. Her sleek dark pageboy framed a heart-shaped face that wouldn't have looked out of place in a silent movie.

Even, just now, to the wide eyes.

"What?" Lucia asked. Pansy was hardly the wide-eyed type. She'd been cool under fire, literally, when a sniper had taken out Jazz's office window, and nearly Jazz herself. It took a lot to get a reaction from her.

For answer, Pansy held out a FedEx envelope—the stiff cardboard kind—and opened it to take out a red envelope. She held it in two fingers, carefully, as if it were a dead roach. "For you," she said. "Do you want it, or do we make the shredder people happy?"

In Lucia's experience, it was always better to make an informed choice. "I'll take a look," she said, and Pansy crossed the room with it and handed the crimson paper over. Lucia examined the outside of the envelope, but as usual there were no clues to the naked eye. A plain red envelope, like a greeting card. Her name block printed on the outside. "Who sent the FedEx?"

Pansy checked the label. "GP&L."

"Not specifically from Borden or Laskins."

"Nope. Mailroom. Could have been anybody."

Lucia nodded and turned the envelope over. It was sealed. She took a sharp letter opener from her drawer and slit it carefully across the top.

She had just put the letter opener down when Pansy yelled, "Stop!"

She looked up. Pansy was staring down into the open FedEx envelope, and her face had taken on a death-white pallor.

"Don't open it," she said.

Chapter 5

"What is it?" Lucia asked. She didn't move a muscle, though her heart had accelerated into a fast, nervous rhythm.

Pansy looked pale enough to pass out, but her voice was steady. "Just put it down on the desk and step away. Now."

It was too thin to be an explosive device, but there was something in Pansy's voice that warned Lucia not to argue. She set the letter, carefully, in the center of her clean desk, and backed up. Pansy stepped forward and laid the FedEx envelope, with infinite care, down next to it.

"Outside," she said.

"What is it?"

"Fine white powder grains in the FedEx envelope," Pansy said. "I think they leaked out of the red envelope."

Lucia was suddenly, acutely aware of her hands. Her fingertips. She rubbed them gently together and felt grit.

Oh, Christ.

"Go," she snapped, and held up her hands like a surgeon preparing to operate. "*Move*. Bathroom. You know the drill—scrub as hard as you can. Go, Pansy!"

"But you—"

"I'll be there in a second. McCarthy!" She yelled it, full-throated. He emerged from his office, half-glasses still in place. "I need you to dial the phone," she said. "I may be contaminated."

The glasses came off. "Contaminated how?"

"Envelope," she said. "Powder." She struggled to keep cool on the outside; fear was strangling her, making her breaths shallow and fast. "Dial this number for me and put it on speakerphone." She recited it from memory. He punched it in, short stabbing motions, and stepped back as it rang. And rang. And rang….

"Pansy?" Manny Glickman's cautious voice.

"No, Manny, it's Lucia," she said. Absurd, how useless she felt, unable to use her hands; she was holding them in midair, acutely aware of the tingling in her fingertips. Imagination, most likely, but, *God*. "I need you to get over here with some kind of testing kit. We may have been exposed to something hazardous. A fine white powder in an envelope."

Silence. A long one. She felt sweat beading on the back of her neck, under the thick fall of her hair.

"Have you called anyone else?" Manny asked. "FBI? Postal inspectors? The cops?"

"No. Just you. I want your opinion first."

"How many people handled it?"

"Just Pansy and me. It's FedEx."

"Lucia, I understand you don't want to jump to conclusions, but testing for anthrax isn't instant. You let that FedEx courier continue on his way, you could endanger hundreds of people. You need to call the FBI, right now. I'll come, but you need to call. It's probably nothing, but just in case. Report it."

He was right. She hadn't thought about the courier, and she should have. "I will," she said. "Manny—"

"Did Pansy open the package?"

"Yes."

"Ungloved."

"Yes."

"And you?"

"I opened the inner envelope."

He hung up. She looked at McCarthy, who raised his eyebrows.

"You want me to find the number for the FBI?"

"Yes. Ask for Agent Rawlins. I know him."

"Fine." McCarthy locked eyes with her. "Go. Scrub."

She did, elbowing through the bathroom door to find Pansy still at the sinks, scrubbing with handfuls of thick, milky soap. Lucia used her own elbow, to turn on the hot water—thanks to whatever industrial designer's foresight had caused them to put in long-handled faucets—and began to do the same.

Pansy was crying. Not noisily, just silently leaking tears that trailed down her face and splashed into the roiling water in the sink.

"It's going to be all right," Lucia said. "We're all right."

Neither of them believed it, but Pansy gave her a shaky smile.

Lucia scrubbed until her hands felt raw.

When she and Pansy emerged from the bathroom, McCarthy was right outside, pacing. "FBI's on the way," he said. "They're getting to the FedEx driver and they've alerted the regional sorting center to back-trace. Agent Rawlins is sending a team, and Hazmat's coming, but it'll be a while. I told them about Manny. They're okay with him working the scene, providing he's careful and he leaves everything in situ."

They would be, Lucia thought. Manny had an even higher credibility within the FBI than to the outside world.

"I got hold of the building maintenance people and shut down the air ducts. They're finding the mailroom people and getting everybody together for testing."

She nodded. It sounded as if he'd done everything she'd have done, plus a step or two more. Authority and decisiveness came naturally to him, even after two years of enforced subordination. She was shakily relieved; she liked being in command, but at this particular moment, it was good to have someone else there.

"Look, I know you're worried, but chances are this isn't anthrax or some other pathogen. Ninety-eight percent of these kinds of things turn out to be jokes. Carelessness. Somebody spilling their baby powder on the desk. You're going to be okay."

"I know." She gave him a fast, reassuring smile. "Although I think my manicure is beyond saving. Did you lock down the office?"

"Yeah." He held up the keys, which he'd evidently found in Pansy's desk. "FBI will be here any minute."

"Manny will be here first," Pansy said. "Trust me."

Pansy was right.

Manny arrived in just under fifteen minutes, dragging a wheeled case full of stuff. He was a big, unkempt man— not as unkempt and wild-eyed as he'd been when Lucia first met him, but Manny was no one's poster child for stability. He wore a black T-shirt with FORENSICS on the chest and a huge white fingerprint on the back. Obviously not standard issue from any agency, but probably as official as he had, these days. He'd trimmed his bushy hair recently, and the blue jeans he had on didn't look too ancient. All in all, a much improved Manny Glickman.

A more focused one, as well. He mumbled a hello to Lucia, gave McCarthy a genuinely delighted smile and a handshake, and held Pansy off from a full-body hug with a warning gesture. "Clothes," he said. "Off and in the bag." He handed her a yellow plastic sack marked with a red biohazard symbol. "Put these on." He'd brought blue jeans and a red sweater, as well as a pair of comfortable-looking flat black slippers and, in a separate plastic sack, what looked like underwear. "I got them from your place."

She nodded.

"Everything in the bag, understand? Rings, watch, necklace, earrings. Underwear. Everything. Nothing that touched you stays on."

Pansy's eyes filled with tears for a second, and then she blinked and pasted on a grin and said, "You just want to get me out of my panties." Before he could answer, she took the sack and pile of clothes and headed for the bathroom.

"Where is it?" he asked Lucia.

She nodded toward her office.

"I didn't have any clothes for you, but I brought scrubs and booties."

"Thank you," she said gravely. "The FedEx envelope and the red envelope are on my desktop. No other papers there, thankfully."

"Red envelope?" Manny raised his eyebrows.

"I slit it open, but Pansy stopped me before I could do more. I don't suppose there's a way we can take a look...?"

"What if there's something in it to aerosolize the substance? Even a paper clip and a rubber band would be high-tech enough to spread a cloud of powder."

That was a scary thought. She nodded mutely, took the scrubs and ducked into Jazz's office to change. The scrubs—maroon—were far from what she'd think of as couture, but they served. Her clothes went into a plastic Hazmat bag, which McCarthy had prelabeled with GARZA in big block letters.

She hated the booties.

"Cute," McCarthy said when she came out. She gave him an ill-tempered glare. "No, honestly. I've always had this nurse thing."

"Shut it, McCarthy."

"I've got this pain right—"

"You don't want to know where you're going to have a pain if you don't shut up."

He grinned. She perched next to him on the reception desk, bootied feet swinging aimlessly, pulse still driving fast. McCarthy's attempts at humor were soothing, but not soothing enough.

Pansy reappeared from around the corner, Hazmat bag in hand. "Where's Manny?" she asked. McCarthy nodded to the closed office door. "What do we do with these?"

McCarthy checked that the names were clear on each bag, and then bundled both into another, larger one. He labeled that one with both their names and the date. Evidence handling was something he was obviously just as good at as managing in a crisis. Lucia wished he'd let her do it, but could understand why he was keeping her exposures to a minimum. Still, waiting was hard. Her hands—freshly scrubbed—felt cold. She rubbed them on her legs to warm them, saw McCarthy watching, and gave him a quick smile to show that there was nothing wrong, nothing at all; being exposed to a hazardous substance was an everyday occurrence.

The phone rang. It was Jazz.

"The FBI is there," she said breathlessly. "Bastards aren't letting us in the building. We're downstairs."

"I didn't want you to come, Jazz," Lucia said.

"Yeah, well, I came anyway. Borden, too. What do you want us to do?"

"Call Laskins, get him out of bed if you have to. Find out what GP&L sent us. Get them to fax over a copy of the text, if they sent it in the first place. I can't get to the red letter to read it."

"Which might be the point," Jazz said.

"True."

"Still…if the opposition could get to the envelope to doctor it, why not take the message? Why not replace it with one of their own and skip the anthrax scare? They have to know it would draw attention."

"All good questions. I don't know. I don't even know that there was an original message in the first place. All I know is that there's a FedEx envelope that came from GP&L's mailroom."

Jazz made a frustrated sound, like sandpaper rubbing stone. "But you're all okay, right?"

"It takes up to seven days to manifest anthrax symptoms," Lucia said. "Ask me in a week."

Manny came out of the office. He was carrying a square black case that was sealed with more bright yellow tape.

"Hang on," Lucia said to Jazz, and pressed the phone against her chest to muffle it. "Better get moving, Manny. The FBI's downstairs. They know you're here, but if you want to avoid questions…" Which she knew he did. Manny would always choose to avoid questions.

His face was wet with sweat. "Yeah. I'd better get this sample back to the lab. Sooner I get the tests started, the sooner…"

She nodded. Manny paused, gazing at Pansy. She tried

for a smile, and he looked as if he badly wanted to touch her, but neither of them managed to pull it off.

"See you," he said, and headed for the stairs. Pansy's gaze followed him. Lucia got back on the phone with Jazz.

"Manny's coming out," she said. "He's got a sample of the powder. Maybe you can ride herd on him…?"

"Done," Jazz said crisply, and hung up. That was Jazz: minimum talk, maximum effort.

"So," McCarthy said. "What do we do now?"

"Anybody want coffee?"

It took hours. Not a surprise; Lucia was well accustomed to the pace of investigations. But it still rankled. She was tired, exhausted from adrenaline, and starving. To her disappointment, the FBI hadn't exactly stormed the building. Agent Rawlins was present and accounted for, but he'd only brought one other agent and two technicians, one of whom was on loan from the Kansas City PD. One Hazmat suit, which none of them bothered to put on.

"So," Rawlins said, and pulled up a chair next to Lucia as his men got to work. "Who's out to kill you this week?"

"Agent Rawlins, you wound me."

"Can't say as I'd be the first, ma'am."

"Cut the folksy bullshit."

He had a lived-in face, too many lines for his young age, and the bright hair made him look tired. His dark brown eyes didn't give away much except his general intelligence. Rawlins liked to pretend he was a hayseed. Lucia knew better. The man had graduated top of his class from Quantico, had piled up a string of high-profile cases and was in the running to be moved up to D.C. on his next rotation. If ever a man was going to make it out of the FBI bush leagues, it was Agent Rawlins.

He nodded, rubbed his big hands together and looked down at the floor. "Want to tell me how this happened?"

She told him the facts, as briskly as possible.

"I won't ask who has a grudge against you, because I know damn well that the list is about as long as the phone book. Including a couple dozen drug dealers and some very unhappy terrorists from the old days." He looked up, directly into her eyes. "You know who the envelope's from?"

"Gabriel, Pike & Laskins," she said. "Our attorneys."

"I'm the first to believe lawyers are evil, but why would they want to kill off their own clients?"

"I doubt they would. Anybody could have slipped an envelope into their FedEx bin at their offices. Wouldn't be too difficult."

"Good enough." Rawlins nodded. "You get a lot of correspondence from these lawyers?"

She smiled thinly. "A fair amount, yes. Legal matters."

"Mind if I take a look?"

"It's privileged."

"Miss Garza, you sound like a guilty party."

"I sound like someone who understands how you work. You're on a fishing expedition, Agent Rawlins."

"Am I close to catching anything?"

"Not even a minnow."

He smiled and looked away, toward the office door.

His tech was coming out, holding a sealed bag marked EVIDENCE, with the standard biohazard symbol on it. Rawlins gave him a thumbs-up and stood.

"The lab's backed up," he said. "Might take a few days to come back with a result on this. My advice—close down until we get back to you. Take vacation."

"You're checking the air handlers in the building?"

"We're taking swabs. My guys are doing field tests, but just so you know, field tests aren't that reliable. False positives in a lot of cases. The lab's got some kind of growth medium it uses that can give us a determination in twenty-four hours."

"Once they get to us."

"Yeah. Once they get to you." It was unspoken, but he knew Manny would get to them first. Of course.

"Your techs already did field tests, right? What did they say?"

Rawlins was impossible to read. "Like I said, field tests aren't really reliable. They're just indicators. We don't base any kind of decisions on what they say."

McCarthy, who'd sat quietly through this entire conversation, said, "Listen, friend, I haven't even been out of prison for one full day yet. Don't make me assault a federal agent. I'd like to spend at least one night in a decent bed, watch a little television…so please, answer the nice lady's question."

"I can't comment."

"What are we, the friggin' press? Right," McCarthy said. "Guess I'm on my way back to Ellsworth." He stood up. Lucia did, too, getting between him and Rawlins; she didn't like the vibe that was cooking the air between them. *Dammit, nobody told me that Jazz was the calm one of their partnership...*

"Back off, Ben," she said, and put a hand flat on his chest. She felt the contact like a physical shock, felt the tension in his muscles, and lowered her voice. "Ben. Please. Let me handle it."

He hesitated for about a second, then lowered himself back into the chair. Next to him, Pansy looked paralyzed with fright.

Rawlins said, "The field test kit showed positive for anthrax. But the field test kit shows bullshit results about thirty percent of the time, so I wouldn't get too excited just yet. Besides, both of you made all the right moves, even if the results are reliable. It's going to be okay. You barely had an exposure."

Pansy nodded. Her face was the color of old ivory, her eyes stark and scared. Lucia felt her fingers tingling again, and knew it was just nerves, just her mind playing tricks on her.

"Thank you, Agent Rawlins," she said. "Can we go?"

"We're going to take you to the hospital as soon as we're done here. By the way, this place is going under seal until we get the results back from the lab. After we find out, either way, you're going to want to line up a biohazard team to come in and do a thorough cleanup. Just in case. Good for business, anyway. It'll make those potential clients feel safer."

McCarthy looked as if he wanted to commit a federal crime. Lucia took Rawlins's arm and walked him a few feet away before she said, "Do I need to get Pansy on any treatments?"

"The two of you should be on prophylaxis, just to be safe. I've made a phone call. You'll be going to Saint Luke's. They're already set up for you. They'll start you on antibiotics. You can discontinue them if the tests show a negative."

Reality was starting to set in. She could feel it as a fine trembling in her nerves, a slight hazy edge to the familiar surroundings. "And if the tests show positive?"

"Antibiotics for thirty days, at least. Maybe sixty, depending on if you start to show any symptoms. Look, Lucia—" He stopped. One of the techs was motioning at him from down the hall. "Be right back."

He walked away, had a short conversation and came back. "Interesting news. My guys tracked the FedEx. Guess what? It doesn't exist."

"Sorry?"

"Officially, this tracking number doesn't exist. It never entered the FedEx system. Label looks genuine, but it must be a mockup. Pretty good one, too." He moved past her toward Pansy, who looked up at him with a determined expression. "Was it the regular FedEx guy today?"

"No. His name's Jim, but it wasn't him. It was a woman."

"We're going to need to sit you down for an Identikit, okay? We want to know what she looked like." He glanced back at Lucia. "FedEx didn't make any deliveries today to this office."

Pansy looked, if possible, even more pale.

"Let's get you guys to the hospital," Rawlins said.

Chapter 6

Saint Luke's was exactly as much fun as Lucia expected. She thought that she probably could have walked away, anonymous in her booties and scrubs, before anyone thought to look for her, but she didn't. Loyalty to Pansy won out against an atavistic desire to just get the hell out, and besides, McCarthy was there, looking sardonic and grim. The nasal swabs were exciting, and the industrial-strength shower and shampoo even more so. Fresh medical garb awaited at the end, but this time she wasn't alone; both McCarthy and Pansy had been given hospital couture as well. McCarthy's hair was damp and sticking up in points. Pansy looked well-scrubbed and a little less scared.

"Doxycycline," the doctor said, and handed over a giant bottle to each of them. "Take it as indicated. If your tests come back negative, you can discontinue it immediately, but if not, keep taking it. No skips. Continue to the end of the regimen, no matter how good you feel. Tell us immediately if you get any symptoms."

"Symptoms?" Pansy said faintly.

"Fever's the first sign," he said. "I want to see all of you in three days, sooner if you have even the slightest rise in temperature or start feeling under the weather. Clear?"

"If we get symptoms—" Pansy began.

"Then you check in here, and we start you on an IV antibiotic course. But we don't even know that what you've been exposed to is dangerous, and even if it is, we certainly don't know that you came into contact with any significant amount, or contracted anything from it. Lots of don't-knows and ifs in there." He shrugged. "Just relax. Chances are you'll be fine."

He wasn't the most caring doctor Lucia had ever met, but she appreciated his clear-eyed, blunt approach. Even if he did look barely old enough to have graduated from high school, much less completed any kind of medical school.

His eyes met hers, and she was surprised to find that he wasn't nearly as young as he looked. Not inside, anyway.

"Good luck," he said, and held out his hand. She shook. He had a firm grip, soft, strong fingers. "Three days, back here, or I send the FBI to handcuff you and bring you in."

"We'll be back."

And that, it appeared, was that.

Ten minutes later, Pansy's cell phone rang. She unfolded it. "Hello?" Her face brightened and took on a little color. "Manny! Any news?" Pansy, Lucia was amused to note, was like watching the news with the sound off. "Oh. Okay."

Obviously, no results yet, but then she perked up again. "Yes! Yes, fine…"

When she hung up, Lucia said, "You're going over to his place."

Pansy paused in the act of putting her phone back in her purse, obviously surprised. "How did you know?"

"Remind me not to put you undercover, Pansy. And besides, I think I know Manny well enough to know that he's not going to allow you to go home alone. Since he's working, he'll want you there, where he can watch out for you."

Pansy blinked and smiled. "Kinda nice, isn't it? Having somebody care?"

"Yes." Lucia, on impulse, reached over and took her hand. "You may have saved my life, you know. I don't forget that kind of thing. Anything you need, Pansy, I'll deliver."

It wasn't an idle promise, and Pansy must have known it. She squeezed Lucia's fingers, and nodded.

"I'd better get moving," she said. "He's sending a car for me. Knowing Manny, it'll be a Bradley Fighting Vehicle, with a full squad of off-duty marines."

Lucia smiled a goodbye and let her walk away. Pansy looked small and fragile, but there was a core of inner steel in her that Jazz must have sensed the first time she'd met her. A fighter, that one. She'd been cool and calm when she'd spotted the problem, and not many people could have handled it with such grace.

"What about you?" McCarthy. He was standing next to her. Some people appeared ridiculous in scrubs, but he managed to carry more gravitas than the doctor who'd just walked away in his official lab coat. Light blue suited Ben, she thought.

"I guess I'll go home," she said. "I don't imagine I'll be able to sleep much."

He nodded and opened the plastic bag they'd given him for the contents of his pockets. All he had was a wallet she supposed was left over from before his incarceration, some keys, and the assorted motel keycards that Omar had procured. Rawlins had asked for his gun, and hadn't asked to see the permit. She'd have to see if she could borrow a gun from Omar for McCarthy.

Omar. She'd forgotten about him. She'd have to call and tell him to take a few days off—or better yet, see if he could trace the fake FedEx. Pity she hadn't opened the red envelope all the way. She dearly wanted to know what they'd had to say. Whoever *they* happened to be.

McCarthy fished the keys out of the bag in his hand and shook them lightly with a bemused expression.

"What?" she asked.

"Just thinking. Jazz put my car and apartment stuff into storage, but I guess I should pick up the car, at least. Most of these keys don't mean much anymore. Apartment's gone. Office—well, I don't think they were saving my desk in the squad room. Anyway, I think I'll pick up the car, then head for the motel." He still wasn't looking at her. "Unless you want to grab some dinner. You've got to be hungry by now."

"Starving, actually. We could eat, then I could give you a ride to your car." She smiled slowly. "Besides, I'm the only one who's actually armed, I believe. Unless you're hiding a gun somewhere I don't want to know about."

"I don't like to boast about my weapons." He dropped the keys back in the bag and followed her out.

Her car was downstairs, in nonemergency parking. They got in and she drove silently through the moderate nighttime traffic to Vine Street. Odd that she didn't feel a need to talk, and even odder that she didn't feel awkward with his silence. He was thinking, she sensed.

"Where are we eating?" he asked, as she slowed and turned into the parking garage.

"Best pizza in town," she replied. "Delivered. Sorry, but I can't stand being in these scrubs another moment. We can pick up your car after."

He didn't comment, just raised his eyebrows a little. She key-carded into the parking garage and found her spot, then led the way to the elevators. They let them in the lobby, which was vast, cool, and had two security guards on duty.

"Ms. Garza." The first one nodded. "Evening. Should I even ask about...?" He gestured at her clothes.

"Mr. Marsh, I'd rather you didn't," she said. "This is my friend Mr. McCarthy. Ben, they'll need your driver's license. Nothing personal. This is a high-security building."

"How high-security?" McCarthy asked, and handed over his license. Marsh scanned it in and handed it back.

"Can't talk about that," he said, and smiled. He was a huge man, intimidating when the situation called for it, but generally good-natured. Lucia liked him. She especially liked that he never let anybody he didn't know pass without ID. "Let's just say Ms. Garza here isn't the most high-profile resident we've got."

"Jagger and Clapton both keep apartments here," she said. "For when they come to town."

"You're kidding. To *Kansas City?*"

"Home of the blues." She shrugged. "You'd be surprised. This place has millionaires, CEOs, a few movie stars. I'm lucky they let a peon like me in the door."

"You're good to go, Mr. McCarthy," Marsh said. "Check in before you leave via intercom. Elevators won't work without a passkey or us releasing one for you."

McCarthy was looking at her as she slid her passkey into the slot in the apartment elevators and pushed the button for the sixth floor. "What?" she asked.

He shook his head. "You must be loaded, living in a place like this."

"Let's say I have resources." Not that she was particularly proud of how she'd come by them. The elevator rode smoothly up to six and dinged arrival, releasing them into a corridor with gleaming white walls, original artwork at regular intervals and deep plush carpeting.

"Jagger live next door?"

"He has his own floor," she said, and led Ben to the second door on the right. Two key locks. Once she'd ushered him in, she flipped on the lights and went to the control panel to shut off the intrusion alarms. The blinking lights went from red to a steady, soothing green.

"Damn," McCarthy was murmuring. "So I guess breakfast at Raphael's was just par for the course for you."

She glanced around, seeing it through his eyes. A sleek, modern kitchen in black and golden woods; a panoramic view past the dining table. A balcony out past the living room, overlooking the city. It was comfortable and classic, and it had virtually nothing of her personality in it.

"Looks like a really nice hotel," he said. "This how you live?"

"Pretty much," she said, and went to pick up the phone. She called the pizza place and ordered two large pies. McCarthy, it seemed, was a meat-lover. She wasn't much surprised. Hers remained, of course, vegetarian.

"Make yourself at home," she said, and picked up the TV remote from the low coffee table. She tossed it to him, and he fielded it without hesitation. "You said you missed TV. Have at it."

She walked past him and grabbed clothes from the closet before making her way to the bathroom to change. She heard the TV start up as she was pulling on a black knit top. Baseball, it sounded like. *Men,* she thought, and smiled. Her hair needed brushing. She took care of it and thought about applying makeup, but it seemed ridiculous at this point. She looked tired, but she'd come by it honestly, and no amount of concealer was going to help.

You realize, she told her reflection, *that you're thinking about makeup and appearances when you're about to eat pizza. With an employee, no less.*

Unsettling. She shook her head, tossed her sleek

black hair back over her shoulders and went out into the apartment.

McCarthy was on the couch, feet up, watching—yes, she'd been right—baseball.

"Beer?" she asked. He turned to look at her, and kept looking. "I assume beer and baseball still go together."

"Sorry," he said, and muted the sound on the TV. "It's been awhile."

Whether he meant baseball or something else was open to interpretation. He stood up and joined her in the kitchen as she opened the refrigerator and pulled out a cold bottle. Imported beer, the only kind she willingly drank. She popped the cap with an opener and handed it to him, opened a soft drink for herself, then clinked their bottles together. "To surviving another day," she said.

"Amen."

They tipped bottles and drank. McCarthy was still watching her, but his eyes closed when the taste of the beer hit his tongue. Sheer ecstasy, from the look on his face.

"Wow," he said, when he put the bottle down on the counter. "It really *has* been awhile. And obviously, you know beer."

"I try." She took down two plates. "You want to tell me anything?"

"Like?"

"Like your theory on why the evidence exonerating you showed up so conveniently when it did?"

He took another sip of beer. Stalling for time.

"Didn't seem very convenient to me," he said. "Considering I'd already had the crap beaten out of me."

"Maybe they decided you'd suffered enough."

"Let's just say that little things like compassion don't enter into the equation for the Cross Society. And I mean that literally, by the way."

She slid onto a bar stool and sipped from her bottle. She hadn't offered a glass; he hadn't seemed to mind. "I don't think I understand."

"What Simms does—you understand about him, right? That he's looking at alternate realities, not just telling the future?"

"Excuse me?"

McCarthy shook his head.

"Oh boy. You'll need a lot of beer, somebody smarter than me and some kind of consulting physicist." He shrugged. "Okay. There's this thing called string theory. Don't ask me how it works—I'm just a cop, okay? But the idea is that there are a whole bunch of realities all layered up against each other. Every decision everybody makes, there's a slightly different chain of events, right? Take six billion people times about a billion decisions—good, bad or indifferent—and you get how many potential realities we're dealing with here. The thing is, most of these decisions end up being meaningless, in the great scheme of things. They cancel each other out, and such. So instead of sixty fazillion realities, you get some manageable number, like a couple of million that simultaneously exist in the here and now."

Lucia listened, thinking hard. Mostly, she happened to be

thinking that she'd never really believed the unlikely story of the Cross Society, or Max Simms, though Jazz seemed to have come closer to buying it, and Jazz was hardly the credulous type. "So, Simms supposedly can use all this theory to predict the future."

"No, Simms is the real deal, he's some kind of savant. He doesn't need theory to do what he does—he just sees it. Like some psychic in the circus."

"Then why the physics explanation?"

"That's what where the Cross Society comes in. They made what he does scientific."

"Uh-huh. And Eidolon...?"

Ben flipped a hand in assent. "Started out the same way, but Eidolon took it further. Has to do with predictive math, or something. Both the Cross Society and Eidolon can track decisions and look at the different outcomes. Only problem is, once playing god gets to be a multiplayer game, it gets nasty. Eidolon actually came first, by the way. It got a ton of defense department money, and Simms actually worked with a staff of high-level physicists to develop a computer system that could do what he did. That was his mistake. He created himself right out of a job. Then he founded the Cross Society to do the same thing, once he realized Eidolon was going to manipulate events to their own advantage. Counter of a countermove."

"And when Eidolon wanted him gone..."

"The new CEO made sure that he was taken out of the picture. I figure Simms should have been killed, but he managed to work the decision tree enough that he only got convicted and sent to prison. You'd better believe that Eidolon's been working hard to keep him there, or better yet, make sure he dies behind bars."

"How do you know all this?"

"I was in early." McCarthy shrugged and turned his beer bottle in neat, precise circles. "Simms wanted people in the Cross Society who could carry out orders, not just sit around and talk theory. I was…" He fell silent for a few seconds, eyes hooded. "I was supposed to help them make things better. But I figured out pretty fast that wasn't how it worked. You start out fighting the good fight, but pretty soon you're just fighting for your life."

"And you didn't agree."

He took a drink, then another. "I didn't say that. I'm no saint, Lucia."

"If you agreed, then why did the Cross Society put you in prison?"

"I told you. I refused to carry out an order."

"To stand by and let Jazz get killed."

His shrug was so small it could have been interpreted as fidgeting. "Hey, even a total bastard's got limits."

"So what's changed? Why let the evidence come to light to get you out?"

"Why the hell do they do anything? Their spreadsheets or Simms or whatever told them I could do something for them."

She nodded. Silence fell, broken by the clink of their bottles on the black marble counter. It seemed eerily quiet, here above the city, in this hermetically sealed building.

The buzz of the intercom made both of them jump, though McCarthy tried to look nonchalant about it.

"Pizza," she said.

She kept the gun handy anyway.

The sound McCarthy made at the first bite of pizza was like a man in the throes of—well, ecstasy. "Oh, God," he murmured. "That's just…unbelievable. Sorry, but you've got no idea how many nights I thought about—"

"Pizza?" She kept her voice cool and amused. "I'd imagine there were other things to think about."

He chewed and swallowed. Gave a Cheshire cat smile. "Pizza's the one I'm willing to talk about."

"Careful, Mr. McCarthy. I'm not on the menu."

"No question about that. Shit, I can't even afford the pizza." He blinked, and before she could feel even the first impulse to take offense, said, "And I didn't mean that the way it sounded."

She had to laugh, because his expression was priceless. "Don't worry. My dignity is hardly that fragile."

"I meant—"

"I know what you meant. Enjoy the food."

He did, wordlessly, letting out involuntary sounds now and then that strongly reminded her of other things he might have missed, during his time in Ellsworth. Which made her skin prickle and made her pulse thud faster. *No. This is strictly dinner. Nothing more.*

She was good at self-deception. It was why she had always been so damn good at undercover work.

He kept on watching her, as he made his way through his second beer and last slice of pizza, stealing glances when he thought she wasn't looking. She felt them like feathery touches on her skin. Her glass was dry; she debated opening another soft drink, then decided to have a beer herself. She went to the refrigerator to pull one free.

"No," he said flatly, and reached past her to close his hand around hers. She resisted the urge to drive her elbow back into his gut, mainly because the warmth of him, leaning against her, undid all her reflexes. "You're on antibiotics. No beer."

"What are you, my doctor?"

"Depends," he said. He was still pressed against her, his hand hot around hers. "Do you need examining?" His voice had dropped to a low, dark-velvet whisper, warm against the back of her neck.

She needed a whole lot of things, and it shocked her, the depth of that need. How long had it been? Nearly a year, she realized, since that business in Dallas that had turned out such a mess. Not a good memory, though the sex…no, even the sex hadn't been worth that. McCarthy made her body come alive in ways she wasn't prepared to deal with— nerves hot and tingling, skin tight and sensitive to every touch, every breath he took.

She could say no to a lot of things, and a hell of a lot of men. It came to her as an inescapable fact that she simply couldn't say no to Ben McCarthy.

The beer bottle slipped back into its place in the door of the refrigerator, and his fingers moved over hers, warm where hers were cold and trembling. Then he traced the sensitive inner side of her arm, his fingertips drawing a line of heat to her elbow, then around. He brushed her hair back in one slow, feather-soft motion, and let out his breath in a sigh that moved, moist and possessive, over her skin, across her throat. She felt her knees going weak. Her pulse pounded torturously fast. *I can have this. I deserve this. Just this once. I know it's not smart. I don't care.*

Without any warning, he stepped back. Far back. Cold air crept along her skin, an arctic chill, and she felt the goose-flesh he'd given her for entirely different reasons tighten in response. She shut the fridge door and turned to look.

He was walking away, his back to her, beer in his hand. Walking to the windows, where he stood staring out at the city lights and swigging beer as if his life depended on it.

"Ben…"

He tipped the bottle up and sucked down the last of the foam, then set the empty down on a table. He picked up the plastic bag that held his personal items.

When his voice sounded, it was rough and abrupt. Hard-edged. "Do they call cabs, your guys downstairs?"

"I can drive you—"

"No."

She pressed her hands to the hard marble of the countertop and willed herself—*commanded* herself—back to some kind of professional demeanor. There was nothing she could do about the rate of her breathing, or the flush in her cheeks, or the dilation of her pupils. But she could ignore it. "Yes," she said. "Yes, they can call a cab for you."

"Set it up, would you? I need—" He swallowed convulsively and drew the back of his hand across his mouth. "I need to pick up my car. It's getting late. And even though this motel promises to keep the light on, I'd better…" He was at a loss for words. She could sense the turmoil in him. He made an effort to put some nonchalance back in his voice. "Besides, I probably have some television viewing to catch up on. Any suggestions?"

She briefly entertained a few suggestions, but they were anatomically impossible. "You seem to enjoy baseball."

"Yeah, love it. Baseball, Mom, apple pie, though come to think of it, I always preferred peach…." He was rattled, terribly off balance, and she imagined this was something of a new experience for him. She watched him visibly take control. "You've been really kind to a down-and-out ex-con. Thanks."

It hadn't been kindness. He knew that, and she wasn't willing to humiliate herself by pointing it out. "Any time," she said. Her lips felt numb and cold. "You'll watch your back?"

"Sure. Watch yours. And—" His eyes met hers, blue and limitless and blind with the same yearning she felt. "You take care of yourself. You heard the doc. Any fever…"

"Go," she said. She didn't know why, except that she knew he desperately needed her to order him out.

He nodded and left, shutting the door behind him. She walked to the intercom and pressed the button and told Marsh her friend was coming down, and would he please call a cab.

And then she went to the couch, turned on the television and sat numbly watching baseball—which she didn't even like—well into the night, thinking.

Chapter 7

Morning came ugly and early, with the soundtrack of a ringing phone. Lucia clawed her way out of twisted sheets and found the receiver as she swung her legs out of bed. "Yes?" she said. It came out more abrupt than she intended, but she wasn't a morning person, and nearly everyone who worked with her knew it. What few friends she had knew it extremely well.

"Jazz."

Lucia collapsed back against the pillows and threw her arm over her eyes. "Manny has a result."

"No, not yet, but I figured I'd better ask you what you wanted to do about today's appointments. We have clients coming in at ten, remember? Santos Engineering? The industrial espionage thing?" Jazz was making notes; Lucia could hear the scratch of pen on paper. She felt as if she had a hangover. Her head felt stuffy. *Don't be stupid. It could be anything. You could just be imagining things.* "Lucia?"

"I'm thinking," she said. "Any way we can postpone?"

"Considering the state of our accounts receivable? I'm thinking no. Look, why don't I take it? Let you rest?"

"I'm fine." She wasn't. Didn't feel fine, and that worried her, but she'd had a crappy night's sleep. She didn't have a fever, at least, and that was supposed to be the first sign. "I don't want you out of Manny's place for now. Eidolon—"

"In case you missed the memo, Eidolon came after *you,* unless that FedEx was addressed to 'Whichever Bimbo Opens It First.'"

"Who're you calling a bimbo, *chica?*"

"Who're you calling *chica?* Ah, hell, get up, would you? Have some coffee. Call me back."

Click. Jazz and her smooth social skills. Lucia groaned and considered rolling over in the cocoon of pillows, but she knew it wouldn't do any good.

Shower. She needed a hot, cleansing shower.

On her third cup of coffee, Lucia called Jazz back and rescheduled the Santos meeting for the client's offices, on the condition that Jazz stay strictly at home.

"You're joking," Jazz retorted. "You think I'm letting you roam around by yourself? *Somebody tried to poison you.* Don't you get it?"

"I get it," she said, and checked the headlines on the papers that had been left at her door. "But mail poisoning isn't exactly the world's most intimate crime. It's a leap to go from that to—"

"Excuse me, but these same people—"

"How do we know it's the same people?"

"*These same people* put a high-powered-rifle bullet through my office window and nearly killed me! That's pretty intimate, not to mention direct! Unless you're wearing Dolce & Gabbana's spring bulletproof line—"

"Oh, Jazz, I'm so proud. A year ago you would have thought Dolce & Gabbana made chocolate bars."

"Would you let me finish?"

"No. And I'll tell you why. I'm going to the meeting, and I'm taking Omar with me. You've met him. Is he enough of a bodyguard for you?"

Jazz made some halfhearted protests, but it was mainly from being left out, which she hated. But Lucia meant what she said: until Max Simms or the Cross Society sent word that Eidolon's attention had moved on, and Jazz was no longer a target, Jazz would stay safe in Manny's home. Bunker. Whatever it was.

"Jazz," Lucia said, just when she sensed her partner was about to put down the phone. "Listen—when Manny gets the results—"

"You're the first call," Jazz said. "FBI second. Pansy's still here, by the way, and feeling fine. You?"

Lucia swallowed another mouthful of coffee and willed the aches in her muscles to go away. "Fine," she said. "I feel fine."

Omar showed up downstairs at promptly 9:00 a.m., looking big and mysterious and sexy as hell in his black slacks, black shirt and designer sunglasses, his glossy black hair carelessly curling almost to his shoulders. "Boss," he said in greeting, and uncoiled from his lounging position at the guard station, where he'd been shooting the breeze with Messrs. Tarrant and Valencia, the day shift guards. He slid the glasses up to take a good look at her. "I leave you alone for a few hours, and you go and get yourself infected."

"Yes, Omar, you could have bravely thrown yourself on the FedEx package and prevented all of this." She moved past him to the parking garage elevators. "Cheer up. Maybe you can take a bullet for me today instead."

"Don't get my hopes up," he said.

Downstairs, his gleaming black SUV was parked next to her Lexus. Illegally. "I suppose we're taking your car," she said.

"You hired me for my vast array of skills," Omar said. "Of which guarding parking garages is only one."

"Shut up and get me there."

"Testy! Not enough coffee?"

There wasn't enough coffee in the world right now to banish the headache that was pounding in her temples. She dug two aspirins out of her purse and swallowed them with a mouthful of bottled water, taken from the built-in cooler between the seats. Omar's SUV had all the comforts of first class. She was reasonably sure that should she ask for a hot meal, he'd be able to provide it out of the contents of the secret compartments.

"Headache?" he asked.

"Not enough sleep. And yes, I have antibiotics, and they don't even know what it was in the envelope yet. I'm *fine*." Speaking of that, she dug the antibiotics out and swallowed the next dose. It tasted bitter. She followed it with plenty of water.

He kept silent, wisely. She closed her eyes as the truck weaved through morning traffic to Overland Park. The sun seemed too bright. She checked the air vents and turned the air conditioning up.

Omar refrained from comment.

The meeting was so dull and ordinary that she coasted through it on autopilot. She smiled at appropriate places and delivered the appropriate endorsements of the ability of the private investigative firm of Callender & Garza to find their security leak. Santos was a small company. The leak wouldn't turn out to be some hard-ass spy; more likely, he or she would be a disgruntled midlevel employee, dissatisfied with his or her prospects and pay.

"The truth is," she told Erin Santos, the firm's chief operating officer, "the target is probably so scared of being caught that he or she will confess immediately, if confronted. I'd suggest some blind interviews this week. Half an hour for each of your employees over the course of two or three days. We'll find your mole." An easy five thousand. Jazz would be pleased.

"Well…" The Santos team exchanged barely concealed eager looks. "Can you do it now? Get started, anyway?"

"Sure," she said. It wouldn't take much. Some guesses, some silence, Omar lounging purposefully in the corner. "Give me the most likely suspects first. We might as well work it as a triage."

In fact, it was faster than even Lucia had anticipated. She didn't get any signs on the first two, but the third person in the door had the body language of someone walking to the electric chair. She had a confession within minutes, and was soon giving her report and leaving the board to handle the guilty employee.

Erin Santos was true to her word, and there was indeed a check cut immediately. Lucia accepted it with grave courtesy and just the right touch of distaste. Money changing hands was never to be savored in public, with a client. No matter how happy one might be later at the bank.

In the SUV again, she called Jazz and gave her the report as Omar deposited the check at a drive-in teller.

Jazz was pleased. "What're you doing now?"

"Now," she replied, slipping on her sunglasses against the relentless morning glare, "I think I will go home and get some more sleep."

"Afraid not," Jazz said. Her tone was gruesomely cheerful. "How close are you to the office?"

"Twenty minutes."

"Then swing by, would you? Security has someone there who tried to get in to see us. He seems pretty upset at finding the office shut down. Name's Leonard Davis.... Hey, is Ben with you?"

"With me? Why would he be with me?"

Jazz's tone turned opaque. "Just asking. I haven't heard from him yet."

"No idea," Lucia said.

Omar was already heading in that direction when she hung up the phone.

She put her head back against the cushions and tried to nap.

* * *

There was a gangly young man seated in the lobby of the office building. He was bundled in a big gray sweatshirt and blue jeans, with a baseball cap pulled low. Lucia nodded at the two guards, who were looking tense and unhappy. One of them came to meet her.

"This Leonard Davis guy showed up about thirty minutes ago," he said. "Wanted to see somebody from your firm. I told him the company was shut down for renovations, but he didn't want to leave. Acting weird, I gotta tell you. You want I should call the cops?"

"No, let me talk to him first," Lucia said, and exchanged a glance with Omar. He moved off to the side, apparently lounging, but he had a clear line of fire if necessary. Lucia walked toward the man.

He didn't budge. Didn't even look up until the last moment of her approach. He had a regular face, squarely middle of the dial between handsome and homely. Medium brown hair. Dark eyes, narrow, with no particular impact to them.

"Mr. Davis," she said, and sank down into one of the leather guest chairs on the opposite side of the glass table. "You wanted to see someone from Callender & Garza?"

"Yeah, I did. I didn't think you guys were here—"

"We're temporarily officing elsewhere. What's so urgent?"

He took off the ball cap in an awkward gesture of gentility, and offered his hand. She shook it. "I'm real sorry to be trouble, but I really needed—look, it's my wife. I need to find her, and I was told you might be able to help me."

"Do you mind if I ask who sent you?"

"A Detective, ah, Brown? I have his card somewhere…." He patted his pockets and came up with a KCPD business card. Welton Brown. Lucia recognized the name—one of Jazz's contacts in the department. A detective with a solid reputation. "Anyway, I don't know where else to go. I mean, I've been looking, but nobody seems to have seen her."

"Slow down," Lucia said, and kept her body language friendly and open. "Tell me what happened, from the beginning."

He took a deep breath and put his baseball hat back on. His sweatshirt proclaimed him a fan of the Kansas City Chiefs. Nike cross-trainers on his feet. He looked athletic, and the watch on his wrist was a sturdy, waterproof sports model. No reason at all for her alarm bells to be clanging. He was nothing but vanilla, through and through.

He said, "It's my wife, Susannah. She, ah, she's missing. I mean, she didn't come home from work on Thursday. I went crazy looking for her."

"And you went to the police." Lucia held up Welton Brown's card.

Leonard Davis nodded. "Sure. The next morning, when I couldn't find her at any of the usual spots."

"And Detective Brown recommended you come to us?"

He didn't answer.

"Leonard," she said, and drew his eyes. "Tell me *exactly*

why the police don't think she was abducted. You know I can find out with one phone call if I have to."

He looked down at his cross-trainers. "She might have taken some clothes."

"Money? Did she take cash?"

His hands washed each other, slowly. "She used her ATM card twice that night. But these carjacking guys, they do that, right? They make you get money out of the ATM. That's what happened. They made her do it."

"Does she have a cell phone?"

"Yes. It's off."

"And her car? Has it been spotted at all?"

"No. What about a chop shop? Maybe they cut it up for parts." Lucia wondered if he was thinking about the same thing happening to his missing wife.

"It's possible," she said. "The police have this information on file, if you gave it to them. They'll keep it in the database, and if anything turns up, they'll reactivate the case. It isn't that they don't necessarily believe you, Mr. Davis, it's that there isn't much to go on in this particular instance. You understand, don't you? The police have to focus on crimes that have definitely occurred, not ones that might have happened. The facts you've laid out for me could involve a woman who's gone missing, or a woman who doesn't want to be found."

Davis fidgeted, fingers pulling at the seams of his blue jeans. There were fading bruises on his knuckles, and she focused on them for a second before flicking her attention back to his shadowed face.

"I believe she's missing," he said. "I believe somebody took her and made her get that money. I want you to help me find her."

She sat back, considering him, Welton Brown's card cool between her fingers. Omar was still lounging in the corner, looking as if he was paying no attention, but intent on every movement.

Something was bothering her, but she couldn't put her finger on it. As she thought it over, trying to run it down, her cell phone rang.

"Excuse me," she said, and stood up to walk to a far corner, her back to Davis. Omar would be watching. Not much risk involved.

"Yo." Jazz. "Leonard Davis has two complaints against him for spousal abuse. KCPD has been to his house plenty of times. Sounds like a lively place."

"Have you talked to your friend Detective Brown recently?"

"Welton? No. Why?"

"This guy's carrying his card."

"Probably filed a missing persons on his wife. Ten to one, he's buried her in the backyard. Thinks he's clever. Brown may be using us to keep him busy while he does a murder investigation. That would be his style."

"I don't appreciate having my time wasted."

"Think of it as becoming a cog in the great wheel of justice."

Lucia said something pithy in Spanish, which was a

waste, since Jazz hardly spoke a word. "So why would this guy engage with us, especially for money?"

"Makes him look honest when they dig his wife up from the melon patch."

Lucia turned slightly and glanced over her shoulder. Davis was leaning back now, straightening his baseball cap with his right hand.

And something clicked. Something she was sure Welton Brown must have noticed, as well.

"Keep digging," she told Jazz. "I don't mean in the melon patch."

"Funny."

She ended the call and walked back, slid into the seat and gave him a cool, professional smile.

"How'd you get the bruise on your hand, Mr. Davis?" she asked. He looked down and instinctively turned it palm upward, hiding the damage. "It looks like you got it about the time your wife dropped out of sight."

He didn't glance up at her. She saw the tension in him and felt a sudden shift in the room, as if gravity had subtly altered.

"I got into a fight," he answered.

"Let me put this to you as strongly as I can, Mr. Davis," Lucia said. She deliberately dropped her voice, slowed it, held his eyes with her own. "If you hurt your wife and she is in hiding, I will not track her down for you. Do you understand me?"

"I got into a fight at work. Look, it didn't have anything to do with Susannah, I'd never do anything to hurt her."

She could feel something weighing her down now, a conviction that was drawn from a thousand hints. The way his eyes cut away at the last second. The bruises. The too-direct stare during a denial. Tiny facial tics as he tried to fake sincerity.

She cut him off. "Our rates are a thousand dollars a day."

Davis sat back, mouth open, and then did that lightning-quick shift of his eyes again. "I see. So it's all about the money, right?"

"We work for a living, yes."

"If I give you the money, you'll find Susannah?"

Not, she noticed, save her. Not find out what happened to her. Just, simply, *find*.

She smiled thinly and stood up, settling her purse over her shoulder. "Not for any amount, Mr. Davis," she said. "Because I don't believe you. Either you've killed your wife or you'd badly like to finish what you started. Either way, we're not interested in helping you."

She expected him to grab, because—if she was right—that would be his automatic response. And he did. His hand shot out and closed on her arm. Squeezed—not with crushing force, because he was aware of Omar, who was straightening up behind her, and the security guards behind the desk. But with enough strength to send a hot jolt of agony up through her shoulder.

She didn't let it affect her cool, professional mask. "You'll want to take your hand off of me now, Mr. Davis," she said. "Before something unfortunate happens."

"I said I need your help!" He didn't sound helpless; he

sounded angry. She understood that anger could be a correct response, especially when a loved one was missing. But his anger was off-key. Narcissistic.

"Yes," she agreed, and pulled her arm free. "You did. Now I'd advise you to go look for an attorney."

Seen up close, those eyes were probably his greatest asset. The kind of little-boy eyes that lulled women into trusting, into believing his apologies, into letting down their guard.

His eyes lied better than the rest of him.

He stepped back. "You've got the wrong idea about me."

"Maybe so. And if that's the case, then I will be sincerely sorry. But I can't take the chance."

She nodded to Omar, and walked away to the security desk. The two guards looked attentive.

"Escort him out," she said. "He doesn't come back inside."

"Yes, ma'am."

In the elevator, Omar didn't say a word, but he was watching her with interest. She felt tired. Achy. Wanted to collapse back into her warm, soft bed and sleep for days.

"What?" she asked.

He shrugged as he pushed the button for the parking garage. "Kinda hard on the guy."

"He's had numerous abuse complaints."

"Doesn't mean she's not missing."

"It might mean that she's missing on purpose, and the last thing she needs is us bringing this guy to her doorstep."

"Sometimes I think you don't like people very much," he said.

"People, meaning men?"

Another shrug.

"I like men just fine," she said. "I just like them better when they're not lying their asses off to me."

Omar's dimples flashed as he smiled. "You don't get a lot of dates, huh?"

"Not second ones."

The door creaked open at the well-lit parking level, and Omar went out first, presenting an unmissable target should anyone be taking aim. He didn't even think about doing it. It was his job. She admired that, even while she couldn't quite understand the mentality behind it.

"Clear," he said, after scanning the area. She stepped out from behind him, and they walked quickly toward the SUV.

She had no warning, but suddenly she felt a powerful shove to the left, felt the world tilt, and landed hard on her side. She rolled instinctively, holding her head up to keep from hitting the concrete floor, and landed next to a fat gray pillar. She hadn't thought about drawing her gun, but it was out, both hands bracing it in textbook firing position.

"Easy," Omar was saying. He was still standing out in the open, having executed his first priority—moving her out of the line of fire. He was holding up both empty hands and trying to look as inoffensive as possible, which was odd behavior for any bodyguard, but Omar in particular. Lucia edged forward and peered around the barrier, hunting a target.

A woman was standing in front of him. Thin, fragile, with short dark hair and ivory-pale skin that showed off a lurid array of bruises. Half her face was swollen almost beyond recognition.

She had a gun trained on Omar.

"Easy," he said again, and held his hands higher when she flinched. "Nobody's here to hurt you."

"I need your help," she blurted. There were tears running from her eyes, streaking silver down her face. She slurred her words, thanks to a badly swollen lip. "Please."

It came to Lucia in a lightning flash of comprehension, and she slowly stood up, holstered her gun and stepped out from behind the pillar, hands raised.

"Susannah?" she asked. "Susannah Davis? You don't have to be afraid now. You're safe. We're not working for your husband. My name is Lucia Garza."

Chapter 8

Susannah stood very still, staring at Lucia, and then slowly lowered the gun. As if she'd used the last of her strength to hold it up, she collapsed to her knees.

Omar started to move forward, then stopped and looked back at Lucia. "Maybe you should—"

"I'll help her." She nodded, and moved in to slowly bend down and pull the gun from the woman's unresisting hand. Omar relaxed. Lucia handed the weapon to him and leaned down to take Susannah's weight on her shoulder. The woman was heavier than she looked. Solid muscle. She seemed out of it; Lucia took the opportunity to do a quick pat-down, but found no additional weapons.

"He might have tracked her here," Omar said. "Maybe wasn't looking to hire you at all, just got caught following her and decided to try to make the best of it."

"Very possible."

"Could be trying to get down here to the parking level."

"That'll take a while," Lucia said. "But let's not get cocky. Open up the truck, help me get her inside."

He moved. Together, they got Susannah into the SUV and belted her in. Omar fired up the engine and cruised up the ramp toward sunlight.

As they exited into the white-hot glare, Omar said, "Bend over, Mrs. Davis. Head down. If he's out here, I don't want him getting a look at you."

Susannah slowly, painfully hunched over. Lucia scanned the street through the tinted windows and paused on a green Ford Expedition parked a block away. The engine was idling, and she was almost sure the indistinct figure in the driver's seat was wearing a red baseball cap.

Son of a bitch.

They cruised by. Omar didn't even look toward the other truck, but Lucia was sure he'd noted it. Unless Davis changed vehicles, he wouldn't be able to follow undetected.

"Okay," Omar said, and reached over to help Susannah back to a sitting position. She rested her head against the upholstery, whimpering slightly. Omar's gaze met Lucia's in the rearview mirror. "Hey, boss lady. You know a friendly doctor?"

"As a matter of fact, I do," she said. "Turn right—"

"No doctors," Susannah croaked. "I'm fine. Nothing's broken."

"At least we can get you some painkillers—"

"I'm used to it," she said, and straightened up. Her slurred voice sounded stronger. "Thanks, but no. No doctors. I'll be okay."

"You could have a concussion."

"No doubt about it," Susannah said, with a grimace that might have been meant as a smile. "I was looking for you. Well, your firm, anyway. This detective, he said—"

"Welton Brown?"

"Yeah. I need protection. He said I should talk to you guys. I didn't want—I couldn't say anything about my husband. Not to the police."

Lucia exchanged another look with Omar, who turned left at the light, heading for the freeway. "Detective Brown also talked to your husband."

"Yes," she said, and let her head drop back against the upholstery again. "The story is that I was attacked by a mugger. That's what he told them. I had no choice. I had to agree."

"Because?" Lucia asked. Susannah painfully turned toward her.

"Because I already tried going to the police," she said. "All that happened was that when he got out, which took a grand total of less than thirty days for all three arrests, he took it out on me. I've moved. Hell, I moved here from New Mexico. Look what it got me. You don't know him. You don't know what he does for a living."

Tears shone hard silver in her eyes again, and she blinked them back.

"I need help," she said. "I need time to decide what to do. I have money. I can pay you."

"If you need to disappear, there are shelters—"

"He knows all about them. Believe me, he's an expert at this, and he's got people working for him. They'll find me. I have to use my ID and social security number to get a new job, a new apartment—he catches up. I need somebody who can get me a new life." Susannah's breath hitched unevenly, and she shifted, eyes shutting against some inner pain. "I know things. Things that can put him in prison forever. I just need—I need some time to think about it. Make plans. A few days. I wasn't lying—I have money. I'll pay you whatever you ask, just keep me safe and hidden for a while. *Please*."

Lucia stared straight ahead, thinking. She had contacts who could provide new ID, forged documents, clean social security numbers. Once Susannah's face healed, Lucia had people who could even provide her with some subtle plastic surgery to change the contours of her face. Make her plain or pretty, but different.

Those were contacts she hadn't used in years. A part of her life she'd hoped she'd never have to acknowledge again. But that life had made her what she was now, the way broken bones sometimes mended stronger.

"Maybe," she said. "First priority is to take you someplace safe, so you can rest. You look ready to collapse."

Lucia settled back in the seat, took out her phone and called Jazz.

Omar made the last two turns and slowed the SUV. It was a bleak industrial area, all solid blocks of buildings with grimed windows and blank concrete faces. He slowed to a crawl in the middle of the block. "There?"

It was a warehouse, just like the rest. Three stories, windows on the top floor and a blank front below with three roll-up doors, all rusted and apparently securely fastened.

"That's it."

"So how do we get in, exactly?"

"Pull up to the door."

He turned the SUV up the incline and to an idling stop at the bay door. Nothing happened.

"And?" he asked.

"Wait."

They waited. After three or four minutes of silence, the bay door began to move upward—not slow and creaking, as you would have guessed from the looks of it, but smooth and silent, and much faster than a typical garage door.

"Go. Manny won't keep it open long." And true to her word, the door began to crank back down when the SUV was halfway through. Omar swore and hit the gas, and even so the door barely missed the back bumper of the truck. "Park under the light."

There was a single working light on the ground level, illuminating a patch of bare concrete floor. Everything else was in inky darkness, except for the slight suggestion of a staircase over to the side. Omar pulled the truck up as instructed and put it in Park.

"Engine off," an amplified voice ordered, loudly enough to penetrate the closed windows of the SUV. Omar shot Lucia an amused, questioning look, and she nodded for him to follow instructions. She rolled down her window, and Omar did the same.

"Manny!" she called. "It's Lucia!"

"I can see that." He didn't sound pleased, not pleased at all. Manny Glickman, on his own ground, seemed a lot more commanding. "And before you even ask, the answer's no."

"Manny—"

"No. Sorry. Can't come inside."

Omar opened his door and stepped out, looking around. Lucia sighed and got out, too, walking around to join him. He didn't seem very impressed. "This is it?"

"No," she said. "Believe me, there's a lot more to it than this. Manny, can't we just come upstairs and talk about it?"

"Too many people."

"I can vouch for Omar—"

"No room at the inn, Lucia. Sorry, but that's how it is."

The last of that was delivered in person, an echoing voice from the bottom of the stairs. He shuffled out of the shadows and into the pool of light, looking different from the man who'd taken charge back at the office yesterday. He slumped, which spoiled what might have been an otherwise impressive entrance. Having Pansy in his life had been a good influence, but he was still phobic, still flinched at loud, unexpected noises, and he did *not* enjoy company. Having Lucia, Omar and a strange woman on his virtual doorstep wasn't waking any innate feelings of hospitality.

"Look," he said, "I like you, okay? I like you fine. You come alone, you're welcome. You call for help, I do what I can. But you're coming to my house right now without asking first, and look, you brought *people.* I need you to go."

"This woman's in trouble. Manny, you have the safest place in the city. Put her up for just a few days—"

"No!" he snapped, then looked away. "I'm sorry, but no. I'm not the friggin' Witness Protection Program, here. I do *consulting forensic work.* I took in Jazz 'cause she's family. Pansy…" He tried to come up with a phrase, and failed. "I'm not running a dorm. I'm out of room."

"You're kidding," Omar said, and looked at the size of the ground floor. "Upstairs has to be a couple hundred thousand square feet."

"No."

Lucia held up a hand—not to Manny, to Omar. "It's all right," she said. "Manny, it's your space, I completely understand and respect that. I was asking for a favor. You can choose not to give it. That's all right."

Manny flush faded from hot rose to a dull pink. "I can't. I can't have strangers here right now. Please, Lucia. I need you to go away."

His gaze kept moving from Lucia to Susannah in the SUV, irresistibly drawn, and then snapping back as if what he saw frightened him. It probably did. Manny had some bad, bad images in his head, and a trauma that had hardwired him against ever risking himself again. He didn't like criminal cases, avoided them at all costs, and he put his personal security ahead of most everything else. Including, sometimes, his friends.

Still, he seemed uncomfortable at Lucia's silence. "I don't

mean to be—look, I'm sorry. I know she needs help. But—Lucia, I *can't*." His green eyes held hers, willing her to understand. "I can't."

"I know," she said. "I'm sorry, Manny. That's all right. Can I go up to see Jazz?"

"No."

That, she didn't expect. "You're kidding. Manny? You know me!"

He shuffled uncomfortably. "Okay, come with me. But they *stay here*."

She sighed, and without even asking—or waiting for Manny to demand it—she pulled her gun out of its holster, made it safe and handed it to Omar. It disappeared into his leather jacket.

"I'm all yours," she said. "Omar, Susannah—wait here."

"And don't touch anything," Manny said. "I mean it. *Anything*."

Omar looked around at the utterly featureless space. "I'll try to hold back."

Manny led her through pools of harsh industrial light and velvety shadows to a steel door. This one had a keypad. He covered it with his hand and typed in a string of at least a dozen numbers, then opened the door for her. It made a hydraulic hiss. She stepped inside, he crowded in behind her, and they were in—what the hell was this?—a kind of secured room. Presuming somebody got past the security on the previous door, this room would stop them cold. It was about six feet square, and—she rapped the wall—seemed like solid steel, with some vents in the ceiling.

Manny pointed up. "I can drop knockout gas," he said. "In emergencies."

"You scare me sometimes."

"Yeah, that's what Jazz says, too. But I've never been robbed."

"I'll bet."

Manny edged past her to the other end of the room and slid aside a well-concealed metal panel. Inside was another keypad. This sequence was longer, and was probably— knowing Manny—completely different and randomly generated. She thought about Jazz, coming in and out of here, and knew her partner well enough to realize that, regardless of Manny's instructions, she would have had all of these pass codes written down somewhere. Probably on a sheet of paper labeled Secret Codes.

That made Lucia smile, thinking of Manny's probable reaction if he knew. He'd definitely move. Again.

"Where are we going?" she asked. The door opened, and on the other side was an openwork metal staircase. For a man who'd been buried alive, Manny seemed to have an affinity for small spaces—but, she realized, they were small spaces he controlled. It made a certain cockeyed sense.

"The office."

"Is Jazz there?"

"No."

Two flights of stairs, another key-coded door, and she was in another world. The office was a big, spacious place, all windows on one side, with thick, off-white carpeting. Modern art hung on the walls, and she could tell instantly that it wasn't lithography; those were originals. He seemed particularly partial to the cool logic and simplicity of Mondrian, but he was eclectic. She spotted a Kandinsky, then a Miro. The colors glowed in the soft natural light.

Gradually, she realized that there was furniture, as well— all pale, spare, unobtrusive. A desk with two chairs on either side. A huge expanse of pale oak cabinets.

"Wow." It was all she could manage. Why was Manny never what she expected? He looked as if he might live behind a sewer grate.

How in the *hell* did Manny Glickman, former government employee, have the cash to live like this? Consulting was profitable; it wasn't *that* profitable. Then again, she hoped nobody would ever force her to explain the funds in her bank accounts, or the penthouses in New York and Madrid. Even though she'd come by the money legitimately, if not perfectly honestly…

Manny seemed to relax as he walked to the desk. His shoulders straightened, his muscles loosened. By the time he eased himself into the suede chair behind the desk, he looked only a little worried.

"Sit," he said. His green eyes were level on her as she silently obeyed. "Do you have a fever?"

It wasn't what she expected. Again. "What…? No. No, of course I don't."

He stood up, took a set of keys out of his pocket and unlocked a desk drawer. She couldn't quite see what he'd palmed. He walked over and, with deceptive quickness, slapped his hand over her forehead. For a ludicrous instant she thought, *That's it, he's gone insane, he thinks he's a faith healer,* and then he took his hand away and stared at her forehead intently. She reached up and touched plastic.

"Thermometer," he said. "Disposable."

Oh. She put her hands in her lap and waited, wondering idly what the thing was saying. Manny's expression was unreadable.

He reached down and peeled it off and mutely turned it to show her. The red line had reached a marker that read 100.2 degrees.

"No?" he asked.

Her reflex was to snap back *I'm fine,* but that was stupid, and it was rooted in fear. She swallowed, closed her eyes for a few seconds and considered. She felt hot, but not really sick. Tired. Had a slight ache in the back of her throat.

"All right," she said calmly. "I have a fever. Some muscle aches. I could sleep for a week. But Manny, those aren't necessarily symptoms of anthrax. They're just as likely to be reactions to stress."

He nodded, dropped the thermometer in the trash and returned to the safety of his chair. He leaned back, still watching her.

"You need to rest," he said. "Let the antibiotics work. And go see your doctor, today."

"You have the results of the tests?"

"The culture's still cooking."

"If it's anthrax, what are my chances?"

"Excellent. You got on antibiotics right away. You just need to take care of yourself."

She took in a slow breath. "Does Pansy have a fever?"

He shook his head, and the tension gathering in her stomach lessened a little.

"No symptoms at all?"

"Nothing. I'm watching over her," he said, and went quiet again for a few seconds. "I want to talk to you about Ben McCarthy."

Of course. Manny knew Ben; in fact, he had more loyalty to Ben than anyone except Jazz. "Go ahead."

"You can't trust him."

She sat back, surprised. It clearly cost him to say that; his expression was deeply unhappy.

"Don't get me wrong," he added quickly. "Ben…Ben means a lot to me. I mean, he's— I wouldn't be here if it weren't for Ben. I wouldn't be anywhere. But—" She watched him struggle for words, with no impulse to help him along. "He manipulates people. Women."

She smiled slowly. "Manny, you've just described ninety-five percent of the men I've ever met, if you insert the words *tries to.*"

"No, I mean…" He ran his hand through his curling dark hair and left it looking just a bit mad-scientist. "I don't think he's telling us everything. There's something wrong here, Lucia. Jazz doesn't think so, but I do. You should watch out."

"It's all right if you just don't like him," Lucia said. "You don't have to, you know. You can owe him your life and still not like him."

Something flickered over Manny's face.

"I died," he said quietly, and curled his hands into loose

fists on the wooden top of his desk, as if he wanted to keep them from doing anything foolish. "Seemed like I died, anyway. I was down there in the dark, all that dirt on top of me, running out of air. Screaming until I couldn't scream anymore, with that tape running, the one of his last victim. He tied me up so I couldn't breathe much. So that every move I made pulled the rope tighter around my neck. I had a choice—I could lie there quietly and suffocate, or I could try to get loose and strangle."

"Oh, no, Manny," she whispered. She hadn't known.

"Over forty hours. You know what it's like to run out of air? You get a headache. It just gets worse until it kills you, until you can't breathe, until you're nothing but a gagging animal. And when I tried to struggle, the rope was like his hands, like his hands around my throat." He swallowed hard and wiped his forehead. "All my life I thought I was smart, but he showed me that when you're down in that hole, smart doesn't mean shit. You need someone else. Someone else. Anyone else."

"Manny—"

"Ben dug with his bare hands, you know. With his bare hands, while the other cop went to get shovels. I was dead. He gave me mouth-to-mouth to bring me back. I'm alive because he dug me up and made me live." Manny raised his eyes and fixed them on hers, fierce and angry. "Ben's the hand of God to me. You know how much it costs me to tell you not to trust him? You think I don't *like* him? How do you not like someone after that? I love him, and screw your smug attitude!"

He was angry. She'd never really seen him angry be-fore—scared, sure, but this was different. He stood up, and she did, too, feeling a little worried. But he stalked over to the door and jerked it open. Made a jerky after-you gesture, head bent. She went to the stairs and walked down them, aware of his bulk behind her. There were no code panels on this side of the barriers. Manny could always get out.

She opened the last door and stepped into the cool dim-ness of the parking garage, then turned around. Manny stood right behind her, one hand on the knob, watching her.

"I didn't mean to discount what he did for you," she said. "And if you think I should be careful, then I'll be careful. Thank you."

He nodded once and slammed the door. The code panel's red lights lit up.

No getting back inside.

She went to the SUV, where Omar lounged against the side, smoking, and Susannah waited in the passenger seat.

"Is he going to help?" Susannah asked anxiously.

Lucia climbed in the back when Omar opened the door for her. "No," she said.

Omar flicked a look at her as he started up the truck. She shook her head. She didn't know how to begin to tell him what had just happened, and she wasn't sure she should.

As the big steel door cranked up to let them exit to the street, another car pulled in to block the way from outside.

James Borden got out of the sedan.

He evidently realized it was too late to wave at Manny for admittance, and he sure as hell must have thought it was important, because instead of stopping like any sane person as that massive door rattled down, he dashed forward.

Three feet left. Two and a half...

Borden dived through the gap, elbow banging on the steel door, and came to his feet in a not-quite-clumsy roll. He didn't have the animal grace of, say, Jazz, but then again, he had a lot of arms and legs to work with.

"Manny!" he yelled. "You asshole!"

An intercom came on. "Next time call first." That seemed to be that, so far as Manny was concerned. He *really* wasn't feeling hospitable.

Borden brushed imaginary dust from his suit—he was nicely done up today; hopelessly off-the-rack, but he cleaned up well, considering. His hair had the unyielding, gravity-defying gel look that Jazz found so funny.

Lucia got out and walked toward him. "Looking for Jazz?" she asked. It was pretty much a given.

"No," he said. "I was looking for you."

And it hardly came as a surprise when he pulled a red envelope from inside his jacket. It was a little creased from his acrobatics.

"Let me guess," she said, and didn't move to take it. "You were told where I'd be."

The tips of his ears turned red. "Don't make this hard. I'm just a messenger."

"Just following orders?"

"Don't—hey, who's she?" Borden's eyes suddenly shifted to look over Lucia's shoulder. He was staring at the bruised and abused faced of Susannah, visible through the van's front window.

"Nobody you need to know, unless you're taking on pro bono criminal cases," she said. "Forgive me for being a little cautious, but the last one of those I got came with a toy prize."

"I talked to Laskins," Borden said, and came a step closer. Just a step, because Omar was watching him with that closed expression that meant trouble. "This one comes directly from the Society. Nobody's touched it but me and him. Do you want me to open it?"

She'd feel like an idiot. And a coward. She took the envelope, ripped it open and drew out the single sheet of paper inside.

It said, GET MS. CALLENDER. GO WITH MR. BORDEN. PARK IN THE LOT ON THE SOUTHWEST CORNER OF PARALLEL PARKWAY AND 10TH AT 5:16 P.M. TODAY. LOOK FOR A MAROON CHEVY VAN. WE TRUST YOU WILL KNOW WHAT TO DO.

"Hang on," Borden said, and handed her something else. It was a tiny flashlight, and when she tried it, the light emerged a cool, faint blue. "UV," he said. "Shine it on the paper."

When she did, a sprawling signature appeared. Milo Laskins.

"From now on," Borden stated, "everything we send you comes marked both on the envelope and on the paper inside. Deal?"

"Deal." She stowed the flashlight in the zip case in her

purse, which included keys to her house and car, secondary ID and a thousand dollars in cash. The bare necessities of a life that might require running at a moment's notice. "Do you know what it says?"

"No."

She handed it over. Borden read it, rubbed his forehead as if he wanted to scrub his frontal lobe, and handed it back. "Fine," he said. "Why me?"

"I think only your boss can answer that one." She turned away from him, toward a corner where she knew a camera was watching, and raised her voice. "Manny! I need to talk to Jazz!" She held up the paper.

After ten seconds of silence, the steel door in the shadows clicked and sighed open.

"Just you." Manny's voice rang over the concrete. Then, after a delay: "And, uh, Borden."

Borden grinned. "Hey, Jazz."

Jazz's magnified voice said, "Hey, Counselor. Get your fine ass up here."

Lucia looked over at Omar, who shrugged and got back into the SUV. "I have DVD built in," he said, and looked at Susannah, who had leaned back with her eyes closed. "You like Russell Crowe?"

"I just want to sleep."

"Concussion," Omar said. "No sleeping. Or I take you straight to the hospital."

Susannah opened one eye. The other was swollen to a slit. "You got *Gladiator?*"

"A woman of taste." Omar gestured for Lucia to go.

She shut the door, and heard the *chunk* of locks as he secured it into a minitank.

Then she followed Borden back upstairs.

This time Manny guided them by voice, releasing locks remotely. They entered on a different floor, into living quarters. Pansy was lying on the luxurious suede sofa in the middle of the loft, watching a big-screen plasma television. She had a DVD on as well, and Lucia experienced a moment of envy. Pansy looked rosy, clean and relaxed, and was wearing a fluffy white robe. *If only I could do the same...*

Pansy scrambled to her feet and brushed her dark bangs out of her eyes when Borden and Lucia passed, as if they'd caught her doing something illegal or immoral...like resting. Lucia couldn't hold back a smile. "As you were, soldier," she said. "Believe me, if I could, I'd pull up a couch next to you, robe and all. And we'd share a gallon of ice cream."

"You feeling all right?" Pansy asked anxiously.

"I'm fine. Manny says you're well...?"

"No symptoms." Pansy's pageboy hairdo bobbed vigorously when she nodded. "Um—shouldn't *you* be resting?"

"I will be," she said, "as soon as we take care of some things."

"Uh-huh." Pansy didn't sound convinced. "What can I do?"

"You," Manny said, coming around a low cubicle wall that Lucia assumed separated off the surveillance equipment, "can sit down and relax. Right, Lucia?"

"Right." She threw them both a quick smile. "This won't

take long." She knew Jazz was going to say, in typical fash-ion, "Screw it," and toss the message in the shredder.

Only, of course, Jazz surprised her. First, she was dressed, and well dressed—no badly fitting jeans and floppy sweat-shirts today. She'd chosen another pantsuit, this one in dark red, and a tight-fitting white knit shirt. Cute. The shoes were still more or less a disaster; Jazz was never going to give up her flats when there was any chance of having to pursue a bad guy. Then again, she had enough height to pull it off.

"Going somewhere?" Borden asked, and crossed to kiss her. It was an open, intimate kiss, and brought instant bright color to Jazz's cheeks. "Or just dressing up for Manny? Should I be jealous?"

"Shut the hell up."

Manny's living space held a series of temporary parti-tions in the open warehouse—some low translucent walls, some higher and more private. Lucia let her eyes roam over the entire floor, hunting for something she'd never noticed before—ah, there it was, a door set flush in the wall, with one of those red-lit key code panels. There was another door to his office, from this floor. She'd been wondering. But it made sense, really; Manny would want multiple ac-cess points, all under his control.

Despite the almost Japanese simplicity of the place, Manny's build-outs, where they existed, were luxurious. The kitchen where Jazz sat could have been lifted from a model home, with wood cabinets and glossy appliances, double steel sinks, and a spacious bar area with high-backed stools.

Jazz was at the bar, Borden close beside her. Lucia hopped

up on a stool next to her. "Are we finished with the love talk?" she asked. "If so, there's work to be done."

Jazz rolled her eyes and gestured for the red letter, which Borden handed to her. She read it quickly. "We sure it's genuine?"

"He says so." Lucia demonstrated the new UV toy.

"Who's downstairs?" Jazz tucked a stray lock of blond hair behind her ear, and read the note again. "In the truck?"

"Omar and a new client."

"The wife."

"Yes."

"No sign of the husband?"

"Omar lost him."

Jazz glanced up at Manny. "Better have. You wouldn't believe how he gets if he thinks—"

"Omar lost him," Lucia said firmly. "I'm going to find a place to stash her, and put Omar on bodyguard duty until we can get her in touch with the FBI. She claims she's got incriminating information about her husband, but she doesn't want to deal with the local cops. Not even Welton Brown could convince her. The way she talks, it's probably organized crime. I expect Agent Rawlins will do us another favor, so long as it also looks good on his résumé."

Jazz snorted. "That's Rawlins, all over. Okay, so this thing. Another typical piece of Cross Society bullshit. Go here, wait here, blah blah. *You'll know what to do?* What the hell does that mean?"

"I hope it doesn't involve shooting someone. Again."

"Pros and cons," Jazz said, and tapped the black marble

counter with blunt fingernails. "Pro, we make a quick five grand for doing whatever this is, and more than likely, it doesn't even involve us lifting a finger. Most of these don't, right? We just change events by being there on time. We force other people to make different choices. Like a couple of boulders dumped into a stream."

Lucia blinked. "You understand this better than I do."

"Yeah, I'm frickin' deep that way. Any other pros you can think of? Besides money?"

"It's possible that what we do could help someone. Maybe save a life."

"Or not. I got over the whole idea that we're working for the good guys when they sent me to wait outside while a woman got murdered, just so I could write down an apartment number and testify about it later."

Lucia shrugged. "I said it's possible."

"I'll put that one in the 'maybe' column. Okay, cons. I don't trust these jerks anymore."

Borden cleared his throat. "Standing right here, Jazz."

She reached up without looking and put her hand on the lapel of his coat. Her fingers curled, touching his shirt beneath, unconsciously seeking skin. "Not you," she said. "And we talked about that."

That must have been an interesting conversation, to say the least.

"There's something else," Lucia said. "Neither of us wants guilt on our head when people die because we didn't act."

"That's exactly what they want us to think—that it's somehow our fault. But it isn't, L. And it isn't our responsibility, either. We're not superheroes. Well, I'm not, anyway. I don't know what the hell you do in your spare time. Me, I bowl. I don't want to save the world. I just want to work my cases and save my friends and family and people who come to me for help."

Jazz paused and looked down. A cat was prowling around the legs of her bar stool, weaving in and out, purring. Mooch, Lucia recalled. Jazz's cat. Evidently, Manny didn't run a no-pets dorm. Jazz leaned down and dragged her fingers down Mooch's silky-smooth back; he arched into her touch, purring harder, and flicked his high-held tail as he walked away.

"He seems to like it here," Lucia said.

"He's a cat. What does he know?" But Jazz was smiling. "Sorry. Guess I mountaineered up to the soapbox again." Lucia hadn't been confused. She understood very well that this was Jazz venting her frustrations, not Jazz explaining a decision.

"I understand perfectly what you're feeling," Lucia said. "But our choice at the moment is simple. We have a red envelope, and it's from the Cross Society. What do you want to do?"

Jazz sighed. "Let me get my gun."

She slid off the bar stool and walked to another temporary structure, this one an actual room with four walls and a ceiling, about fifteen feet away across the concrete floor. Her bedroom. Borden followed her. She looked back at him as she opened the door. "You going to help me get my gun?" she asked.

Borden said, "No, I'm going to help you put on your body armor."

"Oh. Okay."

The door shut.

Lucia poured herself a cup of coffee, smiled and waited.

Chapter 9

In the end, they agreed that Jazz and Borden would take his car and head to the location; there were still two hours until the time listed on the Cross Society note, and that was plenty for Lucia to get Susannah Davis settled someplace safe. Someplace not on Manny's property; he again made that clear, in case Lucia had missed any of the first volley of refusals.

The simplest way to hide Susannah was to do so in plain sight. Lucia made use of Omar's credit cards to book a two-room suite at the Raphael Hotel for a week, with the private, if misleading, understanding that the booking was for a movie star recovering from plastic surgery. The star's personal assistant, Mr. Smith, would handle all room service and cleaning requests. No one would be allowed to enter the suite.

The concierge took on a hushed, serious air when he was

given the news, and opened a secured entrance on the side of the hotel. Susannah—swathed in a silk scarf and huge sunglasses from a minimart, and one of Omar's jackets—was escorted inside quickly and silently.

Lucia waited in the SUV. Her cell phone, which doubled as a walkie-talkie, finally bleeped, and Omar's voice said, "We're in. Nice room, by the way. And complimentary champagne. I presume I'm being reimbursed for this."

She hoped that Susannah was good on her promise to pay. "Yes, of course. Keep her away from the windows."

"You want me to call a doctor friend to come take a look at her?"

"Be careful about it if you do. You good to go?"

"Let's see—guns, bullets, Kevlar, fruit basket. We're all set."

"Watch your back. I don't like her husband, and I barely met the guy. I'll set up an interview with the FBI for tomorrow. Maybe we can get this over with quickly and make it their problem instead of ours."

One challenge down. She swallowed a sip of water, felt it burn at the back of her throat, and remembered what Manny had said about her fever. She checked her watch. Still about an hour and a half to go. Might as well get checked out while she could, before…before whatever might happen.

She pulled the SUV into traffic and headed for the hospital. She asked for Dr. Kirkland, and was immediately bumped to the top of the waiting list, which told her something about how worried they were. She ended up exactly where she'd been a few hours before, in a stark E.R. examining room, wearing a flimsy cotton gown, getting stuck with needles. The fever, Kirkland said, was a worry, but they were still waiting for the cultures to be completed, and she was already on doxycycline to combat any infection.

"Rest," he told her. "You understand that's what will kill this thing, if it is a thing, right?"

"Yes." She did understand. And just as soon as she took care of whatever waited at the corner of Parallel and Tenth Street, she'd comply.

Lucia pulled into the parking lot at the corner of Parallel and Tenth with fifteen minutes to spare, and saw Jazz and Borden parked in the shadow of a big industrial building. Backed into a space. Watching as much of the street as possible.

Lucia paid the parking attendant, walked over and slid into the back seat of Borden's rental car. It was clean, except for his briefcase and a well-thumbed Grisham novel. "So," she said, and slid on her sunglasses to cut the afternoon glare. "You kids been behaving yourselves?"

"Not especially," Borden said. "This is what you guys do all day? It's boring."

"I'm sure it lacks the pulse-pounding excitement of legal briefs," Lucia said solemnly. "This is what we do all day. Sit in parking lots and wait for a crime to happen, so that we can investigate it. Oddly, our business model doesn't seem to be working out so well."

The clock on his dashboard said 5:08 p.m. Jazz handed her a sealed bottle of water, ice-cold; Lucia uncapped it and took a deep drink. She was terribly thirsty today. Fever, she supposed. The naproxen had taken care of the muscle aches, but the fever seemed persistent. She checked the time and downed another horse pill.

"Did you get her settled in?" Jazz asked.

"Yes, she's at the Raphael. Omar's on watch. I'll contact Rawlins later and set up a meeting for tomorrow. With any luck, we can get paid and get some gratitude from the local field office."

"Nice." Jazz stretched.

"Don't we look suspicious, the three of us just sitting here in the car?" Borden asked.

"We'd look a lot more suspicious if we were all three making out in the car," Jazz said. "What?" she added, when Borden turned and gave her a wide-eyed look.

"You have no idea what kind of happy place you just took me to."

"Shut *up*."

It was 5:11 p.m.

"Actually," Lucia said absently, "you'd be amazed at what you can get away with doing in a car in the middle of the day. People just don't look. Even when they're parking next to you."

Borden turned to stare at her. Jazz was too much of a professional to do so, but Lucia could feel her grin.

"I'd tell you all about it," she said, "but then I'd have to kill you. National security."

"God, I love my job," he said, and turned back to face the street.

Lucia, at the moment, didn't. She didn't like the fact that

there were so many low rooftops offering firing positions. She didn't like the constant flow of traffic on the street in front of them. Work had just let out, and the lot was full of people on their way home.

Not an optimal situation. She could feel Jazz's tension, and knew she read the situation the same.

Five fifteen.

"Heads up," Jazz muttered.

Five sixteen.

Nothing.

"Come on, come on…" Jazz was chanting it under her breath, probably subconsciously. Lucia kept silent, but she was aware of her increased heart rate, of the sweat trickling down her neck and between her shoulder blades. For all of their banter, this was serious business, and they both knew it. "What the hell are we looking for? Come on, give us something…."

And then, Borden spotted it. "Um, maybe I'm wrong, but isn't that guy getting a shotgun out of his trunk?"

The one in question was a small, thin man dressed in a white short-sleeved shirt, khaki pants, loafers. Business casual. Cell phone clipped to his belt. Thinning brown hair. Gold-rimmed glasses.

A Winchester Model 1300 Black Shadow: Lucia's mind automatically cataloged it. Five shells, if he had one in the chamber, and she had to assume he did. He was getting it out of the trunk casually, as if he were taking out his lunch bag.

"Go," she said, and tapped Jazz on the shoulder. "Take the back."

"Front."

"*Back,* Jazz."

Before she could argue about it, Lucia slipped out and walked briskly forward in long strides, and made a sharp turn to bring her parallel with Mr. Shotgun.

He reached into the trunk and took out what looked like a heavy gym bag, black. From the rattle, she guessed it was filled with ammunition.

She swallowed hard and turned toward him. Her gun was out and held unobtrusively next to her side, in line with the seam of her pants. Safety off.

He looked up as he slammed the trunk lid. For a split second she saw his eyes, and they didn't match anything else about his perfectly ordinary exterior. Those eyes were full of *nothing.* Dark holes, gravity wells that consumed everything around him. The darkness inside this man wanted to kill.

Jazz was behind him.

"Hi," Lucia said. "Going somewhere?"

He started to bring up the shotgun, and for a split second she thought, *God, no, he's really going to make it.* But then Jazz kicked the bend of his legs from behind, he pitched forward on the asphalt, his mouth opening in shock, and dropped the weapon. It skidded to a stop at Lucia's feet. She put a foot on top of it as Jazz jumped on the man's back, pressed a knee into his spine and twisted his arms behind his back to snap handcuffs on.

It took five seconds. Five seconds of precise, well-coordinated action. Jazz looked up, and her blue eyes were blazing, her face glowing with excitement.

All that changed in one split second.

Lucia didn't hear the shot, only felt the hot burn along her arm, the kinetic force rocking her to the side. She saw the spark of a bullet hitting the metal grille of a car fifteen feet beyond.

And then Jazz was moving, moving *fast,* and Lucia's body was following suit while her mind was still processing data. She hit the pavement and rolled into the thin cover of another car. *Angles*…the bullet had come right past her, hit the grille of the car at a flat angle. Someone on the ground.

A second shooter.

All that information passed through her mind in a little under a second as she slid beneath the car and twisted to get her gun out in front. With both hands around the grip, she scanned the street. A few people were starting to react to the single shot, but most had probably assumed it was a backfire, somebody dropping something….

A pair of feet started walking toward the man lying hand-cuffed on the asphalt. There was something about the body language, which was way too deliberate…predatory. He didn't seem to be in any hurry.

Lucia smelled blood. It hit her in a strange wave, that slightly acrid smell. Had somebody been hit? Jazz? No, Jazz had been well wide of the path of the bullet….

Damn. There was blood dripping steadily from Lucia's right arm, and a hot sensation starting to tingle along her biceps. It wasn't that bad, certainly not an arterial hit. The fact that she could feel it so soon after the strike meant it probably wasn't anything more than a graze, and the associated shock was minor.

She had no doubt that the man prowling between the cars, moving so purposefully, was the second shooter. *What the hell was he doing?* She didn't dare move to try to get a better look. Either he knew where she was, in which case she'd see him bend down to take the shot, or he didn't, and she'd rather keep it that way. He stopped circling and advanced to the handcuffed man, who turned over on his side, panting, staring up....

And his head jerked as the bullet smashed through his forehead and exited behind, into the asphalt, with a good portion of his brain, and most certainly his life.

And then the shooter's knees bent smoothly, she saw his body tilt sideways, and he was looking right at her, his finger tightening on the trigger....

She fired, but she knew even as she did so, even as her weakened right arm trembled and threw the shot wide, that she'd missed, and she was a dead woman.

Someone hit his blind side, coming over the hood of a car, and she could have been forgiven for naturally assuming that it was Jazz. Because it would be Jazz, wouldn't it? Only the legs were too long, the body too angular, and in the second heartbeat she realized it was Borden, unarmed, who'd jumped the shooter.

Borden wasn't a fighter. *Oh, Christ, no...*

She could almost sense Jazz moving. Lucia shoved with her toes and slid out from under cover, rolled on her side, and saw the shooter throwing Borden to the ground, turning to aim his gun at him at point-blank range—

And Jazz fired. Two fast shots to the chest, dead center. Blood misted the air for a second longer than it took him to collapse to his knees, and Lucia squirmed out the rest of the way and kicked his handgun aside as he fell.

Borden was silent, panting. He was lying on the ground on his back, looking stunned and pale, and there was blood spattered in small dots on his skin and shirt. She silently offered him a hand—her left—and pulled him up to his feet.

This time, nobody had mistaken the gunfire for backfires; people were running, screaming and dialing 911. But where Lucia and Jazz and Borden were standing, staring down at the bodies of two completely nondescript gunmen, without a clue in the world as to what they'd been doing *here, now,* it seemed eerily silent.

Jazz moved to Borden's side and embraced him, hard and fast, her face pale and her breath racing. He couldn't seem to take his eyes from the dead man at his feet. Eventually, she let go, stepped back and tried for a bitter smile. "This," she said, "is a cluster f—"

"Don't say it," Lucia interrupted wearily.

"Well, it is."

Lucia sighed and holstered her gun, or tried to; her right arm didn't seem willing to cooperate at the moment. Jazz looked up and spotted the blood, and her face blanched. "Oh Christ, L., you're hit."

"Grazed," she said. "Not even bleeding much. Don't worry about it." Sirens in the distance. They were going to have considerable explaining to do. "Maybe we should work on a system by which the Cross Society tells us a few more details," she said. She felt unnaturally calm right now, but knew it would pass. "What do you think?"

Borden looked sick. Sick and scared and anxious, and he gazed from one of them to the other with so much emotion that it seemed to make up for the lack of it in the two of them.

"I didn't know," he said. "I didn't know. They didn't…"

"Tell you?" Jazz finished dryly. "No, really? Wake up, James, they don't tell anybody anything. Not even you."

Lucia took the gun from her right hand and awkwardly holstered it. "Let's get our stories straight."

"You think anyone's going to believe us?"

"Well, at least we have a lawyer present."

Somewhat surprisingly, nobody in the police department seemed inclined to blame them for the shootout. Then again, Lucia noted, Detective Ken Stewart was nowhere to be seen, either. She nursed her soft drink carefully, after downing another aspirin to bring down her again-spiking fever, and wondered what Dr. Kirkland would think of her rest schedule. He wouldn't approve, she imagined.

She, Jazz and Borden were alone in a more upscale interrogation room…one not designed to resemble those on television. This room came equipped with a relatively comfortable sofa in dull green, a television set silently playing CNN, a water cooler, and reinforced safety glass windows and doors. There'd be surveillance, but it would be subtle.

Paramedics had touched up her arm; the passing bullet had ripped a furrow through about a quarter inch of flesh and a bit of muscle. Now that the adrenaline had left, taking its soothing blanket away, Lucia felt cold and exhausted, and she wanted, badly, to sleep.

Jazz poked Borden in the ribs. They were sitting on the couch, but she got his attention and they both moved. Borden wandered over to get a cup of water. Jazz gazed down at Lucia. "Come here and lie down," she said. Lucia was sitting upright in one of the wooden chairs. "On the couch, L. Now."

"I'm—"

"Swear to God, if you say you're fine one more time, I'm going to beat you with a copy of *Martyrdom for Dummies.*"

Lucia mutely went over and sat on the couch, glared at Jazz for a second and then let herself go horizontal with a shameful rush of relief. Borden pulled up another chair, and he and Jazz sat; Borden worked on a palmtop computer and Jazz steadfastly stared at the television screen, watching the news scroll.

Lucia was almost asleep when Jazz announced, "Potential mass murder in Kansas City foiled by private citizens, police say."

"What?"

"It's on CNN." Jazz looked around for a remote control, didn't see one, and got up to change the channel. It didn't change. Only one station. "Great. Sons of bitches have it locked down."

"That's so we don't have people surfing the porn channels," said a new voice. "The cops, I mean. We did that after you left the department, Jazz. Hey, I brought in a friend—that all right?"

Lucia opened her eyes and saw that a big, gray-haired plainclothes detective had entered the room. Ben McCarthy was right behind him. McCarthy crossed the room, trailed his fingers over Jazz's shoulder and exchanged a quick look with her, and then crouched down next to the couch as Lucia struggled to sit up. "No," he murmured, and those fingers moved lightly over the thick bandages wrapping her arm, then up to skim over her hair. "Stay down, okay? Nothing to get up for right now."

"Lew," Jazz said, and stood to shake his hand. "Good to see you, sir."

"How you been, Jazz?"

"Good, sir. Real good." Jazz looked like a bashful school-girl meeting the principal. "Lieutenant Prince, this is Lucia Garza, my partner. We own—"

"I know all about your new business," he said. "Ben's been keeping me up to date. You saw the bit on CNN—it's playing on the local channels, too. Those men you took down, they left notes. They were on their way to the building across the street to take out their coworkers when you stopped them. Apparently, they figured it would be easier around quitting time—lots of confusion with people coming and going. Their firm works until six." He gave Lucia a long look, then Jazz. "We're saying you two were there investigating a separate matter. Now, understand, with you mixed up in a couple of other events the last few months, some people have got their noses in the air. So you need to go low-profile awhile, got it?"

"Yes, sir."

"Detectives took your statements?"

"Yes, sir."

"Confiscated your weapons?"

"Just the one used in the shooting," Jazz said. "I've got another one. Registered."

He nodded. "Good girl. You're free to go. I'd avoid the media if I were you. They're chumming the waters. It's bound to get worse. Your offices are shut down?"

"Yes."

"Hope you've both got unlisted numbers. You're free to leave, all of you. Take the back way out of here, and if you want my advice, consider a few days off. We have any questions, we know where to find you."

McCarthy hadn't moved. He was still crouched next to Lucia, one hand resting lightly on the arm of the sofa. He wasn't watching her, but she could somehow feel his attention focused her way. "Thanks, Lieutenant," he said.

The older man nodded briskly. "It's Captain now, actually. Keep your ass out of the wringer, Ben. Plenty of people gunning for you out there. Ken Stewart's one of them."

"I know, Captain."

"Then all of you, get the hell out of my house. I have to go give a statement on the front steps, that should give you time to go out the back."

He turned and walked away, a big man, physically imposing, with a heavily jowled face and lugubrious eyes.

The kind of old-school cop who showed up all too rarely these days.

Lucia let Ben help steady her. The world dipped and swirled a little.

"Let me take you home," he said.

She smiled faintly. "I was hoping you'd ask, actually."

No media waited at McCarthy's car, or lurked under the bumpers of Borden's rental vehicle. Apparently, they were all out front, listening to Captain Prince give his statement. Ben guided Lucia to the passenger side of his car before she had time to contemplate what she was getting into.

Either the car or the situation.

When he entered the driver's side and slammed the door, she turned her head toward him and said, "You drive a Thunderbird?"

"Yeah, why?" He started it up, and the engine sounded remarkably smooth for something that had been sitting in storage for a couple of years.

"It's just...such a cop car."

"And I'm such a cop."

There was something to be said for that, she supposed, but she'd have guessed that he'd drive something more up-scale. Imported. A BMW, a Lexus, even a Volvo. A boxy Thunderbird well past its prime style era wasn't quite what she'd expected.

It was, however, a smooth ride, and she found herself leaning against the window, eyes shut. Fading. McCarthy's warm hand touched her cheek, and she roused enough to say, "I'm okay."

"Yeah, sure you are. Did you hear from Manny yet?"

"No."

He flipped open his cell phone—how had he gotten one so quickly? Or was it one of those disposable kinds?—and dialed. "Manny," he said, as he took the turn onto her street. She blinked and looked up at the streetlights. Everything seemed surreal in the harsh light. "Pick up, man, it's Ben."

After a few seconds, he glanced at her, shook his head and hung up. "He's there, he's just focused on something else. With you and Jazz gone, hey, maybe he and Pansy—"

"Let's leave that thought right there, shall we?" She closed her eyes again, then opened them as he approached the parking garage. "You need a key card." She dug in her purse and found it. Ben fed it into the slot and the metal gate rolled up to allow the big T-bird entry.

The parking elevators delivered them to the lobby. The lobby procedures seemed endless, from the checking of Ben's ID to the walk back to the upstairs banks of doors. Lucia's knees were ready to fold. She refused to let him see it.

They rode the elevator in silence, watching numbers light up, and as the fourth one took on a frosted white glow, McCarthy turned toward her, backed her up against the wall of the elevator and kissed her.

She was so surprised that for a second she didn't react, too overwhelmed by the sudden heat against her skin. Stunned by the damp, urgent pressure of his soft lips sliding on hers.

And then there was a red-hot flash of lightning through her body, a surge of something so primal that she couldn't name it, didn't think it *had* a name, and she made a sound that wasn't a protest and wasn't agreement and wasn't in the least part of the controlled, cultured exterior she'd created for herself...

...and before she could reach up and grab him, McCarthy was gone. He'd backed off, all the way across the elevator, hands behind him like a guilty schoolboy. Looking shocked.

She didn't say anything. Her lips parted, damp and tingling; her heart pounded deep and fast, like a Taiko drum. He hadn't disarranged her clothes, but they *felt* undone— odd, too tight and too warm.

McCarthy didn't say anything either. He looked like a man on the thin edge of control.

The elevator announced arrival, and she felt the upward movement glide to a graceful halt. The doors rumbled open.

Neither of them moved.

Are you coming? seemed like a double-edged entendre, at best. She took in a deep breath, saw him look at the swell of her breasts as she did, and said, "You should probably go."

He swallowed. She found herself wondering what the skin of his throat tasted like, what sound he would make if she scraped her teeth and tongue lightly over that bobbing Adam's apple. "You're sure?" he asked. His voice was rough-edged and deep, like uncut velvet.

"Yes."

She didn't dare invite him to the apartment. God only knew what would happen if he walked in the door just now.

It's the fever. I'm ill. I'm injured. This wouldn't happen if I weren't already impaired.

Maybe that was what he'd come for. Wild, unrestrained sex, and she'd been half a second from doing it in the elevator, and *God,* it was insane how much she would have liked for it to have happened.

McCarthy smiled slightly, as if he knew what she was thinking—and maybe he did, maybe she was really that transparent—and slid his hand inside his jacket. It reappeared holding a red envelope.

"You *have* to be kidding me," she said. "Two in one day? Are they insane?"

"It could be argued." He held it out to her. When she didn't take it, he gave it an impatient little shake, then sighed. "Look, take the damn thing, shred it, use it for a coaster.... I don't want it anywhere near me, believe me."

She stepped forward, took it and stayed where she was. Close. Close enough to see the hunger in his eyes when they met hers. He was crazy with it; she could feel it coming off of him in waves, and she'd be insane to—

"Come with me," she said, aware that it was most likely that mistake Eidolon had been jeering about in the first place, the one she couldn't help but make because she simply needed it as much as Ben did.

She stepped off the elevator and walked a few steps away before she heard his footfalls behind her. "I'm just making sure you get in bed," he said, and then, a beat later, "To rest. I meant, to rest."

"Of course," she murmured. Her whole body was on

fire, jittering with tension, pulling itself apart with need and denial and caution and wild, ungovernable desire. She couldn't keep a grip on her keys. They fell to the floor, and McCarthy was there ahead of her, reaching down to scoop them up, one hand on her arm to steady her. Even through her clothes, she could feel the slightest nuances of his touch, the firm way his fingertips pressed, the heat of his palm.

She looked at him. He stared straight ahead, his face gone blank again. She couldn't see what he was feeling or thinking, but he didn't let go of her arm. It wasn't a possessive grip, just a light touch. Caring. Distant, almost.

"Ben?" she asked in a low voice. They were at her door. He slid the keys into the first lock and turned it, then the second. He pulled them out and handed them back to her, and looked straight into her eyes.

"You can get the alarm?" he asked.

"Of course. But—"

"Promise me you're going to bed. Promise me."

She reached out, grabbed him by the lapel of his jacket and dragged him one step forward, and then he was kissing her. It was a long, feverish dream of a kiss, and she was against the hallway wall, his body pressed tight against her, his hands doing things inappropriate in a public space, and she didn't care, didn't care….

He pulled back from her with a gasp, and those blue eyes were wild and even more alarmed than they'd been in the elevator.

"Come inside," she said, and opened the door.

He didn't follow her. She could see how much he wanted

to, *needed* to, but he put one hand on the wood of the door-way and braced himself, as if there was some invisible force pulling him toward her. He shook his head. "Get the alarm," he told her in a hoarse, low voice. "Go to bed, Lucia. Please."

He reached in, grasped the doorknob and pulled the door shut with a quiet *snick*.

She felt it like a physical shock, and a healthy compo-nent of disbelief came with it. *He turned me down? Twice?* Lucia Garza had never in her life been turned down by a man she really wanted, not once. Not even the one who'd later turned out to be latently gay.

That bothered her a great deal.

She muttered imprecations in Spanish under her breath, and heard the accelerated beeping of the alarm. In thirty seconds it would sound, and for all she knew, the National Guard would be mobilized. She punched in the code with vicious precision, went to the door and stepped out into the hall.

The elevator doors were closing, and he was gone.

Slamming the door helped. So did violently kicking off her shoes. She felt hot and giddy, and terribly sore, and anger only intensified the feeling of disconnection. She tossed the red envelope—yes, it was neatly lettered with her name—onto the kitchen counter and went around to pour herself a drink.

She paused with the bottle of wine over the fine belled glass, and remembered McCarthy's hand on hers, holding her back from the beer. *Antibiotics.*

Jazz would have cursed and thrown a glass across the room and probably gotten drunk out of spite.

Lucia put the cork back in the bottle, replaced it in its holder, and was extraordinarily careful with the glass, just to be sure she didn't give in to her temper. Then she poured herself a large sparkling water, and took a long, hot bath. Careful not to get the bandage wet.

When she came out, dressed in a thick, white, fluffy robe with her small .38 in the pocket, she settled on the couch, sipping water, stealing glances at the red envelope.

Some days she believed. Some she didn't. Today, having been at the right place at the right time to save uncounted numbers of lives, she was just angry at the entire world for having the gall to do this to her. *Haven't I been through enough?* She had. Beyond any question.

She put the water aside, walked to the counter and dug the UV light that Borden had given her out of her purse. There, on the face of the envelope, was Milo Laskins's bold, flowing signature.

She tore open the envelope to slide the thin sheet of paper out. No powder in it, but that didn't mean it wasn't deadly in its own way.

It read, THANK YOU.

That was all.

She ran the UV flashlight over the note.

The signature wasn't Laskins's. It was a different name, spiky and difficult to read, driven in straight-up-and-down strokes of the pen.

When she finally made it out, she felt a chill bolt down her spine.

Max Simms, psychic and serial killer, had sent her a personal thank-you note.

Chapter 10

She fell asleep on the couch and woke up to a conviction that there was somebody in her apartment.

And she didn't move. *Wait,* she told herself. *Listen.* She heard the steady, near-silent tick of the silver clock on the table, the whisper of the air conditioner, indistinct ghosts of noises from outside the windows....

And there, the scuff of shoes on carpet. The creak of leather as someone shifted weight.

She opened her eyes and stared hard at the window in front of her, focusing on reflections. Something dark moving behind the couch.

Lucia slid the .38 out of her robe pocket with a slow, gentle pull, trying to make it look like the natural movement of a sleeper. He hadn't come closer yet, but she couldn't let him see the gun. If he shot first...

She made her decision and rolled off the couch, gun held

flat, aiming up at an angle where she knew his head would be. Her injured arm screamed in pain, and she flinched, nearly dropped the gun.

Nearly.

"Easy, my lovely. I'm not armed."

A male voice, low and faintly accented. Eastern European. She recognized it a split second before the moonlight revealed a pale face, thick dark hair, a goatee and mustache. Gregory Valentin Ivanovich. *Madre de Dios*...

The last time she'd seen Gregory had been outside a rundown, abandoned factory near Prague, and he'd been shooting over her head to make her escape look good. She'd been barely alive, barely together...and some of that had been his doing, too. She couldn't forget the cold purpose when he'd told her to run for her life or he'd have no choice but to make his shots count.

"Gregory," she said, and tried to slow down the panicked hammering of her heart. "If you start off with a lie, that just continues the same old cycle of disappointment between us." Her voice shook only a little.

He smiled and leaned on the back of the couch. His hands were empty. Gregory had always favored black, and he was drowning in it today—a black knit shirt under a black leather jacket, black slacks. The only hint of color to him was his hazel eyes, and a thin red scar along one high cheekbone.

She remembered the scar. She remembered giving it to him, a wild and lucky swing with a piece of broken glass in the dark. And he'd looked down at her, chambered a round in his Glock, and said, "*Dorogaya,* you must still have fight left in you, if you can do that. Good. You will need it."

He smiled at her now, and she remembered that, too.

"Very well," he acknowledged. "I am armed. But, my lovely, we're both always armed. It's understood. It would be impolite to assume anything else."

"Wouldn't want that." Was she having some kind of fever dream? It would make sense. Half of her worst nightmares featured glimpses of Gregory Valentin Ivanovich. The trouble was, so did half of her other dreams. It was…complicated, yes. Very complicated.

His eyes shifted and focused on her right arm. He couldn't have seen the bandage through the robe, but he would have seen the flinch, and the weakness. "Are you injured?"

"Grazed."

"Ah. Yes, I followed the afternoon's heroics. Very stirring." He shrugged. "Very stupid."

"Thanks. So would you care to explain how you come to be in my apartment without an invitation?"

"Would you care to get off the floor while we discuss it?" he asked, raising those thick eyebrows.

No point in keeping the gun on him; Gregory would do as Gregory pleased, consequences be damned. She nodded and stood up, cinching her robe tight again and dropping the gun back in her pocket. "I'm assuming this isn't a social call," she said. "Since social calls don't usually require breaking into a person's apartment in the middle of the night."

"Yes. High-security apartment, very nice. I approve. I have one like it in Chicago, you know, only mine has a better view." No point in asking how he'd defeated that security either; he'd just smile and ignore the question. He'd defeated it the same way she would have, by simple and logical steps, and a terrifying amount of innate ability. She'd have to go over it later, trace back his modes of entry, see how he'd bypassed the systems....

"*Dorogaya*? Are you with me?"

She felt a hot burn of embarrassment that he'd seen the lapse. *Damn.* It wouldn't do to show him weakness. "Get to the point."

He pushed away from the couch, crossed his arms and walked to the wing chair nearest the windows. He settled in, legs apart, watching her. He nodded to the couch. She sat, knees together, hand still in the pocket of her robe. Just in case.

"You know, of course, who I work for?" he asked.

"That depends."

"On...?"

"What day of the week it is, and your mood."

He laughed. A good, warm chuckle. His eyes never wavered, and the wolf in them remained unamused. "My dear Lushenka, I cannot believe they let you quit the business. What an asset you were. So amusing. But yes, you are right, of course, I have been known to be...less than consistent, since Mother Russia turned me out as a whore. To answer your question, today I work for the Cross Society."

"Lovely. We're coworkers. What do you want?"

He tapped a finger on the curling edge of his smile. "There is a need for secrecy."

"Meaning what, exactly? You know something I don't?"

"I know many things you don't, *zolotaya*. Many, many things. For instance, I know that you will get another red envelope tomorrow."

She said nothing to that. He might very well know it to be true.

"I also know that tomorrow, the Cross Society has arranged that someone close to you will die. Possibly you do not care that your new friend—her name is Jasmine, yes?— suffers an accident, but I know you well enough to know that you *do* care about your own survival. I have seen in the past how hard you will fight for it."

"How do you know what's going to happen tomorrow?"

He shrugged. "How does any of this become known? They tell me. Simms tells them, or they calculate it on their little machines. I don't know which it is and I don't want to know. The process is unimportant. What *is* important is that their information is rarely wrong."

"And they sent you to tell me this."

He didn't answer.

"They didn't send you. You came on your own." She felt something curdle in the pit of her stomach. "What's going on?"

"A very large game. A game of the world, and men trying to control it. Villains and heroes, but my love, which are you? Do you know?" He shook his head. "You stop a killer here, abet a killer there. It's no different than the game you hated before. Don't you see?"

"We stopped a child killer not long ago. We stopped a

pair of potential mass murderers today. I wouldn't say we're not doing good."

"Yes, of course. There should be statues in the square in your honor. But you have no idea how small your victories are, or how many killers the Society decides not to stop, for its own purposes. Once you play God, how do you decide where to halt? Who to kill? Who to allow to live?" He gave another shrug, this one more heartfelt. "This is why I go where I am told, and where I am paid. It is easier than trying to be moral and upright."

In his own way, Gregory Ivanovich was pouring out his heart. Lucia sat very still, listening, watching him, not quite believing the experience. His hand had, after all, been on plenty of triggers; he'd seen more than enough cruelty and blind stupidity in his life. He'd been lauded, and betrayed, often enough to be realistic and cynical about both.

He'd stood in the dark and hurt her for money, once upon a time. And then he'd cut her bonds and whispered in her ear, "Run for your life," and fired over her head....

"What are you trying to tell me?" she asked. Her voice, despite her best efforts, wouldn't stay steady.

"I have told you. Unless you take steps to prevent it, someone close to you will be killed tomorrow. And sooner or later, it will be your turn. You are a Lead, they tell you, and yes, there is importance to what you do, or do not do. But not only importance. *Power.* And power corrupts what it touches."

"I don't—"

"You and your partner, Jasmine. You become one of the

key points on which events turn. And you can't be controlled. They are learning this. It is not a lesson they like."

The sick feeling in her stomach grew worse. "And if we can't be controlled...."

"This is about power. Power requires control." Gregory put his hands flat on the arms of his chair and settled down in it more comfortably. His eyes fell half-shut, and his smile—she remembered it. Remembered that rare expression of approval.

"The Cross Society wants us dead? But the Society put Jazz and me together in the first place! We never would have met if—"

"My beloved, you're not that stupid. They put you together for a reason. Now they want to take you apart for a reason. You're just tools to them. And given our similar histories, I'm surprised that you didn't consider that from the beginning."

She was silent, staring at him. Aware of a lot of things, suddenly—of the fever still burning inside of her, a heavy feeling in her lungs, the carefully hidden trail behind the FedEx that had delivered something deadly to her offices. It could have been Eidolon, trying to throw suspicion on the Cross Society. It could just as easily have been the Cross Society using a double-blind. *They hadn't sent it through Borden.* Maybe Borden was still too valuable to them. Maybe James Borden, with his heart lost to Jazz Callender, wasn't going to play their game anymore, especially if it turned deadly for his friends.

Any of it could be true.

Or none of it.

"So," she said after a quiet moment, "what do I do?"

He shrugged. "I leave that to you. But were I you, and did I care anything for your friend—which I do not, you might note—I would be sure to stay alert during the morning hours of tomorrow. Events would conspire, as they say."

"Tomorrow morning. It's that specific."

"I imagine it's more specific than that, my love, but that is what I heard. Or, more accurately, overheard."

"So you're telling me you came here to warn me out of the kindness of your heart. For old times' sake."

He laughed. Not a chuckle this time, a full-throated bray of amusement. "Oh!" he gasped, when he got some control again. "Oh, *zolotaya,* you never fail to amaze me. You know what *zolotaya* means, yes?"

"Gold."

"In Russia, wealth is endearment, and you, my *zolotaya,* are beyond measure. I've always wondered if you would marry me someday. Would you?"

"No."

"As I thought. I am bereft." He stood up, and she got to her feet as well. The important thing with Gregory, as with all beautiful wild animals, was to never take your eyes off him. "Will you let me tell you one last thing?"

"I don't see how I can stop you."

"I don't think they want you dead yet, although I think soon they will. No, I think they want you frightened, and alone, so that you will do what they say. I don't think they understand what a silly hope this is."

"They don't know me," she said.

For just a moment, there was something other than the wolf in those beautiful eyes. "That is entirely their loss," he said, and the comic-opera Russian was gone. "Take care. I've done as much as I can for you without inconveniencing my own plans."

That was as much truth as she could ever hope to expect. She inclined her head slightly. He bowed his a fraction less.

And then he left.

She sank down on the couch, not bothering to lock the door after him—there didn't seem much point—and thought about things one more time.

Sometime in the middle of it, unexpectedly and without drama, her body simply decided that it had had quite enough of the stress, and sent her into a deep and dreamless sleep. She didn't know how long it lasted—not long enough for morning to arrive, at any rate—and she woke to the insistent electronic tones of a ringing phone.

It was Manny.

The anthrax culture was positive, and Jazz was on her way over.

Lucia was dressed when Jazz arrived, and was putting her hair up in a ponytail to keep it out of her face. It was a practical habit she'd developed over the years, a sort of ritual for going into battle. And she knew it was a battle now, whether that was likely to be obvious or not. She had just put on her shoulder holster when the bell rang.

"No way," Jazz said flatly when Lucia opened the door.

"You've got to be fucking kidding. You think you're actually going somewhere, other than to the hospital? Manny called, didn't he? You were supposed to pack a bag."

"Sit. I have things to tell you."

Jazz didn't, but Lucia wasn't in any mood to wait for compliance. She started with the red envelope on the counter—Simms's creepy note of gratitude—and saw a flash of genuine irritation come over Jazz's face. *Of course. She's the one who pulled the trigger. Why would he thank me?*

But when comment came, it wasn't about the details. "I got one, too," Jazz said. "Courier brought it. You wouldn't believe the full-out paranoid lockdown that went into effect when Manny saw the van drive up."

Lucia could only imagine, and shook her head in wonder.

Jazz was still frowning at her. "Look, that doesn't explain you being out of bed and ready to rumble, okay? If there's any work that needs to be done, *I'm* doing it. Not you. You're flat on your back for the duration, getting good IV antibiotics. Doctor's orders."

"Not yet. I've got things to tell you—"

"Sit. Down."

Lucia put up her hands and sat. And truthfully, she hadn't slept well, or woken up that way, either. She still felt hot and sore, but at least the tickle in the back of her throat had died to a memory, and her lungs seemed clear. Surely she'd be worse, if this was going to go badly.

"Jazz," she said. Her partner brushed shag-cut blond hair back from her eyes and bustled around the kitchen, bitching about overpriced, overcomplicated appliances. Her black

T-shirt was tucked in and clung to her curves; whether Jazz recognized it or not, she had a gorgeous, elegant line to her. Broad shoulders, curving hips, a not inconsiderable bustline. More than that, she just looked...strong. Strong and—now that she'd abandoned the ill-fitting men's flannel shirts and baggy jeans—female, without being in the least feminine.

"This thing's broken," Jazz said mutinously, staring at the high-tech coffeemaker. Jazz preferred one-button models. Lucia was reasonably certain that hers could navigate a spacecraft to Mars, if adequately programmed.

"No, it isn't," she said. "It's just temperamental. Jazz, I need you to listen to me for a minute."

Her partner paused in the act of spooning grounds into the filter. "Yeah?"

"Something happened last night."

"McCarthy brought you home." Jazz snapped the filter basket shut and punched buttons. Nothing happened. She slapped the coffeemaker with an open palm, frowning. Lucia sighed, got up and pressed the right button. The machine began a soft chuffing. "Yeah, I know. You can skip the details."

"No. No, Ben—didn't stay. He just saw me home. Something else happened."

"What?"

"I had an unexpected visitor."

That drew Jazz's total attention. "Here? I mean, I know it's not Manny's Fortress of Solitude, but it's got ambassadorial security. Who?"

How could she explain it, exactly? "It was someone I once knew. His name is Gregory Valentin Ivanovich—"

"I remember the name. You saw it in the files about the Cross Society."

Lucia blinked. "What?"

"The first day we were in Borden's office, and you jimmied the lock on his file drawer. Ivanovich's name was on a list of people employed by the Cross Society. You said he was somebody you recognized."

She barely remembered it. Jazz, it seemed, had a rare gift for memory. "Gregory came to warn me that the Cross Society means to set us up. Set you up, I mean. This morning."

Jazz took it with a shocking lack of surprise, and a shrug. "I don't doubt it," she muttered, and came to sit next to Lucia. "I'm not exactly a good little soldier. I mean, come on. Wouldn't they rather have people who follow orders, in something this complicated? You start knowing too much—"

"You start questioning the right and wrong of things. Like we've already done."

"Like Borden does, too." Jazz frowned at the coffee-maker, which didn't really deserve it, since it was doing its job. "That's why you're strapped? Because you think our buddies at the red envelope factory are out to get me?"

"Yes."

"L., I've been assuming that from the very beginning," she said. "Makes no difference if one of your oh-so-mysterious ex-boyfriends shows up to point a spotlight at it."

Lucia smiled wearily. "The only difference is that he was very precise about it being this morning."

"You trust this guy?"

She considered that very carefully. "In certain specifics, yes. And I think he was telling me the truth as he knew it."

Jazz raised her eyebrows. "Huh. That sounds not very convincing." She looked toward the coffeemaker, which had started filling the carafe. "That thing have a sensor so you can take the pot out and it won't pee all over the burner?"

"Yes."

"Figures." Jazz filled two cups and put the carafe back in place. The machine continued its puffing, hissing work. She carried the cups over and handed Lucia one. "Listen to me, okay? I don't care what kind of doomful signs of the apocalypse are on the horizon. You're going into the hospital and you're going to rest. End of story. Now go take off the gun and pack your bag. Consider me forewarned. You know for damn sure I'm always forearmed."

Lucia eyed the time. It was going on 9:00 a.m. now, and Gregory had been quite specific. Morning. Assuming he had been truthful, and that came down to her instincts.

"I'll stay with you until noon," she said. "No negotiations, *chica.* I mean it. I'm not letting you run around unchaperoned. Three hours won't make any difference. They can strap me to the bed and give me whatever they want this afternoon."

"Lucia…"

Jazz, she saw, was close to exasperation. Lucia reached

across and captured her hand. Jazz's fingers were slack with surprise.

"You shot someone yesterday," Lucia said. "The second man in a few weeks."

Jazz's eyes flew up to meet hers. "What the hell does that have to do with anything?"

"Is that why you're mother-henning me?"

"No, dammit, I'm mother-henning you because you need it! Because you—you did the same thing for me. Remember?"

She did. She remembered Jazz, white around the lips, barely able to move after surgery to remove a bullet, determined to try to go about the business of her life.

She stared at Jazz for long seconds, and then said, "My life is my own, Jazz. As is yours. But please, let me do this one thing before I give up control. All right?"

Jazz swallowed, looked away and nodded. "We keep it to a minimum, then. Far as I'm concerned, we don't do anything that puts either one of us in danger. We can hang out here and watch TV until noon—"

The telephone rang. Jazz's eyes went dark and shadowed, and she grabbed it before Lucia could reach for it. "Yeah," she snapped. Her body language shifted, from resistant to cautiously open. "For me? You're sure? Okay. I'll be right down."

She hung up and looked at Lucia, who frowned. "Down for what?"

"Delivery. FedEx, for me."

"Let's consider the last FedEx I opened, shall we? *Carefully.*"

"It's like the lotto. Can't win if you don't play." Jazz grabbed her jacket and swung it on to hide her shoulder holster. "You stay here. I'll be right back. No fair having ninja fights while I'm gone or anything."

Jazz was gone before she could protest. Lucia, resigned, went to the intercom and buzzed the security desk. "Mr. Tarrant? My friend is on the way down. I want extra attention while she's coming and going, all right? There could be trouble."

"Yes, ma'am," he said. "We'll keep a close eye."

That was all she could do to protect Jazz at the moment. She pulled out a small carry bag and stuffed in sweatpants, underwear, tank tops, comfortable soft things that wouldn't bother her if—as she anticipated—the doctors did indeed tie her down for the duration. The bathroom necessities went into the side pockets, and after a second she put in the collapsible combat baton that Jazz had given her as a partnership gift, and professional-strength pepper spray. She'd have to surrender the offensive weaponry, but...

She heard the front door open and close, and made her way back that direction. Jazz was standing there, frowning.

"You're not gonna like it." Jazz held up the FedEx envelope and removed a red envelope with the air of an actress about to announce an award.

"You've *got* to be kidding me."

"Yeah, I wish I was. But I checked it out with your little light thingie." Jazz handed it over. "It's to both of us."

It read, IMPERATIVE YOU GO IMMEDIATELY TO THE RAPHAEL WHEN YOU RECEIVE THIS MESSAGE. TAKE MS. GARZA.

"So much for our plan to stay put," Jazz said. "Didn't you stash Susannah Davis there?"

"Yes. But there's no need for us to go. Omar's with her."

They exchanged silent stares, and Jazz nodded. "Call him."

She dialed Omar's cell number. It rang to voice mail. She hung up and dialed the hotel's main desk and was put through to the room.

No answer.

She didn't have to say anything. Jazz's face was grim with understanding.

"You think—" Lucia began.

"I'm trying not to." Jazz looked down at the paper Lucia was still holding. "I can get Ben to go with me."

"No. If anybody goes with you, it's me. I told you, Ivanovich said there was an explicit threat." Lucia got up, retrieved the UV light and ran it over the message. It was signed, again, by Max Simms. "Simms sent this, not Laskins. You tell me, does he want you alive or dead?"

"Who the hell knows what that creepy guy wants? Look, *you're* not going. And if you're not going and I'm not going, what are we going to do? Hide here like a couple of rabbits?" Jazz looked fierce, in fighting mode. Razor-edged and glittering with menace. "I don't hide."

There was a strange joy in it. And it was catching, driving back the sickness and leaving purpose in its place. "You're right." Lucia checked her purse for its usual load of lethal supplies. "Both of us go. You can put me in intensive care at noon."

Jazz looked wary. "You're not going to let me stop you, are you?"

"Laughable. Would you let me stop you?"

Jazz's jaw worked, chewing words, and then she spat them out, rapid-fire. "Fine. You so much as flutter an eyelid, I'm calling an ambulance, and you get carted out like a little old lady who slipped in the shower." That was Jazz's way of expressing affection.

"I'm fine. Quit staring like you expect me to fall over and froth at the mouth. I'm not contagious, and I feel all right. I'm not impaired." The gnawing headache hardly counted. The heavy tickle in her lungs could be nothing more than suggestion, she told herself. "As I recall, I let you go along on our first case together when you still had a bullet wound. So please, let's not discuss fitness."

"Lucia!" Jazz grabbed her by the shoulders. Lucia instinctively brought her forearms straight up and knocked the grip loose, which startled them both. "Damn. I'm not trying to beat you down, you know."

"I know. It's been—an odd couple of days. I'm sorry."

"You're entitled." Jazz stepped back, but she hadn't lost the frown. Her hands were fisted at her sides now. "Look, this is serious. We could be walking into anything. I need you sharp. You could walk into a bullet the second you open the door. You really ready for that?"

"Yes." Lucia met and held the stare. "I'm ready, Jazz. I've got your back."

Whatever Jazz saw, it seemed to satisfy her. She reached into her black leather jacket, took out her gun and checked the clip—an autonomic reaction for her, like breathing.

Lucia bent over to put on her shoes.

Jazz raised an eyebrow. "That's what you're wearing? You know, I always think practical when I'm planning for some kind of fight."

Lucia nodded and reached down to zip the sides of the low boots. "These are practical. Flat heels, ankle support and steel toes. And yet stylish."

"Huh. I need to take you shoe shopping." Jazz glanced down at her Doc Martens, which looked exactly like the work boots they were. Lucia gave her a full smile and checked the position of her .38 in the holster at the small of her back, then took out the nine millimeter resting in the shoulder holster. Jazz mimed a desire to see it. Lucia handed it over.

"Wow," she said, and turned it right, then left. "Ruger P95? This new?"

"Absolutely." Lucia reached out and took it from Jazz's hand, then slotted it securely in her holster. "You know, you're amazingly easy to distract with things that can hurt people." She donned her leather jacket—brown, not black; she hated to match her partner—and picked up her purse. "After you, Jazz."

"You're sure you—"

"We've been through this." Lucia met her eyes levelly. "I

put Omar there, and I didn't think to warn him. Consider how that feels."

Jazz didn't blink, and for seconds, Lucia thought she'd failed. She knew she wasn't likely to be able to take Jazz in a straight fight—Jazz had a gift—but she'd been hoping that she wouldn't have to try.

"Fine," Jazz abruptly said. "But one cough out of you, and you're at the hospital. In restraints. And I tell them you need a colonoscopy, too."

"Deal."

It was inevitable, Lucia realized, that after a pronouncement like that, she'd fight the urge to cough the entire way down in the elevator.

Chapter 11

Jazz—through some sort of divine intervention, Lucia assumed—had persuaded Manny to loan her his enormous black vehicle. The Hummer wasn't just a gigantic SUV, of course, it was customized to Manny's particular paranoid standards. Lucia knew it had bullet-resistant glass, and no doubt Kevlar in the frame; she wouldn't be surprised if it featured a rocket launcher somewhere in the accessory package.

It also had a staggering arsenal in the back. For a totally nonviolent individual, Manny believed in preparation more than many Boy Scouts.

Jazz drove, of course. Lucia was just as happy to let her; she couldn't imagine piloting the thing around without scraping off a few bumpers from the tiny-looking cars around them. It was a little like steering a cruise ship through a sailboat regatta.

Lucia kept busy watching the street around them, alert for any sign that Eidolon, the Cross Society or anyone else might be intent on following or intercepting, but she didn't spot anything that tripped an alarm. Of course, if it was Gregory, or someone as skilled, then she probably wouldn't know until the bullets began flying.

Jazz slowed as they passed the Raphael's main entrance, and took the next turn. Service entrance and non valet parking. She parked the Hummer carefully and finally asked, "Ready?"

"Of course."

"Watch your ass."

Before Lucia could reply, Jazz was already out the door, climbing down to the parking lot. Lucia hurried to catch up, and scanned the lot as they moved to the back dock. The door was propped open, and a chef was smoking a cigarette outside; he was a big fellow in his white uniform, made taller by the trademark hat. Jazz nodded pleasantly to him, and he nodded back. He didn't try to stop them.

The service elevators—like service elevators everywhere—were a great deal more lived-in than the fancy ones used by the guests, and were big enough to move grand pianos without feeling cramped. Jazz pushed the button for five, then six.

"You take the fifth floor," she said. "Come in through the stairwell. I'll go straight in."

"No," Lucia said instantly, and had to think fast to come up with a reason. "Susannah knows me, she's never seen you. It'll be less confusing if I make the direct approach. Right?"

"Fine." They watched numbers crawl. "How do you feel?"

"Do you want me to manufacture a cough?"

"Heh. No."

"Then let's just get this done so I can go to the hospital."

At the fifth floor, Jazz stepped off, heading for the stairs. Lucia pulled her P95 and held it at her side, and edged back into the far corner of the elevator as it dinged arrival.

She risked a quick glimpse down the hallway. Clear. It was a long way to the room, exposed all the way. No help for it.

She left the elevator and started walking, constantly scanning the closed hotel room doors. Nothing stirred. She heard televisions from one, a hair dryer from another. Voices, muffled and indistinct.

The room they'd been given was in the discreetly secured section, beyond a manned concierge desk and behind a key-carded door.

The concierge's desk was empty.

The door clicked open. Beyond, the hallway was wider, and more opulently appointed, with antique hall tables and original artwork on the walls. And the lights were lower.

No sign of the concierge here, either.

She paused at the stairwell and opened the door. Jazz stepped out. "Any trouble?" she asked.

"None. You?"

"There's a few blood drops on the stairs. Could be anything—a kid having a nosebleed. Or could be something.

No way to tell." Jazz, Lucia noticed, also had her gun out and ready. "Which one?"

Lucia mutely nodded at the right door. They moved into position on either side, communicating silently, and Lucia knocked twice and said, "Omar? Open up."

No response. She held up the key card. Jazz nodded, all business, and shifted her weight to be ready to move.

The card clicked in the lock, and the door opened at a touch, swinging back with silent ease. Lucia beat Jazz to entry by a split second, taking the low line, unable to see much for the shadows. The curtains were drawn.

"Lights," Jazz said, and hit the switch with her shoulder.

In the blaze, the blood looked very, very bright.

Omar lay on the floor, sprawled and lifeless, next to an overturned armchair.

His throat had been cut. Lucia gasped in a breath, felt her body constrict with the shock. A wave of unreality swept over her.

"Focus," Jazz said softly. "Stay with me, L."

Omar was dead. The cut was deep, one slice, right to left. The standard for a right-handed killer facing him. She wanted to reach over, press her fingers to his neck, even though she knew it was illogical to feel for a pulse. This had been done at least a couple of hours ago. Omar's lovely dark eyes were open, and dry. Gregory? It could have been, but even Gregory might find it in bad taste to come visiting a few minutes before killing her friend. No, she didn't think so. Gregory wouldn't have made this much of a mess.

"Lucia!"

She blinked and focused on Jazz's stark, pale, set face. "I'm here," she said. "Take the next room." Her voice sounded far away, but normal.

Jazz nodded and went into the bedroom. Lucia averted her eyes from Omar's body and scanned the closets, the bathroom, under the furniture. She was almost convinced Susannah was gone, dead in a ditch, when she heard a stealthy hiss of breathing, quickly muffled.

"Susannah?" She turned and looked at the far end of the room again. Nothing there. An elegant Queen Anne desk and chair, a big-screen plasma TV, the sweep of long maroon velvet curtains…

It couldn't be that easy. She couldn't be hiding behind the curtains. Not even kids did that anymore, did they?

And then she spotted it. It was tough to see, and designed to be that way, no doubt. A privacy screen of the same material as the wallpaper, blending seamlessly into the fabric of the wall.

Lucia moved around, giving it a wide berth, and came face-to-face with Susannah Davis, huddled against the wall, trembling. Bruised face averted.

"Got her!" she called, and reached out to touch Susannah on the shoulder.

She had just enough reflexes to jump back out of range as the knife slashed wildly at her. *Don't shoot her,* some part of Lucia's mind screamed, in time to stop her finger from tightening on the trigger. She danced backward, holstered the gun as she went, and executed a perfect roundhouse kick that sent the knife flying out of Susannah's hand to thud against the velvet drapes.

The knife was bloody. Omar's blood.

Lucia lunged forward, batted aside Susannah's flailing hands, and wrenched one arm up behind her back. Susannah cried out. She felt hot and damp with sweat against Lucia's chest, and Lucia was overcome with a wave of disgust and anger that made her want to pull that arm up until it snapped.

Instead, she kicked the backs of Susannah's knees and got her down flat on her stomach on the carpet.

"Jazz!" she yelled, and snapped handcuffs around one of Susannah's wrists, then the other. "I've got her!"

Jazz reappeared at the door, gazed down at Susannah coolly, and said, "I think you'd better take a look in here."

"Now?"

"Now. Bring her."

Lucia removed her knee from the center of Susannah's back and hauled her upright; the woman's battered face was spattered with blood, pale where it wasn't stained or abraded. Her eyes looked dim and shocked.

The lights were on in the bedroom, and there was more blood. Not Susannah's, obviously; not Omar's, who'd unquestionably died in the next room. No, this was...

Leonard Davis, Susannah's abusive husband. He was facedown next to the bed. Hard to tell how he'd died, but Lucia bet it had been from the blade of some knife. Whatever wounds he had must be in the front; his back looked untouched, except for the fact that his pants were halfway down his pale butt.

Rachel Caine

"What happened?" she asked, and looked at Susannah, who was staring at Leonard as if he might rise from the dead at any moment.

"I don't know how he got into the room," Jazz said, "but I can walk you through forensics. He got the drop on Omar, probably by threatening to kill Susannah. I'm betting he had a knife at her throat."

She looked at Susannah, who didn't even seem to know Jazz was talking.

"Omar misjudged him, got too close—maybe he was trying to get her out of the way. One fast slash, straight through both carotid arteries. From the arterial spray in there, I'd guess Omar was standing when he was cut. He must have gone down immediately, and was dead in about thirty seconds. Meanwhile, Leonard dragged Susannah into the bedroom." She indicated the scuffs on the carpet, clear drag marks from the doorway to the bed. "Then I guess he figured he'd get some last fun in before he killed her, too."

Susannah shuddered in a deep breath. "I let him in," she said. "Omar was in the bathroom. I let him in by accident. It wasn't Omar's fault."

They both stared at her in silence for a few seconds, and then Jazz cast a pointed look down at Leonard's body. "He took Omar out, but not you? How's that work?"

"He put the knife down when he was unzipping his pants," she said. "He didn't think I had the guts. I never have before."

Lucia raised her eyebrows in silent question to Jazz.

"Yeah," Jazz answered quietly. "That's more or less the

way I read it. Omar died first. There's a trail of blood drops from the other room into here. Hubby died with his pants unzipped. There's a void in the blood spray on the bed. That's where she was, on the bed. Which confirms the story, pretty much."

Lucia swallowed hard and resisted an urge to kick Leonard Davis's unresisting corpse.

"Better call Welton Brown," she said to Jazz. "We're going to be here for a while."

"So much for our low profile." Jazz sighed. "Susannah stays in cuffs until the cops say otherwise," she said. "I mean, I told you how I read it, but Brown may see it differently. Better keep him happy. We're already in deep shit."

Lucia nodded, led Susannah to a chair and sat her down, facing away from her husband's body. Jazz got on her cell phone.

It was going to be another long day, no doubt about it, and the hospital was—once again—going to have to wait.

The police took Susannah into custody for questioning, and kept Jazz and Lucia in interrogation for the better part of four hours. The only good thing about it, from Lucia's point of view, was that the clock safely ticked over well past noon, and the deadline, so far as Gregory had described it, had passed.

And if it had been Ben and Jazz going into that room? Jazz would have been the one to find Susannah. And that knife would have gone across her throat just as easily as Omar's.

Lucia's eyes felt grainy and sore, and her whole body ached. Hard to tell whether it was due to the infection, the antibiotics fighting it, or plain, garden-variety exhaustion.

Welton Brown had not been happy to find two murders in his lap after having pointed Susannah Davis in their direction. That really wasn't good, since Brown was one of the few detectives with whom Jazz had stayed on good terms. A private investigation firm needed the cooperation of local police.

But Lucia was too sick and too tired to do any fence-mending, and when Brown dismissed them, Lucia was only too glad to go.

"You're going straight to the hospital," Jazz said, once the police car had dropped them off in the parking lot of the Raphael. This, Lucia thought mournfully, was one hotel that she wouldn't get any cooperation from in the future. A pity. She really liked the ambience, and the sense of history.

The hospital visit was exactly what Lucia had anticipated. She had a fever—no surprise—and an elevated white count. They gave her a course of IV antibiotics, which took the better part of two hours.

"I'd like to keep you here for the next few days. We really need to keep an eye on that fever," Dr. Kirkland informed her earnestly, as they unhooked her from the IV.

"I'll do it myself."

"If I send you home, I want you to *rest* this time, all right? Your partner told me you've been working. This is *not* optional, Ms. Garza. Rest, sleep and take your medications. Are we clear?"

"Crystal." She swallowed and forced a smile. "How bad is it?"

He stared at her for a long few seconds before he said, "It could be very bad. But with rest and medications, you can beat it in about a week. You didn't have a massive exposure, and your immune system is strong."

Jazz looked as if she was holding back an "I told you so" with all her strength.

"I'll drive you home," she said, and walked Lucia out to the parking lot. The Hummer looked gigantic, like the *Queen Mary* in a pool full of paddleboats, and Lucia couldn't imagine how she was going to summon the energy to climb up into the cab.

She paused, one hand on the door, because she felt someone watching her.

There was a boxy blue sedan sitting a few parking spaces down the row, and someone was standing next to it. For a tired, disorienting second she thought it was Omar, and then her mind and her eyes cleared.

Ben McCarthy.

He didn't move, and he didn't approach them. He'd either done some shopping or located some of his clothes in storage; he was wearing a knee-length coat against the night's chilly breeze, something in a warm amber that glowed in a passing car's headlights.

Lucia nodded toward him. Jazz turned to look, and walked over to join him. Lucia checked the parking lot. You could never be sure anything was completely safe.

McCarthy was listening to Jazz recount the scene inside

the hotel room when she joined them, and the look he threw toward Lucia was unreadable. When Jazz stopped—she had a cop's terse delivery, nothing but the bare facts—he said, "Omar didn't strike me as the kind of guy to go down without a fight."

Lucia felt something clench hard inside. She'd been avoiding thinking about Omar. "It had to have been fast. Very fast."

"Son of a bitch. I liked the guy."

She felt the guilt like a lead ball in her throat. She kept swallowing, but it didn't go down. Metallic taste in her mouth. She felt sick and hot and utterly undone.

"So the cops are keeping the widow Davis for a while?"

"A few more hours, anyway," Jazz said. "They'll decide whether or not to charge her, depending on her story. But my guess? This Leonard guy, he was a cold-blooded killer. Cold-blooded enough to cut Omar's throat and decide to rape her afterward. Probably would have done the same for her when he was done. Seemed to me like he had practice at that kind of thing."

McCarthy folded his arms. He was watching Jazz, but Lucia could feel part of his attention fixed on her, warm as a spotlight. "You guys okay?"

"I need to make arrangements for Omar," Lucia said dully. "He's got family back East. I need to call—"

"Let me," Jazz said. "How many times do I have to tell you? *Rest.* Take your pills and rest. That's your job now. You give me the numbers. I do the calls."

Lucia nodded.

"Yeah," she murmured. "I should go home."

"I'll take her," McCarthy said. With no particular emphasis, just simple words. He and Jazz exchanged a look—another one that Lucia couldn't read, whether it was complicated partner-language or just a malfunction of her own normally competent abilities—and he opened the passenger door of his car. "You get home, too, Jazz."

"Been a busy couple of days for a guy straight out of prison," she observed.

"Yeah, you two should talk. You make Navy SEALs look boring."

The upholstery of McCarthy's old car felt luxurious, soft as down to her tired body; Lucia struggled for a while to stay awake, but minutes disappeared, and she had no memory at all of the drive. Just the warm sensation of McCarthy's fingers stroking her cheek, and his voice in her ear saying, "Let's get you upstairs."

Her knees gave out as she was leaning against the wall in the elevator. McCarthy caught her without a word and picked her up. She wasn't heavy, but she knew she wasn't that light either; she murmured a protest, but there was something so seductive about being cradled against his body, her arms around his neck, her head on his shoulder. He carried her the short distance to her door and let her slide back to her feet.

Close together. Breathing the same air.

He leaned forward and pressed his lips gently to her forehead. A kiss of peace, not passion, although there was that, too, in the tense set of his body, in the light in his eyes. "Get inside," he murmured against her skin. "Take care of your-self. I'll check on you tomorrow."

He started to pull away. She grabbed his collar to hold him in place. "Promise me something first. Promise me that—if something happens to me—you'll look after things. After Jazz. After—even after that bitch who got Omar killed."

Something Susannah had said nagged at Lucia, but she was too tired to make the connections. She was running on instinct, not thought.

"Nothing's going to happen to you."

"Anthrax," she said flatly. "Something's already hap-pened to me. The stuff can be deadly. I could be dead—"

His fingers touched her lips. Light, but unmistakably a hush. "Don't say that."

"Just promise, okay?"

"I promise."

She thought he'd kiss her. She could see he wanted to, could *feel* it, but he stepped back as she opened the door, and let her go inside.

"Rest," he said. "That's what you need right now."

When she looked back, he was already walking away, el-egant in his tawny coat, hands in the pockets. She wanted to call him back. Wanted to sleep in his arms, stretched against his warmth. Wanted the sheer animal comfort to keep the fears and the memories at bay.

Instead, she shut the door, locked it and set the intrusion alarms for instant alert.

She managed to strip off her guns before she fell on the bed and sank into a sleep so deep it seemed eternal.

She couldn't wake up. Couldn't. She tried, because she knew she should; she felt the danger, but her whole body was sluggish and unresponsive. Inert, heavy flesh, weighing her down.

Dreams. Terrible dreams, full of twisted, screaming bodies, and blood, and friends—old friends dying. She wanted to cry out, wanted to scream, wanted to *stop this,* but there was nothing she could do, nothing but witness and grieve. Endless dark mazes and corridors and cells and *run for your life* and the shots ringing out over her head... *Gregory Ivanovich, please, help me.... I'll make it worth your while.*

Flashes of light.

Smeared voices, nightmarishly slow. She didn't understand them. Was this the past? Was it Prague? Had she never really run, her bare feet sliding over cold concrete blocks and leaving footprints of sweat and blood...oh *Dios,* was she still there? Were they asking...?

She felt the white-hot burn of drugs in her veins. Slow fire, screaming through her body.

Nothing. Sleep. Dreams.

A feeling of cold on her skin. Her body being lifted, moved. More nightmares, hands on her, moving her legs up and out. A sense of cold invasion that made her flinch and want to weep.

More drugs.

Darkness.

Chapter 12

She woke up in the hospital, with an IV in her arm and an oxygen mask on her face, and for a panicked moment she thought, *I'm dying.*

Didn't feel that way, though. In fact, she felt a lot better. Sore and weak, but better. Her mouth was dry as old paper. She cleared her throat and tried to sit up.

"Whoa!"

A face, looming over the bed. Jazz, looking delighted. Behind her was James Borden, all angles and smiles. His hair was creatively mussed, and his clothes looked lived-in. So did Jazz's, but that wasn't remarkable.

"Look who's awake," Jazz said, and reached for her hand, and the warm pressure of her fingers felt nice. Felt real. "How you feeling?"

Lucia nodded slightly and tried to talk. No good. Her voice wasn't even a hoarse croak. She gestured toward

the pink pitcher of water on the stand next to the bed, and
Borden hurried around to pour some for her.

Water, after such a long thirst, tasted like a revelation of
the divine. Lucia whimpered with delight and swallowed
until the cup was dry.

"Better?" Borden asked. He refilled it. "You've been out
awhile. Couple of days." Some silent conversation between
Borden and Jazz passed over her head. "You remember
anything?"

"No." That was a word. A small one, and it sounded
rough, but it was a recognizable word. Progress. "Pansy.
All right?"

"Pansy's fine," Jazz said. "Never even got a sniffle or a
fever. No infection at all. No other victims reported, either.
Looks like you were the lucky one."

"What happened?"

"What do you remember?" Jazz asked.

"Going to sleep, after—after the hospital. Tired."

"Nothing else? You're sure?"

Lucia swallowed another ball of fire that seemed to
be clinging to the back of her throat. "Dreams, maybe.
Nightmares."

"But you don't remember leaving your apartment."

The fragile sense of well-being shattered. "I—left?"

Another look passed from Borden to Jazz, Jazz to Borden.
Lucia was still fuzzy, the world still indistinct, but even so
she didn't care for the way they were avoiding her questions.

"Yeah," Jazz said softly. "You left. At least, that's what
the security logs say. You entered the code to disable the

alarm, and you just—vanished. No sign of how you got out of the apartment."

This wasn't right. Couldn't be right. She hadn't felt well enough to leave. She remembered setting the alarm for instant alert and stumbling off to bed.

There was, of course, another way out of the apartment that wouldn't appear on the security logs—her own Manny-inspired precautions—but why would she run away? And why wouldn't she remember it? "Where did you find me?"

"We didn't," Borden said. "You were missing for four days. And on the fifth day, you were found sleeping in a supposedly unoccupied room at the Raphael."

"What?"

"Yeah," Jazz said grimly. "I'm not a woo-woo girl, but I'm not ruling out alien abduction."

That was impossible.

Lucia didn't remember anything from the moment she'd fallen asleep on her bed, fully clothed, to waking up here.

Nothing. Just dreams, and those were fading fast.

"Where was I?" she asked. Her voice was faint and weak, and Jazz looked at Borden again, this time for support.

"Honest to God, L.—I wish to hell I knew. The only good thing anybody can tell us is that you were being treated for what was wrong with you. IV antibiotics, just like they would have done here, apparently. You're weak now, but you're on the mend. Fever's gone, no sign of infection from the swabs they took, and you're not even going to want to know about any of that swabbing business, believe me." Jazz blew hair off of her forehead and grinned grimly. "Trust you to end up kidnapped by renegade doctors."

"Renegade doctors whose heads I'm going to mount on my trophy wall."

"Yes, bwana. I'll carry the elephant gun."

Four days. Four missing days. Six, if she'd been unconscious here since they'd found her. Almost a week of her life gone into a black hole.

"What about Susannah?" Omar, dead on the floor, hands open, throat cut. "Do the cops still have her?"

"No. They let her go. McCarthy's watching her," Jazz said. "Although believe me, it's been a challenge keeping him from being here twenty-four–seven. Look, I've been thinking…maybe the Cross Society decided they owed you one. Considering that it was their fake red letter that got you in trouble in the first place."

Eerily possible. Gregory Ivanovich had defeated her security once. He could have done it again. *And carried me out?* If he'd used her emergency exit, he could have done it.

"I'll deal with that later," she whispered. "What about Susannah? You said they released her?"

"Forensic evidence proved out her story. Her husband's prints were on the knife, hers overlaid his. So she picked up the knife after he did. So yeah, KCPD released her." Jazz cleared her throat. "Problem is, she's already had one attempt on her life since they let her go. We had to step in again."

McCarthy. Omar's bloody corpse flashed in front of Lucia's eyes again. "Anyone—" *McCarthy* "—hurt?"

"No, the shooter tried for a sidewalk hit. McCarthy got her behind a car in time. No damage."

"No red envelopes?"

"Evidently, saving *her* life isn't important." The grim set of Jazz's face told Lucia what she thought about that. "I chewed Laskins a new asshole trying to get Simms to tell us what happened to you. No comment from the jailhouse psychic. He'll put himself out for strangers, not for his own. Bastards, all of them. I'm sick of this fucking circus."

Lucia smiled faintly. She could well imagine Jazz on the phone with Borden's boss, reading him the riot act. Laskins wouldn't have been pleased. For all she knew, Jazz might have hopped a plane to California, where Simms was jailed, to try the psychic in person.

Borden was looking elsewhere, deliberately taking himself out of the conversation. She wondered if Jazz had considered the ramifications of having him in the room, and then realized that Jazz nearly always considered the ramifications. That was part of the contradiction of the woman. She was impulsive and rash, and she also saw consequences coming a mile ahead. That didn't mean she allowed them to dictate her course of action.

Lucia cleared her throat again. "She's still with him? With McCarthy?"

"Yeah. He put me in charge of finding you." Jazz shrugged, eyes glittering. "Called him every night to tell him that I hadn't. And every night, he told me that I'd better find you, or it'd be my ass."

"You did find me."

Jazz nodded. "Yeah, tripped over you getting admitted to the hospital. World-class detective, I am. But on the bright side, guess I get to keep my ass."

Lucia drank more water. Borden raised the pitcher inquiringly; she shook her head. "I wish I knew what—what happened." Because anything could have. That was a disturbing void in her life. "When can I get out of here?"

"When you can gnaw through the straps," Jazz said. "I want you here until you can kick ass and take names."

That, Lucia thought, would take nothing more than a decent meal, a walk around the building and a fresh set of clothes.

Because she was so very, very ready to kick ass.

It took something more than an afternoon—a day and a half, to be exact—for the various doctors to present themselves and sign off on her release. She'd grimly demonstrated her ability to walk, eat, drink and pee in sufficient quantities to get everyone off her back.

Ben McCarthy didn't show. She kept expecting to turn around and see him walking through the door, kept expecting to feel his presence behind her. Didn't happen. But then, she reminded herself, he was working. Doing her job, in fact.

That didn't stop her from feeling irrationally annoyed about it.

She felt weak, but it was the kind of weakness that only movement and exercise would cure. She started off by scorning the wheelchair and taking the stairs, with Jazz and Borden clumping along behind her.

"Did you bring me a gun?" she asked Jazz before they hit the ground floor exit.

For answer, Jazz jumped down to the landing, reached in the inside pocket of her leather jacket and pulled out Lucia's P95 and shoulder holster. Lucia ran through the checklist on the gun, ratcheting the slide, examining the clip, ejecting the bullet in the chamber and reloading. Everything worked smooth as silk.

"She cleaned it for you," Borden said.

Jazz shrugged. "No big deal." Then she grinned and nudged him with her elbow. "Besides, nude girls cleaning guns turn him on."

"More than I needed to know. From both of you." Lucia removed her coat and put the holster on, settling the gun snugly against her ribs. While she was putting the coat on again, Jazz pushed past her to reach the door first.

Protecting her, Lucia realized. She blinked, smiled slightly and followed.

Once again, Manny had given up his Hummer to the cause; Lucia was starting to like the damn thing. It certainly gave one a feeling of security, riding high above traffic. *It also presents a fine target, and it's easy to follow.*

Jazz wanted to take her straight home, but Lucia wasn't having any of it. "Has Susannah said anything about her husband's business yet?"

"Not a word. Ben's been working on it, but she doesn't seem to trust anybody. Why? You want to take a run at her?"

"Absolutely." Mostly, she had to admit, she wanted to see McCarthy.

"And you don't think you should be, you know, resting…?"

"Apparently, I've been resting for almost a week. The last thing I need is more sleep. I need to think and I need to move. It's time to get into this thing, Jazz. I have a hunch that it's larger than we can see right now."

Jazz took the next right turn. "Far be it from me to get in the way of your hunches." She sounded amused, but not dismissive. Progress, of a sort. "I'm going to keep digging. Somebody had to see you being carried into the Raphael. You damn sure weren't walking on your own."

Borden said nothing. He had a laptop computer open, and he was typing away.

"Counselor," Lucia said. He looked back over his shoulder at her, eyebrows raised. "Shouldn't you be in New York?"

"Actually, GP&L is considering opening a branch office here," he said. "I'm fact-finding. We have seven corporate clients here, not to mention some other vested interests. And the air travel's getting old. They don't even feed you anymore on the plane."

"Tragic," she agreed, straight-faced. "Was this your idea, or your boss's?"

"Mine."

"Sure about that?"

He lost the friendly smile. "Meaning?"

"Meaning, are you sure that you're not doing the Cross Society's work instead of your firm's, setting up here?"

"They're not mutually exclusive."

"I'm not so certain."

He blinked and turned around even farther. The laptop was in danger of sliding to the floor. "So you think we're the villains now? Is that it?"

"We?"

That wasn't Lucia speaking. It was Jazz. Borden looked at her, stricken. "I mean…"

"Yeah," she said. "I get what you mean. Your loyalty's still with the Society. *We* means people who aren't in this car."

"Jazz—"

It was a lost cause, and Borden knew it. He turned to face the road.

It occurred to her that he'd be updating Laskins about what they were doing, and through Laskins, the Society and Simms. But she couldn't tell Jazz to turf him; she could see how important he was to her, and truthfully, she liked Borden. She liked his off-center smile, his quick intelligence, his wit, the passion in his eyes when he looked at her partner.

But she didn't like what he represented, at the moment. And she wasn't sure she liked him knowing where Susannah Davis was hidden.

They pulled into an apartment complex parking lot—not a complex Lucia was familiar with, more of a cheap, run-down establishment. The paint was peeling, and even the spring flowers in their landscaped beds looked cheap and struggling. It was the sort of place drug dealers rented, and hookers, and people who couldn't afford better. The sort of place where people averted their eyes from their neighbors and hoped that the noise in the apartment next door wasn't a felony being committed.

But Jazz's instincts were, as always, sound. It was also a place where women with bruised faces weren't necessarily worth comment.

"Number 317. Some distant cousin's apartment," Jazz said. "He's in jail. I told you before, my family tree has some funky branches."

"How'd you get the keys?"

"It's a cheap apartment." She shrugged. "Keys aren't all that relevant."

When Jazz and Borden started to exit the Hummer, Lucia reached over the seat and grabbed both of them by the shoulders. "No," she said quietly. "Listen. I want to talk to Susannah alone. I don't want an entourage. I appreciate everything you've done for me, but you have to let me do my job now. And Jazz—you're not supposed to be running around like this, it isn't safe. Borden, you're supposed to be keeping her out of trouble, not getting her deeper into it. Right?"

"No way," Jazz said instantly. "I go with you to the door, at least. Don't start, okay? You get escorted. We protect each other. Hell, it's worked so far."

Before she could form a coherent objection, Jazz was out of the truck. Lucia scrambled to follow. Jazz wasn't wasting time; she moved fast and sure, heading for building three. Lucia fell into step with her.

"I let you out of my sight," Jazz said softly, "and you were *gone*. You seriously think I'm going to let that happen again?

Four days. *Four fucking days,* Lucia, and I thought I was looking for a corpse. Not again. Understand?"

They followed the cracked sidewalk in long, no-nonsense strides. The grass was sparse and dry, the bushes more branches than leaves. Some of the residents were making an effort—cheerful lawn furniture on the patios, wind chimes, bird feeders—but most had abandoned hope and lived with closed, sagging curtains, minding their own business.

The apartment was at the top of two flights of stairs that creaked as Lucia and Jazz jogged up. Even had they wanted to be stealthy, it wouldn't have been possible.

They slowed as they got to the landing, and Jazz unceremoniously pushed Lucia behind her and pulled her gun as she stepped forward. Two apartments, both with closed curtains. There was a faded welcome mat in front of 318, nothing but dried leaves in front of the other.

Jazz raised her hand to knock, but the door swung open, and Ben McCarthy was there. He opened his mouth to speak, and then his eyes focused past Jazz, on Lucia.

The look stopped her breath. His lips shaped a word—not her name. It took her a second to realize that it was *God.* A prayer, of a kind.

"Delivered to the door. Want me to wait in the car?" Jazz asked.

Ben tore his gaze away from Lucia to her. "No," he said. "I'll get her home. I don't want you hanging out in a god-damn Hummer in this parking lot. Kind of draws attention."

"Ah, hell, half a dozen guys in this complex drive Hummers."

"Drug dealers."

"Exactly."

McCarthy stilled her with a hand on her arm. "Jazz. I'll get her home safe. Count on it."

She shut up and looked at him for long seconds, then nodded.

"Now get the damn truck out of here. Go."

Jazz glanced at Lucia as she turned toward the stairs. "I'll kill you if you up and die on me," she said, and descended quickly, two steps at a time.

"Inside," McCarthy said, and tugged Lucia over the threshold before she could react. He stayed at the door for a long moment, and she watched him, reading the tension in his body. He had his gun out, ready at his side, and she could tell the precise moment when Jazz was safely in the Hummer, because he let out a held breath and shut the door. The place smelled faintly of old cats and stale cigarettes. She blinked, and her eyes adjusted to the dimness. Except for the welcome sight of McCarthy, she wished they hadn't. The furniture was garage sale, most of it broken, and the carpet was an unattractive green shag that she thought at first was stained, but then decided must have been meant to have a mottled effect. Plain white walls had plenty of damage to give the place that special designer touch.

A giant glow-in-the-dark poster of a marijuana leaf decorated the wall over the sagging couch, and another of a long-dead singer looking the worse for wear. Heroin chic, the entire apartment.

McCarthy finished the last of the dead bolts and turned

toward her. She met his eyes and smiled slightly. "Jazz said you were worried."

"Worried?" Something flashed in his eyes. "Worried doesn't quite cover it, Lucia. Where the hell were you?"

"I don't know." It hurt to say it, and a bubble of panic formed somewhere just below her stomach. "All I remember is going to sleep in my apartment and waking up in the hospital."

"Nothing else?" He took her arm and guided her to the couch. "You're sure?"

"Dreams," she said. "Impressions. Nothing—" She remembered a quick flash. Bright lights, a smothering feeling of panic, her limbs heavy with sedatives. Smeared voices.

Violations.

"I'll find out," she said flatly. "If it's the last thing I do, I'll know what happened to me."

He helped her to the couch, assistance she didn't need but didn't resist. Unlike Jazz, she knew when to control her independent impulses. Instead, she reached up and covered his hand with her own—not to remove it, more a confirmation that she was really touching him. The heat of his skin against her palm, the caress of his fingers...the longing in his eyes.

The care with which he touched her made her shiver. "Jazz said wherever you were, you had medical care. The..."

"Anthrax," she supplied, with a flash of a smile. "You can say it. And it's gone. I don't think Dr. Kirkland would have allowed me out of bed if I hadn't been healthy."

Ben slid his hand from her arm, to fold her fingers in his. "Anything else?"

"What?"

"Did they find anything else?"

She frowned. *Violations.* "No. No, nothing."

He let out a slow breath. "Good." He smiled, heavy on the irony. "Good as it is to see you, I hope you didn't risk your life to come out here to visit me."

She had, mostly. But it wouldn't sound precisely smart to admit it. "I need to talk to Susannah," she said.

He nodded and, without a word, turned around and walked into the bedroom.

Lucia got up from the couch and moved to sit on a battered wooden chair. It looked less likely to harbor fleas than the grimy plaid cushions. It took a few minutes, but McCarthy reappeared, bringing with him a sleep-creased woman whom Lucia barely recognized as Susannah Davis. She looked considerably better. The swelling in her face had gone down, and the bruises were fading to blotches. She'd be pretty when she recovered, if not beautiful.

The scared expression in her eyes had faded, too. She looked different now. Desperation had made her seem honest, but the truth was emerging, and it wasn't entirely reassuring.

"Susannah," Lucia said. "How have you been?"

"All right," she answered, and slid into the chair opposite, across the battered kitchen table. She yawned and pushed her sleep-disordered hair back from her face. "I heard you were missing or something."

"Or something." Lucia let that sit for a few seconds to close the topic. "Someone tried to kill you, I hear."

Susannah looked down at her hands. She was picking at her cuticles. "Well, it damn sure wasn't Leonard." Cold, Lucia thought. Very cold.

"Maybe Leonard's business associates," Lucia said. "Right? You told us in the beginning that you knew things about his business dealings. Maybe they don't want you telling anyone what you know?"

She didn't reply. Her nervous picking continued. She'd had a good manicure once, but it had grown out, and the polish was halfway up her nails. Seashell-pink. When she'd had that manicure done—three weeks ago, at a guess—she'd also had a haircut. The shape was still there, even if she'd done nothing to style it. The clothes Susannah had on weren't her own, but the shoes were, and they were good ones. Not a woman who did her shopping at discount stores, but one who'd taken pride in herself, up until recently.

"Susannah," Lucia said, and drew her eyes in a direct gaze. "You know something. You knew Leonard would come after you, and you were afraid he'd kill you. He or his associates."

Susannah nodded and looked down again, picking furiously at the offending cuticle. She tore off a strip of skin. A bright bead of red appeared in the corner, next to the nail bed.

"You need to tell someone," Lucia repeated softly. "Why not McCarthy?"

The woman gave a mute shake of her head. Lucia made

an intuitive leap, and didn't like where it took her. McCarthy was in the other room, but she couldn't tell if he could hear. She had to assume he could. "Maybe you just don't like him," she said. "You wouldn't be the first."

Susannah's head shake this time was almost a shiver. She knew something about McCarthy. Nothing that would require her to scream bloody murder over being left alone with him, but something. Maybe she'd picked it up at KCPD; plenty of cops might have said things there. A detective willing to take bribes might be the last person she could trust.

"Will you tell me?"

Susannah's fingers stopped moving. Lucia didn't speak; she knew Susannah was arguing with herself, and adding her voice would only hurt.

"He—" Susannah's voice failed, briefly, then came back stronger. "Leonard was working for these people. They had some kind of plan or something—I don't know what it was all about. But he would get these messages, and he would do things for them. The last one...he bought a lot of chemicals. A *lot*. He rented a building somewhere. He said he was starting up a lab."

Ah. "A meth lab," Lucia said.

Susannah gave her an irritated look. "No, it wasn't a meth lab. I know the chemicals for a meth lab, and this wasn't— look, it was different. There were two things they were delivering there. Sodium cyanide and hydrochloric acid."

The skin tightened on the back of Lucia's neck. "Were they opening an electroplating lab? Those are chemicals used—"

"Electroplating? You've got to be kidding! When I say I know what chemicals you use for a meth lab, how do you think I know that? I'm not a damn saint, and he wasn't opening any damn legitimate business. This was something else. Maybe the paperwork says electroplating, I don't know, but it's a lie. Can't you use that crap for something else, too?"

"Possibly." Noncommittal was the best strategy. If Susannah got frightened—more frightened—there was no telling what she might do. "I can check it out if you want. Where's the lab?"

"In SubTropolis," Susannah said.

Lucia frowned. "I don't—"

McCarthy, sure enough, was within earshot. He came to the bedroom doorway, leaned against the frame and said, "Underground business complex. It's huge. You're going to need more than that. A business name, a unit number..."

"I don't know, okay? He didn't tell me anything. When I asked, he got mad." Susannah pointed at her face. "I didn't ask any more questions."

Lucia looked from her to Ben. "We could track suppliers. That could give us the unit number."

"Or we could just give the FBI the information." He nodded at Susannah. "And her."

"I can make the phone call, but without some proof, I don't think Agent Rawlins is going to be giving it much priority. He's overworked. He barely responded when we had anthrax in an envelope." She paused, thinking about it. "I know somebody to talk to, but he's undercover. I'll have to arrange a drive-by meeting. Shouldn't take long."

McCarthy didn't look happy about it.

"How are you going to get there?" he asked. "To your meeting? I can't leave her alone here."

"That's the wonderful thing," Lucia said, and pulled the cell phone from her purse. "If you have a phone and a credit card, you can get just about anything delivered."

"Get pizza while you're at it."

She called FBI Special Agent Roger Cole ten minutes later. Cell phone, not office phone. Two minutes of idle chatting, a simple thirty-second request, and silence from him on the other end.

"Is this going to bite me in the ass?" he asked her. He was in his car. The road noise nearly overwhelmed his voice. "Because I'd like to know how, so I can get my will ready."

"It might make your day, Roger. If I'm right."

"Then you should give me everything you have so I can get to work on it. Or better yet, somebody else can. I'm a little busy. Maybe you've heard, somebody's been playing with funny little white powder in envelopes."

"I've heard," she said blandly; he knew perfectly well who'd gotten the envelope. "This could be connected." A lie, but a nebulous one.

"Yeah?" The road noise lessened; he was pulling over. "Okay, give. What do you have, and why aren't you talking to your red-haired boy?"

"My red-haired boy isn't exactly jumping through hoops for me at the moment."

"Don't be that way. He had four guys on the street looking for you, you know. He was distressed."

"So distressed he hasn't bothered to make a phone call to say hello and interrogate me about what I know? He's got bigger and juicier fish to catch just now. Look, all you have to do is track the shipments of chemicals to a specific address in SubTropolis, and I'll do the rest. If it checks out, it's yours. You get to be the hero." She read out the names of the specific chemicals as Susannah had given them. "Sound like anything to you?"

"Electroplating," he said. "And gas chambers. Fuck. You've done it again, haven't you?"

"Are you going to get me the information?"

His sigh rattled in the speaker. "No. I'll get the info, but I go with you."

"I don't want a full team for reconnaissance."

"Relax. I'll make some calls, pick you up in…" he paused to check the time "…about an hour, okay?"

"Thank you."

The pizza arrived in forty-five minutes, and the driver looked nervous when Lucia met him at the door to hand him cash. She didn't doubt the apartment complex had a bad rep among deliverymen. She added on a considerable tip for his trouble, and hoped he wasn't mugged on his way back to his car.

Two slices later, her cell phone rang. Cole had a unit number in SubTropolis, including an entrance address. He'd even secured a Bureau van labeled as an electrical contractor; it would draw less attention in the SubTropolis tunnels than a private vehicle, especially since so much of the place was fitted out for industrial use.

"Where should I meet you?"

"You shouldn't," he said, amused. "I'll pick you up. Curb service and all that crap. Address?" She gave it. "Right, I'm close. Five minutes. I'll honk twice."

As she hung up, she realized that both McCarthy and Susannah were staring at her. "He's a decorated FBI special agent," she said. "I can vouch for him. He's the last person you need to worry about."

"Lucia, I don't like this," McCarthy said. He leaned back in his chair, frowning. "You just got out of the hospital, for Christ's sake. Let Jazz check it out."

"Jazz is looking into where I was taken while I was unconscious. That's not something I can put on the back burner. I need to know."

"Jazz hasn't slept in a week," he said softly. "You know that, right? She's catnapped a couple of times, when she fell down from exhaustion, but she's been living on coffee and Vivarin. Give her a break. Hell, give both of you a break."

"Hydrochloric acid and sodium cyanide?" Lucia asked, and raised her eyebrows. "What if they release it on a bus, Ben? In a shopping mall? You remember the Tokyo subway attack, right?"

He said nothing, just shook his head.

"I'm going," she stated. "We're just going to check it out. If it's a legitimate operation, then no harm done. If not, the FBI will have a leg up. It's the best way to handle it. If it does turn out to be hinky, Susannah, you'll be in witness protection so fast the carpet will smoke on your way out the door."

She didn't look happy. "I don't like it here. Wouldn't it be better if I was someplace safer now? Someplace more—I don't know—fortified?"

"You've been fine here for days. You'll be fine another few hours."

Lucia got up and washed her hands in the kitchen sink, wincing at the state of the hygiene. McCarthy was going for drug-dealer authenticity. She hoped he'd changed the sheets, at least.

"Hey." He was behind her, close and warm, his voice low in her ear. She turned to face him. Behind him, the TV flipped on. Susannah was surfing listlessly through the channels, her face lit by the flickering glow.

"I know I don't have to say it, but for God's sake, would you be careful?" he asked. "You and Jazz, you're killing me. I was better off in prison. At least I didn't have friends to worry about."

She met his eyes. "Friends," she repeated softly. The sound from the TV was covering their conversation. "Is that what you want?"

"Of course not. Fresh out of prison, remember? But wanting more isn't all that smart between us right now. You're not—" He sucked in a breath and inclined his head, hiding his expression. His voice went very low in his throat. "You're not some cheap lay, okay? And I'm not going to use you that way. Or let you use me."

Oh, God. That was—powerful. She pressed back against the counter to keep from wrapping herself around him.

He raised his head and met her eyes.

"Do we understand each other?" he asked. "No matter what, I'm not going to use you."

She nodded. She wasn't sure she could actually speak at the moment.

"Okay. Then don't get yourself killed, or I'll be very disappointed," he said, and moved out of the way. She didn't go. She reached out, took hold of the scooped neck of his wifebeater, and pulled him toward her.

It was a long, slow kiss this time. He moaned, low in his throat, and put his hands on her, sliding them warmly up her shoulders, her neck, burying his fingers in her hair. She was glad she'd let it out of the ponytail.

Two honks sounded in the parking lot. His lips looked damp and hungry, and she brushed hers against them one more time. "I have to go," she whispered. He nodded. "I'll be back soon."

He stepped away and let her leave the kitchen, then stopped her with an outstretched hand at the apartment door and checked through the peephole before flipping the locks and swinging it open. When she looked back, the door was closed and locked, the peephole dark.

He was watching her go.

She followed Jazz's excellent example, taking the steps fast, and saw the electrician's van idling in the parking lot twenty feet from the sidewalk. She crossed to it without incident, she checked for Cole's familiar face before opening the passenger door.

Cole was a medium guy—medium height, medium weight, medium complexion. He'd disappear into a crowd of two. He'd chosen the vehicle well; the paint on the exterior was sun-faded and the contractor's logo and information were chipped. Cole himself was wearing a denim shirt, blue jeans and a tool belt that had just the right wear on the leather.

She wouldn't have given him a second glance, and Lucia knew herself to be more paranoid than most.

He put the van in gear without any words being spoken, and pulled out of the parking lot and onto the road.

"Sorry," she said, and indicated what she was wearing, which wasn't exactly appropriate to the occasion. "I haven't been home."

"Yeah, I heard you were in the hospital." He gave her a long look. "How are you?"

"I'm fine. Any word on the origin of the anthrax strain?"

"Came out of a lab in California, and believe me, somebody's ass is cooking on a grill right now. Rawlins is pissed. He really doesn't like terrorists."

She grinned. "And you do?"

"I spend a lot more time rubbing shoulders with them. Hard to get a real hate going when you've met their wives and kids. You know you have to do it, but sometimes it gets hard."

"Probably the same for them."

"Yeah. It is." He glanced out the back windows of the van. "You armed?"

"Always."

"Good. Not that I figure we'll need it, but I don't want to get caught with my tool belt down, if you know what I mean. Your source was right, by the way. These guys are ordering in big amounts of sodium cyanide, and their next-door neighbors are shipping in hydrochloric acid. I can see why you're not fond of the combination. It'd make a hell of a nice hydrogen cyanide cloud. In an enclosed space, it could kill hundreds, maybe thousands. Arrowhead Stadium's right down the street. The volume of gas we're talking about, you set it off in a place like that, you could count on major results."

"God," she whispered reverently. "How easy would it be—?"

"The stadium? Not very. I mean, we're talking about a lot of chemicals here, very high profile, and chemicals are bulky to move around. But you look at some of the high-rise buildings in the city? Pump some of this into the air handlers, and you're talking big numbers of bodies." Cole considered it, his light brown eyes distant as he rubbed his chin. "Unless they're making a hell of a lot of gold chains and pimping up the hubcaps of half of the country, I can't see how they could be using everything they've ordered."

"So we take a look."

"Wrong," he said. "I take a look. You watch my ride. Looking like you do, I don't think anybody's going to believe you're apprenticing as a cable puller, so you'd better keep out of sight."

He wasn't being judgmental, just practical. She nodded and settled herself in the grimy seat. It occurred to her that she should call Jazz, but truthfully, she didn't want to. She knew she was pushing her luck. Fresh from the hospital and already taking risks? Jazz wouldn't approve. Loudly. At length.

As if she'd conjured up a connection telepathically, her cell phone rang. She exchanged a quick glance with Cole as he turned the van down Eldon Road, heading toward the railroad tracks. The entrance to SubTropolis was just ahead.

Lucia pulled her phone out and flipped it open, and winced as static blasted her eardrum.

Wind noise.

No, *jet* noise. Someone was calling her from a plane.

"Hello?" She couldn't hear a damn thing. The connection was terrible, and the van she was in was rattling as well. She blocked her other ear and concentrated. "Hello? Anyone there?"

The answer, if there was one, was lost in the dull thump of the van's tires going over railroad tracks. There was a line of vehicles passing through the SubTropolis gates, most of them 18-wheelers. Cole slowed the van to a crawl. She listened for another few seconds, but the connection cut out.

"Anything important?" he asked.

"Couldn't tell," she said. She checked the caller ID, but as she'd expected, it was an air phone. "I hope not."

They edged forward slowly. When they got to the guard

station, Cole presented ID that Lucia didn't doubt was absolutely authentic. The guard waved him on, and they passed into a tunnel.

She'd expected it to be dark, but SubTropolis was surprisingly bright. The tunnel was huge and well-lit, the limestone it was carved from reflecting the brilliance.

"These guys have got some balls, setting up something down here. This place has everything. Post offices, restaurants, hell, they keep film reels somewhere. A few billion in inventory stored down here, at least. Not exactly low-profile."

"Maybe that's the point," she said. "Hiding in plain sight." She leaned over to look past the front seat at the empty, seemingly endless stretch of tunnel. "How far do we have to go?" It was too late to realize that she didn't like this kind of place, with the weight of so much rock over her head as they descended. Her palms were getting damp. The ceiling, high as it was, seemed oppressively heavy.

"Long ways," Cole said, which was not reassuring. "We make a right up ahead at Huspuckney Road, then a left on 8800."

She was starting to seriously regret suggesting this, not so much for the potential danger ahead but for the uncomfortable feeling of claustrophobia that she was battling. Stupid. She was in a van, which should have been much more claustrophobic than the spacious tunnel they were traversing.

But she could get out of the van. There were only two ways out of the tunnel: forward and back.

"You okay?" Cole was watching her. She nodded and

forced a smile. "You'll let me know if you plan to freak out, okay?"

"Remember who you're talking to," she said. "I don't have a reputation for freaking out."

"Yeah. Those are the ones you have to worry about."

Mercifully, he left her alone. She found that closing her eyes didn't help, so she finally resorted to clinging tight-lipped to the seat, fingernails digging in to the bending point.

They slowed. "All right. It's up ahead. Here's the drill. I'm going to get out and scout around, you stay in the van and monitor. I'll keep my walkie channel open. I get into trouble, you wait until I give the code phrase, which is 'electrical short.' Okay?"

"Yes," she muttered. "Fine. Absolutely."

He gave her one last assessing look as he pulled into a parking spot off the road, next to a rough-textured limestone pillar, and jammed the van into Park. "We good?"

"Fine," she repeated. "I'll be okay. You go."

He shook his head, clearly not believing her—smart man—and got out of the van. She climbed out of the passenger seat and into the murky dimness of the windowless back, where even someone staring in the window would have trouble spotting her. He nodded, locked up and sauntered toward a big industrial building that looked oddly lost in the cavernous open spaces. This was just so weird. She caught herself breathing too fast, and deliberately slowed down. Biofeedback. She'd survived traumas and tortures; she could survive a short visit underground.

Cole even walked like a working man—as if tired, in no particular hurry. He picked something overhead and traced it with a stare as he walked, clearly intent on his own business; he had some kind of handheld device in his grasp. She could hear the crunch of his work boots on rock as he walked to the back dock of the warehouse. It was labeled J&J Electroplating—Warehouse and Distribution Center. No trucks were lined up just now. Cole climbed the steps and opened an unmarked door. It closed behind him.

"Hey!" Not Cole's voice, someone else's. It came from the walkie-talkie she was holding. He'd already been challenged. "What are you doing in here?"

"You guys having trouble with the plugs?" Cole asked. "We have a fault report."

"No, we don't have trouble. Try someplace else."

"You sure you don't want me to check it out? You got a faulty plug, you could get a fire." Cole knew just how to work it, she thought; he sounded conscientious but not concerned. The subtext was his body language—he'd be ready to move to the door, convincing the subject that he wasn't at all eager to be on their property. "Hey, your call. I can write up the report, but buddy, your insurance company could nail your ass to the wall, you don't check out a fault report."

"Where you need to go?"

"In there." Cole might be choosing at random, or he might have seen something. "Line goes right in, see? Up there?" He'd be pointing at something nobody could possibly see or understand. She suppressed a grin. *Beautiful.*

"Wait here."

Footsteps faded away. Cole didn't say anything, but she heard him moving around. It seemed like a long time, but as she watched the sweep of the second hand on her watch, she realized that he'd been inside only two minutes, going on three. Probably not enough time to—

"Hey, I told you to wait!" The voice was startlingly loud.

"Sorry, man, I'm just trying to do my job, here. I got to get through twelve buildings. You know how big this place is."

"We checked it out. Everything's fine."

"Okay then. I'll write it up. Anything goes wrong, though, you—"

"Yeah, insurance, whatever. We're closing up."

"Have a good one."

Cole was on the move, heading for the door.

"Hang on a second," said the other voice. "What's your name?"

Lucia slid her gun from its holster and put her hand on the door handle.

"Frank. Frank Scarabelli. Here—here's my ID, okay? I don't want no trouble or nothing. I'm just—"

"Doing your job, yeah, we heard. Listen, hang out a second, okay? I'm gonna make a phone call."

"Okay," Cole said. He sounded thoroughly disgusted. "You guys get an electrical short, it's no skin off my—"

She was out of the van, gun at her side, before he finished the sentence. Her knees felt weak, her whole body not quite in tune, but it served to get her across the exposed parking lot and behind one of the massive white limestone pillars. She sucked in two deep breaths, then finished the run to the warehouse dock. Up the six concrete steps to the flat staging area. The walk-in door was closed again. All but one of the garage doors were down. The one on the end was clanking shut.

I won't make it, some part of her thought, but she didn't allow that to stop her. It wasn't a matter for thinking. She kicked off her shoes and crossed the distance in long runner's strides, moving as silently as she could.

The door was clattering down. There were two feet of clearance left.

Lucia hit the concrete and rolled, tucking elbows and knees, and she felt hard steel and rubber grab her for a heart-stopping second. But then momentum won and she was inside. The door rattled irritably shut with a boom just an inch behind her.

She was panting and shaking, but there was no time for fear now. She was exposed. There were three men at the end of the hall, one smaller, two larger. Cole was the smaller. This end of the dock was in relative shadow, which was in her favor.

Should have called for backup, she thought, but she doubted that wireless signals would make it through the solid limestone roof. She'd need a land line, and by that time…by that time, she'd have gotten another friend killed.

She rolled up to her knee, gun trained steadily on the group at the far end of the hall, and then to her bare feet. The concrete felt ice-cold. She gained the concealment of a big industrial trash bin and risked another look to assess the situation. She was close enough to see faces now, and catch fragments of words.

Cole still looked bland and harassed. "Guys, this is stupid. Look, let me get the hell out, you call whoever you want to fix the damn electrical—"

The biggest one hit him. One quick pop, not telegraphed, and it took Cole full in the face. Blood spattered. He went down, and the man was already moving his right foot in a bone-breaking kick.

She couldn't afford caution. Caution would get Cole disabled or dead, and she couldn't take these men playing by FBI rules. This would have to be done Jazz-style.

Lucia stood, braced her shoulder against the wall and kicked the big rubber trash can at its wheeled base. It screeched indignantly and rolled at an angle across the exposed space to slam into one of the metal doors, then tipped and crashed onto its side.

Both of the suspects spun to look. Both drew guns.

Lucia braced her right hand with her left and sighted.

"Freeze!" she yelled. They moved fast, too fast, and a bullet exploded part of the concrete next to her arm.

She pulled the trigger twice without flinching, and the first shooter sank down on his knees, swaying. The gun slipped from his hand and spun across the concrete. Cole, his face a mask of blood, scrambled after it and kicked the man's side to dump him on his face. The other man dropped his gun and voluntarily went down, hands on the back of his head.

"Dammit!" Cole screamed. "Are you hurt? *Lucia?*"

"No," she said calmly, and walked forward. "If you call an ambulance, you can probably save this one. I think I missed his heart."

Cole—normally so cool and insouciant—looked shocked. She raised her eyes to his, and saw him flinch a little. Seasoned FBI, and he flinched. But then, he didn't know her, did he?

Nobody did.

"Better call it in," she said. "I'll check the rest of the building. These can't be the only bad guys in the place."

"I'm going to hell for this."

"Yeah," she said grimly. "I'll save you a seat."

Chapter 13

There were, in fact, seventeen other people in the building. She didn't have to shoot any of the others; intimidation worked well enough. She herded them into an unused freezer room and locked them up tight.

She was sitting against the door, listening to them batter at it, when Cole came to find her. He'd wiped some of the blood off his face, but that was a broken nose, no question, and it was beginning to swell. He'd have black eyes, too. That had been a hell of a first punch.

"What are you going to say when they get here?" she asked, when he was seated on the concrete with her, back against the door.

"Planning on throwing myself on the mercy of my superiors," he said. "Fuck, Lucia. I ought to know by now that if you're involved, it ain't exactly a fact-finding mission. I mean, I've heard enough stories."

"Stories," she repeated. She felt tired, liquid, as if her body might just drip away.

"You know."

"I don't."

"Is it true what they say about what happened in Prague?"

"What do they say happened?" The door behind them rattled with a particularly violent kick. It felt good, rather like a massage.

"Two dozen terrorists, a cache of nerve gas, and you were the only survivor."

"It's not true." It wasn't. There was Gregory Ivanovich, after all. Turncoat and torturer and savior and traitor. God alone knew what he was now, but she had no doubt he knew where she'd gone during the past week, and what had happened to her.

Cole made a doubtful sound. "You should have declared first, by the way."

"Declared what? I'm not FBI. The government doesn't pay me. And in the kind of work I used to do, declaring yourself was stupid." Which was as close as she intended to get to reliving the past, even with Cole. "If I'd taken the time to chat, they'd have killed me. You also."

He sighed and dabbed at his bleeding nose. "Man. I'll be lucky if I get a posting in Antarctica after this."

"Cheer up," she said. "I think you just averted a major terrorist act. Also, there seems to be a clean room behind that door. Biohazard suits hanging from hooks in the airlock. You might have even found the source of the anthrax."

As the sirens came closer, they sat in silence, surveying

the big white room with its drums of chemicals and—most ominously—pressurized tanks marked with Poison labels.

"So," Cole said. "If I get my ass fired over this—"

"Always a place for you at Callender & Garza, my friend. Provided we're still open, since we've shot more people in the past couple of days than the KCPD has shot in a couple of years. It might pose a problem."

He shook his head. "You'll be okay. You're a survivor."

They both froze at a sound outside, from the direction of the door, and without any discussion got to their feet and moved to stand on either side of the single doorway to the room.

A hand holding a gun crossed the threshold.

"Freeze!" Lucia yelled, and spun away from the wall. Cole did the same, bracketing the newcomer from an obtuse angle, taking a low line.

"Police!" the other man screamed at the same instant, and Lucia held off on the trigger just by a split second as she recognized the ragged, unshaved, red-eyed face of... Detective Ken Stewart. "Drop the guns, dammit. Drop them!" he ordered.

"FBI," Cole said calmly, and showed his badge and credentials without wavering his aim. "Detective Stewart, right? KCPD?"

"Yes." Stewart stopped trying to cover both of them, and focused solely on Lucia. "Drop it!"

"Jesus! Drop yours!" she retorted hotly. "You know who I am!"

He cocked the hammer on his gun, an unnecessary and

theatrical gesture. "First shot cripples you for life. *Drop it now!*"

"That isn't necessary," Cole said.

"If she's not FBI, she drops the goddamn gun!"

There wasn't much choice. Getting into a pissing contest with Stewart wouldn't do her any good, even if she won. Lucia made the gun safe and put it down on the ground. She took a step back from it, hands still raised, as Stewart gestured.

"You got here fast," Cole said. "Ambulance on the way?"

"I had a tip. Yeah, paramedics and squad cars should be a couple of minutes." Stewart looked around the place, and focused on the banging of the steel door. "Suspects in custody?"

"Custody would be a stretch, but they're contained," Cole said. "One wounded in the back room, one not wounded and hog-tied like a son of a bitch because I don't like him very much. Other than that, we've swept the place and the rest are in there."

"Okay, good." Stewart, after a long moment, holstered his gun.

"Can I pick up my weapon now?" Lucia asked.

"No," Stewart said. "Over there. Sit down and wait." He picked up her gun and shoved it in his coat pocket. "Move it, Garza." Behind him, Cole made an apologetic shrug.

She kept her hands up, walked to the corner and slid down to a sitting position, resting her hands in her lap. Stewart stared at her for a second or two, as if considering handcuffs. She could hear the eerie wail of sirens outside, and wondered wearily how long it would take to untangle this particular mess.

If she looked tired, Stewart looked...sick. Pale, red-eyed, twitching like an addict. Was that possible? Was he, in fact, an addict? No, surely drug tests would show it. She was being uncharitable, purely because of his prejudices against Jazz. He was probably just sick.

Should have shot him, she thought. It came from a part of her that she often denied existed—cold, calculating, the voice of a survivor.

"You received a tip?" she asked Stewart neutrally. "You've never been here before?"

He gave her a glare. "No. Why?"

Anthrax sent to her office.

Ken Stewart, following her from McCarthy's hearing.

"No reason," she said, still neutral, and watched him sweat.

There were, by the last count she heard, enough chemicals in the warehouse to kill tens of thousands, and maybe more if delivered accurately. And she'd been right about the clean room. There was a neat little bottle of white powder. Anthrax. Enough for a dozen lethal mailings, at least. From the envelopes they'd found in the process of being addressed, they'd been intended for the local FBI offices, as well as other government buildings.

If Ken Stewart had contemplated killing her and Cole— and she had no doubt that he had—he lost his chance as the worker bees from KCPD took over. She and Cole were quickly whisked off to a local FBI establishment. It was an improvement over the police headquarters isolation room. The FBI facility came with fresh coffee and more comfortable chairs. She caught a glimpse of Susannah Davis being brought in, at one point, escorted by Ben McCarthy.

Lucia heard Jazz's voice even through the soundproofing.

"—son of a bitch!" Jazz finished bellowing, just as the door opened again, and Agent Rawlins came in. His ears had turned red, though he was keeping a carefully blank expression. Jazz was right on his heels, as dynamic as he was controlled. She'd been messing with her hair, and it stuck out in unruly spikes. Her face was flushed and vividly animated. When she saw Lucia, she charged forward and dropped into the empty chair next to her.

"Hey," she said, without looking.

"Hey," Lucia replied. She felt a smile tugging at her lips and sternly exiled it back to its waiting room. "So. How's it going?"

"So-so. You were supposed to take it easy, as I recall. Have a talk with Susannah. Lay low."

"Change of plans."

Jazz sat back and folded her arms. "You put *another* guy in the hospital, and that's the best you can come up with? *Change of plans?*"

Lucia shrugged. "I shot in defense of the life of an agent of the FBI. Which I'm pretty certain is covered under self-defense. Isn't it, Agent Rawlins?"

He pulled up a chair, too, on the opposite side of the table. "Do you want legal counsel, Ms. Garza?"

"You're kidding."

"I don't kid about things like that."

"Am I being charged with something? Bringing a clue to the attention of the FBI, perhaps? Is that criminal these days?"

Rawlins was furious. "From anybody else, I could accept ignorance as an excuse, but you know better. You know better than to come to some agent off the books and put him in a dangerous situation."

"Agent Cole was only trying to establish—"

"He was grandstanding, and you were helping him, and you both nearly got yourselves killed. Which in itself doesn't distress me, but now I've got about twenty people to investigate, the clock's running, and for all I know the major players have hopped a plane to Brazil. So you'll forgive me if I'm not pleased with the outcome of this little fishing expedition."

"Agent Cole," Lucia repeated, "was only trying to independently establish the truth of what our witness was saying about the chemicals. And if you've got twenty people to check out, then why are you wasting time with me?"

Jazz didn't bother to suppress a snort. "Wow. Gotcha, Agent Redhead."

He glared at her.

"Rawlins," she amended blandly. "Sorry. Pet name. I find red hair very sexy. It's distracting."

With a mighty effort, he ignored her. "So your information came solely from this witness, Susannah Davis. Is that right?"

"Yes," Lucia said. "Cole verified that there had been shipments of chemicals to the SubTropolis address. He was just confirming that the operations weren't really doing electroplating before bringing in a full team on the operation."

"Cole can answer for himself. You shot a man."

Lucia raised her eyebrows. "Agent Rawlins, I shot someone who was about to put your agent's ribs through his lungs!"

The door opened again. Agent Rawlins frowned in irritation as a woman—FBI, by the well-scrubbed look of her—stuck her head cautiously inside.

"Attorney's here," she said. "He's demanding to see her."

Rawlins swiveled his eyes back toward Lucia. "I thought you didn't want a lawyer."

"I don't think I ever actually said that."

She expected Borden, but when the female agent disappeared, the door opened wider, and a silver-haired man in an expensive suit walked in. His briefcase cost more than an FBI agent's monthly salary, Lucia felt sure. The suit was European, hand-tailored and impeccably elegant.

Milo Laskins, senior partner at Gabriel, Pike & Laskins, nodded briskly to Agent Rawlins, set his briefcase down on the table and handed over a card. "I represent Ms. Garza and Ms. Callender," he said. "Please explain to me why they're being detained."

"They're not being detained. They're—"

"—assisting you in your inquiries, to coin a British phrase?" Laskins didn't bother to sit. He gave the impression he wouldn't be staying long. His silver hair gleamed in the dim lighting, and so did his diamond stickpin. "Please, sir, I didn't graduate from Harvard yesterday. You're on a fishing expedition, trying to find something to level a charge against my client, who was, by the way, attempting to save the life of one of your own."

"She put him there in the first place. I don't like private investigators using my people to do their dirty work."

Laskins's white eyebrows rose, giving his electric-blue stare even more impact. "And if she hadn't called you in on a potential terrorist threat, I can only imagine how much difficulty she'd be in right now. She received suspicious information, and turned it over to the FBI. She offered to assist the authorities in their investigation. In the course of the investigation, she came to the aid of a federal officer in the performance of his duties and was unfortunately forced to wound one man participating in a suspected terrorist conspiracy. Do I have the facts straight, Agent Rawlins?"

Rawlins's ears were red again, his face masklike. "More or less."

"You have all the information my clients possess in this matter. You have Ms. Davis, who was the source of the information in the first place. You have the location, and you have the players involved. Am I to assume that you have everything you need to conclude your investigation for the moment?"

"For the moment."

"Then I believe I'll escort my clients home at this time. As you know, Ms. Garza has recently been ill. Ladies…?" Laskins hadn't even opened his briefcase. Lucia had seen dazzling lawyering before, but this had set a land speed record. She stood up, Jazz close behind her, and followed Laskins out of the interrogation room.

Rawlins didn't say a thing. He said it very loudly.

Outside, the other FBI agents stared, but didn't stop them. McCarthy was waiting nearby, arms folded, leaning against the wall. When he saw Lucia he slowly straightened, hands falling to his sides. There was something in his eyes she couldn't read, except that it was strong, and it was all he could do to look casual under the pressure of it.

"All in one piece?" he asked.

"Still," she confirmed.

Laskins's hand closed on her upper arm in a viselike grip. "Downstairs," he said, and all of the smooth civility had disappeared from his voice. "Move it."

"Hey!"

He'd grabbed hold of Jazz, too. Lucia could have told him that wouldn't go over well, but not even Jazz was willing to start a physical confrontation in front of several rapt FBI witnesses. Laskins herded them to the door, tossed his visitor's badge on the receptionist's desk, and then steered them out into the elevator lobby. McCarthy followed.

Jazz yanked free as soon as the office doors closed. "Boy, you'd *better* not put your hands on me again, or—"

"Or what?" Laskins snarled. He was scary, for an old man. "Shut up, the lot of you. You're coming with me."

Lucia felt a weary flare of anger. "Or?" she asked. "Because I'd very much like to go home now. Can't your obligatory lecture on responsibility wait until tomorrow?"

"No," he said, and stabbed the elevator button with a fore-finger. His jaw muscles were so tense she was surprised he could force words out. "Tomorrow is too late, Ms. Garza. *Today* may very well be too late. As I said, you're coming with me, and if you resist the order, then I have people who will enforce it."

"People?" Jazz laughed out loud. "Damn, this I gotta see."

The elevator doors opened, and Gregory Ivanovich gave them all a wide, lovely smile. The wolf was back in his eyes. "Do you?" he asked Jazz, and gestured politely for them all to get in the elevator. "Perhaps better if you don't see."

He was holding a gun. Gutsy, Lucia thought, considering that just feet away were six armed FBI agents.

He had the gun focused unwaveringly on Jazz's head. "In the elevator, my dear," he said—not to Jazz, to Lucia. "I would hate to have to create a mess all over the federal agents' lobby to make my point. *No!*" he said sharply, without shifting his gaze, as McCarthy moved forward. Ben instantly stopped. "You know I mean it. One at a time, into the elevator. My lovely Lucia first."

She moved in and took the opposite corner. She knew of no one with more iron concentration than Gregory; she'd seen him hold a target in the middle of a firefight, waiting for just the right second to pull the trigger. McCarthy seemed to have realized it as well; he came next, hands well away from his body. Laskins followed, standing behind Gregory.

Gregory smiled very slowly at Jazz, and made a tiny little gesture with his empty left hand.

She walked in, eyes still locked on his, full of fury and challenge. He held the stare as he released the Hold button and the doors rumbled shut.

It was a long ride down. Nobody spoke. Jazz never blinked. Neither did Gregory.

"Your name is Jazz, yes? Like the music?"

She kept on staring. He returned the gun to his shoulder holster with the fast, elegant gesture of a stage magician, about one second before the doors opened.

"You're crazy, *dorogaya*. I like that in a woman."

"You and me," Jazz said grimly, "are going to go a few rounds. You know that, right?"

"I look forward to the opportunity."

Laskins pushed forward, leading the way. McCarthy grabbed Lucia's arm. "Stay here," he whispered. "Go back up, get Rawlins—"

McCarthy was wrong. There was no chance—not even a small one—that if she went back upstairs the FBI could protect her. But that wasn't what made her step out to follow Laskins. It was Gregory Ivanovich, who knew her as well as anyone alive, putting two fingers to the back of Jazz's head and miming pulling a trigger.

She didn't know what Laskins would do, but she knew Gregory. All too well.

Chapter 14

There was a big black limousine in the parking lot across the street and it held all of them comfortably. Or uncomfortably, thanks to the tension in the passenger compartment. It was a long, silent ride, but the landmarks were familiar. Lucia exchanged a quick look with Jazz, who raised her eyebrows and widened her eyes. Lucia shrugged.

The limousine turned down the slope of a parking garage, and parked on the top level, next to the elevators of… their own office building.

"You're kidding," Jazz said flatly.

"You may be assured, Ms. Callender, that I'm deadly serious today," Laskins said. "There's nothing I'm finding remotely amusing."

Gregory Ivanovich hustled them into the elevators and upstairs. The doors had been opened wide into their office suite, and all the lights were on. No one there. At least,

Lucia thought, Pansy hadn't been caught up in this mess. That was some comfort.

Laskins opened the doors to the big conference room, with its long, gleaming table and recessed lighting.

It was full of people, who were chatting among themselves in a pleasant buzz of sound. Twelve—no, fourteen of them. Sixteen, counting Laskins, who took a chair at the table, and Gregory, who leaned against a wall, seeming entirely at home. Lucia scanned the other faces quickly. Laskins was the very image of a successful lawyer, but there was a tired, unkempt-looking woman who might have come straight from tending her kids. A tall, thin black man who wore glasses and looked like a professor. A slender, well-dressed young woman with understated jewelry and the unmistakable aura of wealth.

The buzz died down as everyone's attention focused on the newcomers.

"Let me guess. The Cross Society," Jazz said, just as Lucia was about to. "Wow. Imagine how impressed I am. No, go on. Just imagine."

The stay-at-home mom smiled. She was the only one who did.

"Not the entire society, obviously, merely a few key players," Laskins said, and shut the doors. "Be seated, the three of you."

"Where's James?" Jazz asked.

"James?" Laskins echoed, as if he'd never heard the name before. Lucia felt a twinge of anxiety, and saw it in Jazz, as well.

"James *Borden,* you asshole. Where is he?" When Jazz got scared, she got belligerent.

"Mr. Borden is on an errand. It's quite an important one, actually. Be seated, Ms. Callender. We don't have a lot of time."

Gregory stepped forward and pulled out a chair. He performed an extravagant comic-opera bow. Lucia tried to send Jazz a message in a last, quick glance, and slid into an empty chair on the other side of the table. McCarthy took the one next to her.

Gregory bowed again, even more comically.

Jazz gritted her teeth and sat.

"What in the hell is this, Laskins?" Lucia asked. For answer, he held up his hand. Gregory stepped forward and put something into it.

A red envelope.

"This," he said, "is a duplicate of what went to Ms. Callender earlier in the day," he said. "It was waiting for her when she arrived back at her temporary home in Manny Glickman's warehouse. Go ahead. Open it, Ms. Callender."

Jazz just stared at him. Didn't reach for it. After a long enough pause that it became clear she wasn't about to comply, Lucia reached over and took it. She opened it and took out a single white sheet of folded paper.

On it was written, DO NOT ALLOW LUCIA GARZA TO CARRY THROUGH WITH THE INVESTIGATION OF J&J ELECTROPLATING.

No letterhead, no signature. Lucia looked up at Jazz, who

returned her stare without flinching. There was something fierce in her eyes.

"Did you get it, Ms. Callender?" Laskins asked.

"Yes," Jazz said. "I got it."

"Then why did you fail to follow instructions? Do you not yet understand the seriousness of the situation? When you fail to follow our instructions, people *die*."

"Yeah, and guess what? When we *do* follow your instructions, people die," Jazz said. "I'm sick of operating in the dark. No more of these mysterious bullshit messages from nowhere. You want to enlist us in your army of do-gooders, you'd better damn well convince me how holding off on busting a bunch of terrorists is *doing good!*"

"It's not your job to question how or why we give these instructions!" Laskins bellowed. His face had gone entirely red, so mottled Lucia was afraid he was going to clutch his chest and hit the floor.

"Bite me!" Jazz screamed. "You guys treat us like trained monkeys, and you know what? We can make our own decisions. Isn't that why we're so damn valuable to you? Because what we do *matters?*"

"Yes," said the thin black man, farther down the table. He'd helped himself to a cup of tea, Lucia saw. By the looks of other cups around the room, they'd also started the coffeemaker. They'd certainly made themselves thoroughly at home. "Yes, you do make your own decisions. And you have no idea how much chaos that creates, do you? Presumptions are made about how the time stream will run—they have to be made, or we'd never be able to predict any outcomes at all. You are a fulcrum upon which events turn. And when you don't do as we've asked, you upset everything."

The hausfrau next to him laughed apologetically. "You've lost them, Jeffrey." She put a plump, motherly hand over his and gave Lucia a warm smile. "You have to imagine the scope of what we're talking about, ladies. It's not just an ei-ther-or proposition. It's like the biggest pinball game you can imagine, with a hundred thousand balls in play, and a mil-lion flippers, each of which has a simple decision to make. Do or don't. You see, it was a simple decision we made on your behalf—don't move on the terrorist information. In connection with about fifty other simple decisions, it cleared the way for something important to happen. However, now all of that is unclear again, the ball randomly bouncing. We can't control what we can't foresee."

Lucia looked around at all of them, all the quiet faces, ranging from scowls to smiles. "You're all...psychics? Like Simms?"

"Oh, no." The man called Jeffrey sipped his tea and looked put out at the question. "There are only a handful of genuine psychics in this world, you know. Fifty or so, in any generation—"

"Sixty-two as of last week," murmured an old, creaky gentleman two chairs down. He blinked at Lucia benignly from behind thick, magnifying lenses.

"Edgar, it doesn't matter. I wasn't trying to be precise, I was—"

"Precision is important," Edgar said. "I wouldn't want our new friends to think we weren't precise. My, no."

Jeffrey shot him a grim look. "As I was saying, I could give you the exact mathematical equations about how we derive the existence and location of these people, but I doubt it would mean anything to you. To put it simply, we are a kind of clearinghouse. In addition to Simms, who founded our organization, we maintain facilities in which quite a number of precognitives are housed and cared for. They give us predictions—some, as many as hundreds each day. We feed these into a sophisticated mathematical model, and from that, we see the shape of things to come. Not in detail, you understand. In generalities. The psychics themselves are specific, but in combining their prophecies you lose the—the details. You understand?"

Lucia exchanged a fast look with Jazz. *Why isn't Borden here?* She couldn't tell if Jazz was thinking about that; her partner looked closed and coplike, utterly unreadable. Just like McCarthy, next to her. How much of this had he heard before? How much did he believe? Not enough, obviously, if he'd finally broken with the Society and gotten himself tossed in jail for his troubles.

"Yes, I understand," she said, although she was fairly certain that she didn't. "You get hundreds of predictions a day. Somehow you create scenarios out of blending all of them together, to show you the future."

"No," Laskins said. He'd recovered some of his calm. His color was a hot pink instead of deep red, and he'd seated himself again. "Not the future. A—sketch of the future. A rough outline of it, with some details in place to give it structure and scope."

"And if you don't like what you see," McCarthy said, "you just figure out which pinball levers to push until you get what you want."

It was as if they'd forgotten he was there. All eyes turned toward him. If he felt the weight of it, he didn't let it show; he was reconfiguring a paper clip into steel origami, and he kept right on doing it.

"What they're not telling you," McCarthy continued, "is that they're all about the greater good. Excuse me, the greater good as they see it. So if a couple hundred people have to die in an upcoming terrorist attack, well, those are acceptable losses if that still takes us down the path they want us to follow."

"People die," said a young woman dressed in ill-fitting blue jeans over a skeletal frame. Her arms were frighteningly thin, as if she'd just come from a prison camp. But since her skin had a tanning-salon glow, Lucia was fairly certain that it was the gauntness of fashion, not famine. "You can't make decisions like this based on individuals, it makes everything worthless. You have to take a wider view than that."

"I'm sure that's a great comfort to the dead," Lucia said. "That they died for a reason."

"Everybody dies for a reason," Laskins said. "We just try to make it a better reason than random chance."

"That apply to all of you, too?" McCarthy asked. They looked surprised. "No. Didn't think so. That's just for the rank and file, right? The chorus? The spear carriers? The guy on the left, in the back row, whose name we never know? It's okay if *he* dies for a reason. Not if your own kid does." He got up, staring at them in bitter contempt. "I told you before, I'm not playing your game."

The gaunt woman smiled cynically. "So you've told us," she said. "Have you informed your friends that we provided the information that got you out of prison? In return for your cooperation?"

McCarthy slowly bent over and put his hands flat on the table, staring at her. If looks could kill... Lucia shuddered at what was in his face. She'd thought Gregory had the wolf in him, but this was something else again.

"I'm not working for you." He said it softly, but it was loaded with meaning. "You have no idea what it costs me, but I'm not doing it. Do you understand me? You can send me back to prison. You can kill me. *You can't make me do what you want.*"

"I think you'll find," she said in an even softer whisper, "that it no longer matters, Mr. McCarthy. You've served your purpose. You're Chorus. You're that poor man in the back row whose name we won't remember when you die."

Silence. Lucia felt her whole body trembling with the tension of it. There was something terrible being said, something awful in Ben's face.

"What did you do?" he asked, and suddenly all that control was gone, and he was moving, moving *fast,* screaming. "*What did you do, you bitch?* You were just supposed to take care of her, you weren't supposed to—"

He went over the table. The woman stumbled backward, terror written all over her face.

"No!" Laskins yelled, and then it was a melee, and when it was over, McCarthy was on the carpet, facedown, panting, with Gregory's knee in his back. "I will not have this, do you understand? This behavior is unacceptable!"

"Unacceptable!" McCarthy's voice broke. "You fucking bastards, you have no idea what you're doing, do you? Ask Simms. Ask Simms if you don't believe me."

Silence. The assembled members milled around, and some of them returned to their chairs. Laskins looked around the room, then cleared his throat.

"Unfortunately, we can't do that," he said. "Max Simms broke out of his prison three days ago. We have no idea where he is at this point."

The thank-you messages Jazz and Lucia had gotten had been signed, in invisible ink, by Max Simms. *They don't know that,* Lucia thought, and met Jazz's eyes.

Jazz smiled slightly. Not a nice expression. She was furious, and she wanted to hit something, anything.

The fact that she hadn't, that she'd let McCarthy be taken down without jumping in with both feet, was significant.

"What do you want?" Lucia asked. "Why are we here?"

Laskins seemed to forget about McCarthy for a moment to focus back on the two of them.

"You're here for the same reason we all are. Because if you weren't, you'd be dead," he said. "And really, we can't have that happen. Not just now. Now if you don't sit quietly, I'm going to have Mr. Ivanovich handcuff and gag you."

"What are you waiting for?" Jazz demanded.

"Something terrible." It was one of the other Cross

Society members, a sad-looking little man in a gray sports coat. He had a ragged fringe of gray hair clinging to the crown of his skull, and big dark eyes behind round glasses. "Something terrible. I wish we could avoid it, but it's impossible. Something terrible *must* happen."

Gregory Ivanovich let McCarthy up off of the floor and tossed a tangle of zip ties onto the conference table, along with three leather ball gags. Tools of his trade. Lucia felt her stomach clench when she saw them.

"Sit quietly, or I will do it," he said. "You know it, *dorogaya*. Tell them."

Lucia leaned forward and put a hand on Jazz's arm. A light pressure, but Jazz got the message.

McCarthy rose to his feet, breathing heavily, face still red with fury, but he didn't say anything either. After a moment, he took the chair next to Jazz and clasped his hands tight on top of the table. His knuckles turned as pale as parchment.

Silence.

"That's better," Laskins said, and turned to look out the window at the view. "That's better. Now, we wait."

Two hours later, with no explanation, one of the Society members' beeper went off, and some unspoken signal was passed. They all relaxed.

Somewhere, something terrible had happened.

"Take them into the other room," Laskins said to Gregory. "Lock them in. We'll see to them later."

He nodded and made a gesture to get Lucia, Jazz and McCarthy to their feet. The next room was an empty office, and Gregory showed them in with another of his extravagant gestures.

With a gun in his hand, of course.

"No lock on the door," Jazz pointed out. For her, it was a pretty mild tone. Gregory's lips grinned, but the rest of his face stayed entirely still.

"Pretty one, *I'm* the lock," he said. "I'll be sitting in a chair across from the door. By all means, open it. I'm a very good shot, but I can always use the practice."

He pulled the door shut.

"He's bluffing," Jazz said.

"No," Lucia sighed. "He's not. Ben? You okay?"

He hadn't said a word. He didn't even look at her. "I'm fine." He didn't sound fine. He sounded—terrible. "How long you think they'll keep us here?"

"Who the hell cares?" Jazz retorted. She stalked toward him. "You want to explain now?"

His eyes focused on her, then slid away. He walked toward a window, changed course and folded himself into a chair in the corner. Eyes shut.

"Oh, no you don't," Jazz said, and followed him. She stood over him, hands balled into fists. "What they said in there. About the Cross Society getting you out of jail. That was bullshit, right? *Right?*"

He didn't answer. Lucia felt what was left of the strength of fear bleed away, and her muscles demanded she sit. She leaned, instead, trying to look composed. "No," she said for him. "It wasn't. The pictures exonerating you were genuine, but they'd withheld them, hadn't they? They wanted something from you. And until you agreed, they wouldn't release the evidence that would get you out of prison."

"I wasn't guilty," he said. His eyes were still shut.

"I know," she murmured. "Not of those murders."

"Wait a minute. They *did* release the pictures," Jazz said. "So...you agreed..."

McCarthy stayed quiet. Jazz reached down and grabbed the faded shoulders of his open flannel shirt, hauling him to his feet. "You *agreed,*" she repeated, and her voice was deadly quiet. "To what?"

"It doesn't concern you."

"No," Lucia said. "It concerns me. Doesn't it?"

His eyes opened, and even as numbed and tired and betrayed as she was, she flinched from what was in them. Jazz kept asking the question, but Lucia knew full well McCarthy wasn't going to answer her. She walked to the window and stared out, thought about Laskins treating himself to the same view one wall over.

She dug her cell phone from her purse and speed-dialed Manny's number.

No answer.

The office door opened, and an older man walked in. He was slender and stooped, with mild blue eyes and thin white hair. Short, maybe five foot five at most.

He looked sweet and a little lost, and his clothes were too big for him. He smiled at them impartially, closed the door behind him and walked across the room to the bare desk. He sat down in the chair, slid open the bottom drawer and took out a duffel bag. He unzipped it and revealed four military-issue breathing masks.

"You'll need these," he said, and held one out. Nobody moved. "Tick tock, people, tick tock. Let's move."

"Who the hell is this?" Lucia asked in confusion, and she looked at Jazz for information.

Jazz was staring at the man intently and didn't answer.

McCarthy did. He stepped forward, took the gas mask and said, "Meet Max Simms."

And then he put on the mask.

Jazz took the second one. Simms favored her with a beatific smile, then turned his attention to Lucia.

"Max Simms," she repeated. "You're kidding."

"We don't have time for introductions," Simms said, and checked a watch on his left wrist. "Let's see, did I adjust it for the time zone? Yes, I think I did. You have approximately ten seconds to make your decision, Lucia. Forgive me if I don't wait."

Jazz had tugged on her mask. Simms put his on.

Lucia looked at them all, one after another, and grabbed for the last one.

She got it in place as Simm's silent finger count went to three, then to two, then to a single index finger.

Then to zero.

Nothing seemed to happen at all. She felt nothing, smelled nothing except the industrial plastic of the mask and her own sweat. Her breath was coming fast, too fast.

"What the hell is going on?" she asked. The plastic muffled and distorted her voice, but she was pretty sure the others could hear her. Jazz lifted her hands and dropped them. McCarthy shook his head.

Simms said, "Obviously, somebody's delivered gas into this building."

"Lethal?" Lucia's mind went to the drums of chemicals back at the warehouse.

"No. Wait, please."

If anything had happened in the other rooms, there was no indication at all. No sound. The minutes seemed to drag on, and on, and on. Simms waited, watching the second hand of his watch, and then moved to the door and opened it.

Gregory Ivanovich was nowhere in sight. A chair sat empty where he'd been. No signs of struggle.

Simms led them toward the elevators. As they passed the conference room, Lucia slowed and looked in.

Empty chairs, pushed back unevenly from the table. A handprint on the glass, smudging the sunlight. An overturned cup, with coffee dripping from the edge of the table onto the floor.

There were drag marks on the carpet.

She heard the steady chop of a helicopter—no, *helicopters*. She dashed forward to look out of the window just as three large black aircraft gained the sky and headed for the far horizon.

Where had they come from?

"Eidolon," she whispered. Her breath fogged the plastic of the gas mask. "Son of a bitch. You're working with them."

Simms took her by the elbow and silently walked her from the conference room out to the lobby. He hit the button for the elevator and stood with his hands behind his back, bouncing on his toes as if he had energy to burn. He hadn't taken off the mask. Lucia felt sweat trickling down the sides of her face and itched to rip the thing away, but she didn't dare. What the *hell* had just happened? How had Eidolon pulled that off? Not without help, that much was sure...

McCarthy's hand touched hers and twined around it, holding fast. She looked at him, but he was staring straight ahead, face unreadable under the gas mask. She shook free.

Once they were in the elevator and the doors had shut, Simms stripped off his gas mask. Jazz was yelling even before hers hit the floor. "What in the hell was that, you asshole? What the hell is going on?"

"I just saved your lives," Simms said. "Well, Jazz, yours and Ben's. Lucia's survival has always been assured."

"Excuse me?" Lucia tossed her gas mask in a pile with the others. The elevator continued down to the parking level, dinged and disgorged them into the empty structure. No sign of the limousine that had delivered them. Simms looked momentarily nonplussed, and then smiled as a shadow rumbled at the top of the ramp and started down.

Manny's black Hummer, glossy and impenetrable in the light. He was driving.

James Borden was in the passenger seat. He jumped out as the vehicle squealed to a stop, and threw open all the doors.

"In the car," Simms said. "This isn't safe."

That, Lucia thought, was the understatement of the century.

* * *

"You're in on this?" Jazz asked Manny, when they'd piled into the SUV and pulled out of the parking lot. Simms was in the back, with Borden and McCarthy; Jazz and Lucia were up front. Not that Lucia was happy having Simms at her back, but she wouldn't be any happier having him next to her.

Manny shot Jazz a near-panicked look. "In on what?"

"The Cross Society crap. Whatever crack dream conspiracy this is!"

"What?"

Jazz got control of herself, or at least enough to take in a couple of deep breaths. "Why did you show up?"

"Borden said you needed a ride. Jazz, you know I don't like strangers in my car. Who is he?"

Jazz looked over her shoulder at Borden, then at Simms. She turned around and started to answer, but Borden cut her off. "We can talk about this at the warehouse."

"No freakin' way am I taking a stranger to my house," Manny said. He stared at Simms in the rearview mirror. Simms stared back. "No freakin' way."

Simms looked away and said, as if he were talking to thin air, "Ben, how did you locate the unmarked spot where Mr. Glickman had been buried alive?"

Manny braked. Cars honked all around them, and he blinked and hit the gas. Going a little too fast, this time.

"Answer the question, Ben," Simms said gently.

"I followed the leads. I worked the case. So did Jazz."

"Yes, but you had something Jazz didn't, isn't that true?"

"Don't."

"You had luck."

"Not everything is your goddamn psychic powers at work, Simms."

"Not everything," Simms agreed. "And you would have found Manny eventually. But I helped you find him before it was too late. In the nick of time, in fact. Wouldn't you agree with that?"

Silence. McCarthy was staring intently out the window. Manny, on the other hand, was an open book—sweating, shaking, clearly and deeply rattled.

"Mr. Glickman, I'm not a stranger to you," Simms said. "I wish I could have helped you before you experienced— what you experienced. It is not a perfect world, and what I do is even more imperfect than that. But I need you now. I need your help. And I'm asking you to give it even though I know that it's against your nature."

"Did he—" Manny's voice failed, choked off. He slowed and stopped at a light, but Lucia could tell that it was just reflex, not thought. He was driving on autopilot. "Ben, did this guy tell you where to find me?"

McCarthy closed his eyes. "I knew where to find you. He told me *exactly* where to dig. Without that—it would have been another hour, probably."

Manny's eyes filled with tears. Lucia, even though she knew it wasn't welcome, even though she knew he'd flinch, put her hand on his arm.

He did flinch. But not as badly as he might have.

"You don't have to do anything you don't want to,

Manny," Lucia said. "Ever. You know that. Neither Jazz nor I would ever ask it of you."

He nodded convulsively, gulped in a breath and hit the gas when the light turned green.

Simms settled back, content, smiling.

She hated him, in that bright and completely lucid second.

"You know," Jazz said, as Manny pushed together two worktables and unfolded camp chairs, "we ought to just office here. Save ourselves the trouble."

"You couldn't afford the rent," Manny said. He wasn't looking at Ben or Simms. Ben, in turn, seemed to be avoiding everyone. The tension was so palpable it was like a vibration under Lucia's skin.

"Kidding."

"Yeah, well, I'm not in the mood, Jazz." Manny walked over to the part of the warehouse that was designated as his lab, opened a drawer, slammed it, opened another.

He came up with a pistol. A .38, Lucia thought. He pointed it directly at Max Simms, who didn't—of course—look remotely worried or surprised.

"Hey!" Jazz yelped. "Manny, what the hell—"

"Speaking of serial killers," Manny said quietly. "You think I don't know why he went to prison? I know." His hand was shaking. "Give me a good reason why I shouldn't just kill him now."

"Prison wouldn't be kind to you, Manny," McCarthy said. He hadn't moved from where he stood.

"That's it? That's your reason?"

"The only reason I know. Hey, go ahead. Kill the son of a bitch, as far as I'm concerned. None of this crap matters to me anymore."

"Well, it matters to me," Jazz said. "Manny, don't. He can help us."

"Yeah? Like he helped me?"

"He did help you, Manny."

"He could have done it earlier!" Manny yelled, and for a blinding second Lucia thought he'd fire. But then he threw the gun back in the drawer and slammed it and stalked away. "Fuck. Do what you want. I'll be in my office."

He went to the far door at the end of the room, punched in numbers and went through. The door—at least three inches of solid metal—sealed with a solid *thunk* behind him, and the lights on the panel turned bloodred.

"What happened back there?" That was Borden, who was looking furious and ruffled and belligerent. His hair was spiked again, not so much from overapplication of product but from running his hands through it in distraction. "Where are they? Laskins and the others?"

Simms, for answer, checked his watch. He was still looking down at it when he said quietly, "By this time? Nearly all of them are dead. The rest are running for their lives. Unfortunate."

Borden's mouth opened and closed, and he leaned on the makeshift conference table and let his head drop forward. Struggling for control. "Laskins?" he asked.

"Milo Laskins is alive," Simms said. "I don't see any possibility that he'll have to give up his life in the current scenario. However, his days at Gabriel, Pike & Laskins are numbered, Mr. Borden. Your star is in ascendance. Feel free to be grateful."

Borden's head snapped up. His face was stark. *"Grateful?"*

"You had no real affection for those people, and we both know it. You disagreed with them quite a number of times, most recently just today. Let's not have any gnashing of teeth."

"You unbelievable bastard."

"Take a seat."

"Not with you. You arranged this—"

"Take a seat, Borden." Simms's voice snapped with command, and for a second there was nothing soft about him, nothing at all. Lucia remembered Jazz's description of him. *Creepy.* "The rest of you. Sit down. I don't have time for your histrionics."

"What about mine?" Ben McCarthy's voice was soft, and somehow even more intense than Simms's. Lucia looked over at him, but he was turned away, showing her only a hard profile, an angular shoulder, a fist clenched at his side. "You got time for mine?"

Simms met his eyes. "I'm sorry. That was not my choice, Ben. That was never my choice."

"It served your purposes."

"Yes. It did. It does. It will. What you're referring to had to happen. How it happened was *your* doing, by the decisions you made. You knew what the Society wanted from you. You chose to do otherwise." Simms studied him for a few seconds in silence. "How long have you known?"

"They told me, earlier today. Indirectly." McCarthy's lips stretched, baring his teeth, but it wasn't a smile. "They said I'd served my purpose. And we both know what that purpose was, from the very beginning."

"All right, I'm calling bullshit," Jazz said flatly, and slid into a chair next to McCarthy. She leaned on her elbows, staring at Simms. "What the hell are you two talking about?"

Nobody answered her. Borden pantomimed *I have no idea* with a helpless lift of his shoulders.

"About what happened to me when I was missing," Lucia said. "Am I correct? Gregory Ivanovich was behind that, at least."

"He did his part." Simms's yellowed teeth flashed in a smile. "Don't worry. Mr. Ivanovich left and isn't looking back."

"Something happened to me while I was missing."

"You were treated for your illness."

"Something else."

Simms, for answer, removed a sealed manila envelope from his jacket pocket, unfolded it and slid it across the table. Not to her. To McCarthy.

McCarthy didn't touch it. "What is it?"

"Proof. I was hoping we might be able to avoid the unpleasantries, but you seem determined."

"You son of a bitch. You cold-blooded—"

"In private," Simms said. "As you said, it is a personal matter."

McCarthy shoved back from the table and stared down for a few seconds.

"I need someplace quiet," he said. "No surveillance. No cameras."

Jazz looked around and said, "Darkroom. Second door along the wall."

Chapter 15

The darkroom was equipped with red lights—bright enough, but unsettlingly bloody. McCarthy ushered Lucia inside and closed the door, flicked the interior dead bolt and put his back against it. The manila envelope was clutched tight in his hand.

It was close quarters in the room, and even though it was well ventilated, the chemical soup of developer burned her nose and throat. Empty developing trays were laid out, and there was a clothesline of drying prints at the far end of the room, above the table.

"What in the *hell* is this about?" Lucia demanded. Her head was aching from the secrecy. "Why am I the only one who's safe? Ben, you have to *explain this*."

He didn't open the envelope. Instead, he said, "I was approached in prison after I got the beating, the one that put me in the hospital. I knew I was a goner in there, you understand? No way was I going to survive if the Cross Society decided I needed to go."

"You made a deal with them to get out of prison. I know that."

"You have to understand, Lucia. I didn't know you. I didn't know anything about you, except that the Cross Society had picked you. You were a name on a piece of paper to me."

There was a table at her back. The edge of it dug into her spine, low and cold. "Ben—"

"I would have agreed to anything to get the hell out of there. I'm not proud of that. I'm not proud of much in my life, but that was a low point." He tried for a smile, and it came out wrong.

She felt it coming, the way wild animals seemed to sense earthquakes on the way. "Ben, are you saying your alibi was a fake? Did you—"

"Kill them?" His blue eyes were utterly unreadable in this red light. They didn't look blue at all, just empty. "Couple of drug dealers who were responsible for at least half a dozen bodies, and those were just the ones they'd personally whacked? Who'd sold crack to ten-year-old kids and seventy-year-old grandmothers? Who raped when they wanted, stole when they wanted, and ran their block like some kind of prison camp? Or do you mean the girlfriend, who was so high she once sold her own two-year-old daughter to a pedophile to pay off a loan? Who couldn't even sober up enough to call the cops when her kid fell down the stairs and broke her neck, so she put her out with the garbage in-stead? God, Lucia. What do you think?"

There were tears in his eyes. Tears on his cheeks. She couldn't tell if they were from fury, pain or regret.

Or loss, the loss of what they'd nearly had, the loss of possibilities.

She didn't answer.

Eventually, he gave her the truth himself. "No. I didn't kill them, but God, I should have. The pictures exonerating me were legit. Still, the Cross Society would have let me rot in prison for something I didn't do. I figure they arranged the whole thing the first time so that I was in cold storage, so they could have me when they needed me."

He wiped his cheeks distractedly with the palm of his hand. Now that he'd started looking directly at her, he didn't seem to be able to stop. As if he was hungry for the sight of her, and knew this was going to be his last chance.

"They wanted me to meet you," he said. "And they wanted me to get you in bed as soon as I possibly could."

It hit her as funny, because she'd been braced for so much worse. She laughed out loud, involuntarily, and covered her mouth with her hand. "That's it?" she asked, and swallowed lunatic giggles. "That's their big master plan? Get us laid? You didn't even—"

She stopped. All of the humor fell away, down a black hole that didn't seem to have any bottom to it at all.

"I was going to say you didn't even try," she said slowly. "But that's not true, is it? That first night. The apartment. You thought about it."

"No," he said hoarsely. "I *wanted* it. I needed you. I mean, I would have done it if it had just been sex, but dammit, you were—do you understand? I looked at you and I wanted you. Not a lie. I wanted something real, not just—"

She remembered him pulling away and stalking to the window. Drinking his beer in convulsive gulps. *Do they call cabs, your guys downstairs?*

His choice. And again, the second time. She'd asked him back to the apartment. He'd—turned her down. She'd even been surprised by it. Hurt by it.

"I thought that this one time, at least, I could make a decision for myself. But I couldn't. They took it away from me."

"Oh, God. Ben, what's in the envelope?"

"Proof that I'm no longer necessary in all this."

"Show me."

He opened the envelope. There were pictures inside. She saw him look down at them, and he made a sound, an animal groan of pain, and slid down the door to a crouch. Staring at the photos. Shuffling through them. "You bastards," he whispered. "They made these for me. Just to show me how little I matter. How they can take everything away."

She couldn't stand it. She lunged forward and grabbed for them. He moved, lightning-quick, and took hold of her forearms, pulling her down to her knees.

The photos spilled over the concrete floor between them, glowing in the lurid red light. Black-and-white photos, taken from above. Grainy, as if ripped from a surveillance feed.

A woman lying on a white hospital-style bed, wearing a loose gown.

Knees up. Feet in stirrups.

Some kind of medical procedure.

Some kind of...

Lucia cried out and buried her face in McCarthy's shoulder. In his warmth and strength. He kissed the top of her head and rocked her, and she twisted to stare at the photos again, silent now.

The stroking of his hand on her hair was almost hypnotic.

"It's all a game to them. Percentages," he said. "Anthrax to get you sick and vulnerable, and keep you running scared. They'd planned to check you into the hospital and get it done there, but Eidolon kept disrupting things, forcing their hand. I didn't carry through on getting you in bed, but it didn't matter, they had a backup plan. When you finally did collapse, when you were unguarded—they took you."

She stared at the photographs. The details of an invasion of her body, clinically photographed.

"I dreamed," she murmured. "I dreamed of lights.... This was it, wasn't it? It wasn't all treatments for the anthrax. The feeling of violation."

He didn't answer. There didn't seem much point, she supposed. It was right there, in the pictures. The doctors with their tools and their completely scientific rape of her body.

"How many times?" She felt as if there was a huge weight on her lungs, suffocating her. Like the old wives' tale of waking with the cat on her chest, stealing her breath. This could not be true. Could not be happening.

"I don't know. As many as it took to make sure, I suppose." His voice sounded raw. Bloody. "You're just a tool,

Lucia. Just a body and a genetic code and a place in history, standing where they need somebody to stand, for the greater good." The weight of sarcasm he gave the last two words made her shiver. "And our baby's going to be exactly the same."

She stirred and looked up. Her hair had fallen over her face, and she pulled it back out of the way. "*Our* baby?"

He kissed her. Not on the lips, on the forehead. A burning kiss of anguish and apology. "I can't be sure without a DNA test, but yeah. They took sperm samples during the tests in the prison hospital, before they told me what I was supposed to do. That was what they wanted from me. Pretty much all they ever wanted. Their backup plan, in case I— got difficult about things. I guess just anybody wouldn't do. Had to be me."

They sat in silence, surrounded by the fallen photographs, wrapped around each other for comfort, until Jazz rapped on the door and asked if everything was okay in there.

Lucia straightened, wiped her face free of moisture, and forced a smile to her lips. McCarthy, bleached of color by the lights, looked awful. She didn't expect she looked any better. "Nobody else needs to know," she said. "You and me. Nobody else."

"Jazz—"

"No. *Nobody*. Promise me."

"I promise." He gave her a wan, empty smile. "The least I can do."

"No," she said. "The least you can do is think of yourself. Whatever that is. Leave. Stay. Hate me. Love me. Do what's in your heart, Ben. Whatever that is, just do it. Quit making decisions based on what you think I want."

His eyes opened wider, and for a second he didn't move or speak. She wasn't sure if he was thinking or just feeling stunned. And then, without saying a word, he kissed her. A hot, damp, desperate kiss, tasting of tears. Wild, distilled passion. His hands rose to cup the back of her head, urging her closer, and his tongue nudged her lips apart.

She let him in.

Our choice, she thought, with what little conscious thought she had in that moment. *One pure thing. Just one.*

He broke the kiss with a tearing gasp and buried his face in the hollow of her neck. The moan that came out of him moved through her like a holy visitation.

"What the hell was that?" she asked, shaky.

"What I want."

She wanted to stay there forever, in the safe red light, suspended in the warmth of this moment, but she reached down and scraped the pictures together, and slid them into the envelope. He straightened up and put his hands on her shoulders, then her face. Thumb tracing her damp, swollen lips.

"Make it your choice, Lucia. Let them chew on that."

She held the proof of her weakness in her hands, and the proof of her strength in her heart.

"We will," she said.

They were all staring when she and McCarthy returned. Jazz opened her mouth to ask, but Lucia stopped her with a look. "Our business," she said. "It's nothing to do with anybody else. Right, Simms?"

He cocked his head to one side. "As you wish."

"I want this *over*. I want us out of your business, the Cross Society's business, Eidolon's business."

"That's never going to happen," Simms said, "as long as the Cross Society and Eidolon are in operation. Especially now." He gave her midsection a fast but significant glance. She sat down at the table and put the envelope in front of her. A silent reminder of just how high the stakes were now.

"Then we shut them down. All of them."

"You can't," Borden argued. "The Cross Society does do good, you know that! Look how many people you've saved because of the leads they gave you. You can't just—"

McCarthy, who hadn't spoken, turned toward him, fists clenched.

"What, now you want to beat on me?" Borden cried. "Fine. Let's go. I'm sick of your macho cop bullshit—"

"James, don't," Jazz said. For her, the response was mild.

"Yeah, James, don't," McCarthy echoed. "Be a good little lawyer and shut the hell up about what doesn't concern you."

"Back off, Ben." Jazz was up, suddenly, standing between them. "You want to take whatever this is out on somebody, hell, bring it on, I'd *love* to kick somebody's ass today. Might as well be yours. I'm pissed as hell at you, anyway."

"I don't need you to fight for me, Jazz!" Borden spat.

"Against Ben? You're kidding, right?" She held up her hands and backed out of the way. "Fine. You guys arm wrestle for biggest jerk in the room. Let us know who comes out on top. *We've got bigger problems than this!*"

She was deadly serious. The tension in the room cranked steadily higher.

"Now." She turned back to Lucia. "You were saying…?"

Simms, significantly, perhaps, hadn't said a word. He wasn't watching the brewing confrontation. His eyes hadn't left Lucia, but she had a sudden eerie feeling that he was seeing through her, beyond her, into some limitless and terrifying distance.

What did I just change?

"You're a constant," Simms said slowly. "Eidolon would like to kill you, but there's no time line I can see in which you don't survive and—" he caught himself and glanced at the others "—and carry out the task that the Cross Society intended. In other words, unlike the rest of us, your fate is assured, Ms. Garza."

"Meaning?"

"Meaning that you are a fulcrum upon which we can move the world." He looked grim suddenly. Tired, and every moment of his age. "You can do anything you want to do. And I hope you understand how grave a responsibility that is. I created Eidolon to help me understand what I was seeing, to right some of the wrongs in this world. And I learned that when you act with knowledge, fate reacts against you. The more good we did, the more evil there was, as if it was being bred specifically to counter us, like antibodies. I wanted to stop. I established the Cross Society to work at cross-purposes to Eidolon, to try to undo some of the terrible consequences." He sagged further in his seat. "The world works on balance. I understand that now. There can be no greater good, because once it is greater, it is no longer good."

They were all silent, watching him.

"There is something you can do," Simms said. "Destroy it. Bring it down. You are the only one who can do that."

Borden shot up again, eyes wide. "You can't."

"She can. She will. More than that, Mr. Borden, she *should*."

"I can't be part of destroying the Cross Society!"

"Don't have to," Jazz said. "Eidolon's the one who's got the upper hand. We go after them, right, Simms?"

He nodded. "Right."

"Problem solved." Jazz stood up. "L. Ben. Let's get busy."

Borden moved toward her. Intimately close, trying to hold her eyes. "What about me?"

She put a hand flat on his chest. "Your decision," she said. "I love you. I want to be with you. But you have to choose now, because I'm not going to be a cog in somebody else's machine the rest of my life. We're expendable to them, and personally, I don't consider *you* expendable at all."

He hesitated, and with a heart-stoppingly tender gesture, covered her fingers with his own. Jazz was not a small woman, but his hand dwarfed hers.

"Quit," she said. "Quit the damn Society. Please, Borden."

He bent forward and kissed her. A long, thorough, sweet kiss, as if there was nobody else in the room.

"I have to fight for what I believe in," Borden said. "Even

if the guy who founded it doesn't believe anymore. I can't change my heart that easily. I'm sorry."

Jazz blinked. For a second there were tears in her eyes, and in the next, they were gone, drained away, and something hard and unyielding had replaced them.

"Me, too," she said, and shoved him away with an explosion of force. He staggered back, hit the pillar behind him and rebounded. She sidestepped, added momentum with a straight arm across his shoulder blades, and he sprawled facedown across the table. Jazz stepped in, grabbed his left wrist and twisted it up, then patted her pockets absently. "Dammit. Anybody got handcuffs?"

Any of them might have—Ben, Jazz, Lucia—but instead, it was Pansy Taylor, looking rumpled and fresh from bed, wrapped in a robe, who walked in on bare feet and tossed a gleaming set of police issue on the table.

"I don't think I even want to know," McCarthy said.

"Morning." Pansy yawned, and watched as Jazz snapped handcuffs on her former boss. "What's going on?"

"End of the world," McCarthy said. He was still sitting, head propped on his hand, watching as Borden squirmed and struggled.

"Oh," Pansy said. "Just checking. Coffee, then?"

"Yeah, all around. Better get a straw for Borden."

"Screw you, McCarthy," Borden panted. Jazz grabbed him by the handcuffs and got him upright, then seated. "Dammit, Jazz, you can't keep me here like this."

"Sure, I can," she stated. "And later on, we'll talk about

better ways to handle our relationship issues, but for right now? Handcuffs work."

McCarthy laughed. A flush mounted in Borden's face, and Lucia thought that if he'd had superpowers, those handcuffs would be breaking like glass right about now.

But he didn't. *You are a fulcrum upon which we can move the world.* Lucia had the uncomfortable feeling that only one of them qualified today as a superhero, and she didn't like the thought.

"I have to make a phone call," she said.

Nobody commented. Jazz was too preoccupied with avoiding Borden's glares.

Lucia stood up and walked to an emptier corner of the vast warehouse space, away from the lights. Out on the perimeter, the feeling of loneliness increased. It was like leaving the orbit of the Earth, launching out into a cold and uncaring darkness.

She dialed a number on her cell phone, spoke her name very clearly after the beep and left a callback number. Exactly forty-five seconds after she'd hung up, her cell phone rang, and she flipped it open.

"This is an unexpected pleasure, my love," Gregory Ivanovich said. He did sound gratified.

"Did you take the pictures?"

Silence for a second. She might have actually succeeded in throwing him off.

"I captured them from surveillance, yes." No jokes. Gregory knew it wasn't a joking matter. "You know who is the father? I deeply regret to inform you it was not me."

"I need a favor."

She'd surprised him, again. "Are we so close that you should think I would give another favor, *dorogaya?* For nothing?"

"Not for nothing. Favor for favor. Yours to be named later, no questions asked."

"You'd put yourself in my debt?"

"Yes."

He considered it. "From anyone else, I would say that you would be lying to me, and that would be most unpleasant for both of us. But from my dear Lushenka I will grant the possibility you will keep your word. Very well. Favor for favor. What do you want?"

"An electromagnetic pulse device."

If she'd thought she'd surprised him before, she'd been wrong. *This* was surprise, this long stretch of humming silence. He was on an airplane, she thought. Probably riding first class, luxuriating in leather seats, eating beluga caviar.

"So we are trading big favors, I see. Very, very big."

"I need it fast."

"In terms of trading, we are in the blue chips, yes? What could you possibly do for me later that would equal this?"

"I don't know. And the point is, neither do you, until you need it. But you have my word, and you know what it's worth. It's why you call me *dorogaya.* You can take it to the bank."

"Hmmmm." He drew it out into a musical thread. She could hear the smile. "Very well. I can secure one for you. It will not be very large and it will not be very portable.

There will be only one charge in its circuits, so you must fire it exactly where you want it. The radius is less than a thousand feet. You understand?"

"I do."

"Where shall I have it delivered?"

Manny would kill her if she had former Soviet agents drop-shipping weapons to his doorstep. Worse, he would quit. "My apartment. I'll pick it up later."

"You're sure you want such a trail?"

"I trust you can avoid leaving one."

"Always. You will have it tomorrow."

He hung up without a goodbye.

I'm going to regret that, she thought. It wasn't even a question.

Chapter 16

"This," McCarthy said as they sat around the worktable four hours later, eating frozen dinners and staring at computer-printed floor plans, "is a really stupid idea, Jazz. I mean, you've had some stupid ideas before, and God bless you, you've pulled them off, but I don't know about this one. If these guys are as all-knowing as you say—"

"They're not all-knowing," Simms said.

"But you don't know what they *do* know, or when, right?"

Simms shrugged. "Eidolon has more than twenty psychics feeding them predictions. Some of those may sense what you're about to do. But I think they'd likely discount this because it *is* so stupidly confrontational."

"Hey!" Jazz cried.

Lucia patted her on the shoulder. "Stupid is good. Clever would get us killed."

McCarthy smiled, briefly. "Not you, apparently."

"Shut up."

He cocked an eyebrow. "You and Borden, wanting a piece of me today. What's that about?"

"I have better reasons."

The color drained out of his face when she said that, and she wished she hadn't; it wasn't like her to rub it in. The shock of those obscene photographs was still vivid. She'd taken them to Manny's shredder and reduced them to a pile of thin crosscut strips, then run them through an acid wash to destroy any chance of reconstruction. Manny's idea, when he'd finally rejoined them, although he hadn't asked what was on the photos. It seemed likely her expression had told him enough.

McCarthy was mutely waiting.

"Work first." She had more than enough to think about. She wondered if she dared ask Manny to run a pregnancy test for her, or if she wanted to wait until later, until this was over and she was free to walk into a store and have nothing but a normal woman's anxieties. "I'm sorry. Cheap shot."

"It's not like I don't deserve it."

"Guys, wallow in whatever you're wallowing in later," Jazz snapped. "*Focus,* already. This is serious."

Lucia sucked in a deep breath. "We go in through the front door, take the device to the server room and position it. Meanwhile, Manny's guy—" Manny knew guys who could do just about anything "—hacks into the off-site data storage facility and arranges for a system crash there. They may have redundant backup systems—we have to watch out for that. Manny's guy will be monitoring and will kill any off-site systems they try to bring online. Meanwhile, we set off the EMP in their server room. In and out, fast, in the general confusion."

"You're going to get yourselves killed," Borden said. He was sitting at the far end of the table, with his hands handcuffed in front now, not behind. "Jazz, don't do this. You have no idea what you're getting into, you don't. Really."

"You have no idea what we're getting into, either, Borden," Lucia said without looking up. "We've tried it your way. It hasn't worked. Time for a new approach."

He was rubbing his head furiously now, handcuffs clinking together. "Jazz, I'm begging you. Please."

Jazz said, "Manny, you're going to keep him secured, right?"

"Absolutely," he agreed. He sounded depressed. "But I don't like it. I don't like any of this."

"You think I do?" she snapped back, and covered her eyes with her hands, pressing. "I'm sorry. Tired. I want this over, dammit."

"And I want everybody out of my house," Manny said. "So yeah, I'll watch him. I'll do what you need me to do. But when this is over, everybody gets *out*. And you pay me for my time. And we go back to the way things were."

"Fine," Lucia said. Jazz started to protest, but Lucia overrode her. "*Fine.* I have no objection to that. Jazz, you'll be okay here for a while? I need to go home."

Jazz immediately looked alarmed. "What's wrong?"

"Nothing." Everything. "I just need a shower and clean

clothes and a nap. Plus, the item's being delivered to me there. I'll bring it here once it arrives."

"I don't like you going out," she replied.

"She's perfectly safe," Simms said.

"See?" Lucia pushed back from the table and had to brace herself. She felt light-headed from too much caffeine, not nearly enough rest. God only knew how much abuse her body had taken in the past few weeks, but it was starting to make its displeasure with the situation very clear. "A nap is all I need."

"Take it here," Jazz said. "We have an unbelievable bathroom, too. Seven showerheads. Marble tiles. Whirlpool."

It sounded, literally, like heaven, but she needed something that she couldn't get here. Silence. Peace. Solitude.

She shook her head. "I'll go," she said. "Everybody else stays." Jazz opened her mouth. "I mean it, damn you. Follow orders, for once in your life."

McCarthy snorted.

"Manny, can I—"

He tossed her the keys to the Hummer before she'd even gotten the words out. She nodded in gratitude.

"Gas it up," he called after her. "And wash it while you're at it!"

Because, of course, saving the world wasn't work enough.

She was at the steel door when she felt someone behind her, and turned to see McCarthy. He leaned a hand on the metal, another on the wall, boxing her in.

"You really going?" he asked.

"Yes. I really am."

He lowered his voice. "You want to take a test?"

She nodded mutely.

"Can I come with you?"

"It isn't safe. You heard Simms."

"Sweetheart, I've been in danger my whole life. I survived some nights in Ellsworth that you wouldn't believe. I think I can survive a day in your company." He was slowly leaning closer, as if her gravity was pulling him in. "Let me come with you. Please."

She looked over his shoulder. Jazz was studying floor plans and ignoring Borden, and he was staring at her with naked suffering on his face.

"Let me." Ben's breath was warm against her face, his voice an intimate whisper in her ear. He pulled back enough to look into her eyes. "You told me to make a choice based on what I want, not what you want. Well, this is it."

She turned away, opened the door and went down the stairs. She looked back. He was standing at the top, watching her, holding the door open.

"Coming?" she asked.

The door boomed shut behind him as he ran down the steps toward her.

It seemed oddly normal, shopping at the drugstore—picking up a few odds and ends she knew she was running short of. McCarthy silently followed her as she strolled the aisles, and she finally turned to the shelves filled with feminine products.

Pregnancy tests were at the top. She stared at the choices

blindly for a moment, then reached up and took one at random. It looked simple enough. As she was reading the back, she said, "This could all be a lie, you know."

"Yeah. And if it isn't, it probably didn't even work, what they were—doing to you. It doesn't, right? Not all the time."

She added the test to her basket and went to the checkout counter. The clerk didn't make any comments, and neither did she. She wondered idly which was more uncomfortable, buying intimate things like this or seeing a steady progression of them all day. Teenage boys with boxes of condoms. Hell, middle-aged matrons with boxes of condoms. Pregnancy tests.

The clerk met her eyes briefly and smiled. "Good luck."

She led the way back to the vehicle, climbed in and piloted the thing to her apartment.

The apartment was undisturbed. The upgraded security monitors—Jazz's doing—showed no intrusions, but then, if Gregory decided to pay another visit, they probably wouldn't. He'd been the one to come and get her; she knew it beyond any doubt. That first night, when she'd woken on the couch and found him in the apartment, had been his dry run, to test the system. He'd almost warned her then, she realized. Almost.

She locked the door and reset the alarms, and exchanged a silent look with McCarthy.

"You do what you need to do," he said, and went into the kitchen. He pulled a beer from the fridge. "I'll be here."

She went into the bathroom with the box, took off her

clothes and grimaced at the state of her hair and general hygiene. She stepped into the shower and let herself fall into a kind of trance, lulled by the warm water, the floral scents of the shampoo and soaps.

Maybe it isn't true. Maybe none of this is true.

She finished and stepped out of the shower, damp and glowing, and decisively ripped open the package to find the test kit.

Ten minutes later, she stared at the single blue line on the strip.

Oh, my God.

She found herself sliding down against the tiled wall, staring at the plastic holder and the blue line. Such a simple thing, to make so many terrible things real.

She dumped it into the trash can, then followed it with her clothes, for no better reason than she never wanted to wear them again, or see them again. She washed her hands with vicious thoroughness.

She wrapped herself in her soft fleece robe, damp hair straggling down her back, and opened the bathroom door.

McCarthy stood there, holding out two choices—beer and soft drink.

She took the soft drink.

He let out his breath in a long, low sigh and turned away. She thought he was all right for a second, and then he let out a harsh yell, punched the wall with his right hand, then leaned his forehead against the plaster.

"Feel better?" she asked neutrally. She sipped the cola,

grateful for the sweetness, grateful for something that felt normal in this increasingly alien world.

"My hand hurts," he said. "Define better."

"Why did you want to be here?"

"Why did you want me to be here?"

"Turn around," she said.

He did, setting his beer down on the table untouched. She put her drink down as well, and crossed the small distance between them. Neither of them reached out.

"So how does it feel," she asked, "knowing you're going to be a father?"

He laughed. It was a wild kind of laugh, on the edge of fury, and she stopped it cold by putting her hands on his shoulders, then cupping his face. He needed a shave. His beard scraped warm across her palms.

"They took away our choices," she said. "But only for a moment, Ben. Only for a moment. Because it would have come to this, sooner or later, and you know it."

She let go of him, and took hold of the sash that held her robe closed. She untied it with slow, deliberate motions and let the fabric move away, revealing the gap between her breasts, then the inner slopes.

His breath caught, and he reached out to slowly slide the robe across her shoulders, fingers lightly skimming skin, and then down over her arms. She let the robe fall to the floor.

She led him to the bed and put her hands on his shoulders. "Don't move." She'd never seen him this way before, so quiet and yet so tense. It wasn't passivity, it was intensity waiting to break free, and it made her breath grow short, her cheeks burn, her fingers shake. The buttons on his shirt surrendered, and underneath that his chest was defined, not muscular, and covered by a mat of graying dark hair. She ran her fingers possessively through its coarse texture, then down to hook into the waistband of his blue jeans.

He stopped breathing and closed his eyes. Fighting to stay still.

She popped the button loose, and ran her fingernail slowly down the zipper. Teasing. Felt him shudder... He had more control than she could imagine. She remembered him turning away from her, knowing there would be a price for his refusal. Maybe a fatal one.

He'd never expected that they'd abduct her and force a medical rape on her. She had to believe that.

She took hold of the zipper tab and dragged it down, one slow click at a time. He let out his breath in a rushing moan as she put her palms flat on his hips, then pulled on the loosened jeans, sending them tumbling in a heap over his feet.

Well, that answered the questions she'd briefly entertained about his preferences in underwear...not that it mattered now. The briefs followed the pants to the floor. She ran her hands slowly from his collarbone across his chest, down the fluttering muscles of his stomach.

Down.

"Ben," she whispered. "You can move now."

He opened his eyes and she burned in the fire of them, and then that intensity was loose. His mouth was everywhere, finding every untouched place to draw a gasp or a moan, those clever fingers knowing exactly where to press, how to move.

The things he was saying flowed through her, thick and sweet as honey, words shaped on skin. He drove her mad with words, and then they left the hobbles of language behind, and it was only intensity, and passion, and love spoken in flesh.

In the moment of white-hot transcendence she felt herself embrace that spark of life buried deep inside, and wrap the whirlwind around it.

Giving it not just life, but purpose.

Ben collapsed against her, gasping for air, and she ran her hands through his graying curls.

"That," he finally managed to growl, "was not what I expected."

"Not as good?"

"Idiot," he murmured, and put his head back down.

She laughed. After a few seconds, so did he, deep rumbles from his stomach, subsonic waves through her skin.

If Simms could see us now, she thought, and was momentarily chilled by the idea that, just perhaps, he could.

And so could Eidolon.

There was no way to understand right and wrong anymore. There was only good, and she had to seek it.

She turned toward McCarthy's warmth, his love, his sense of safety.

Toward the good.

She woke up fast to a loud buzzing sound, and catapulted out of bed naked, reaching for her gun, before she realized two things. One, the sound was the intercom calling for attention. Two, Ben McCarthy had rolled out of bed on the opposite side, and he had a gun in his hand as well.

They shared rueful smiles, and she kept the weapon in her hand on the way to the keypad, to press the call button. "Yes?"

"Sorry to buzz you so early, Ms. Garza, but there was a special delivery for you. The guy said to tell you that it's a package from back East. That make any sense? I can't read the label."

"No, that's fine, I'm expecting it. I'll be down in a minute, thanks." She turned back to find McCarthy pulling on his briefs, then his jeans. She walked to him without hesitation and stepped into the circle of his arms, her bare skin pressed against his from the waist up. The luxury of it nearly overwhelmed her. His left hand moved lightly up the curve of her arm, and in the morning light she saw a fine lacework of lines around his eyes when he smiled at her. They deepened when she stroked her fingers through the warm mat of hair on his chest.

"No regrets?" he asked her.

"Why in God's name would I have regrets?"

He traced the line of her cheekbone with his thumb. "I'm old, you know."

"Older," she acknowledged. "Didn't slow you down."

"Oh, it did," he said, and dropped a slow, warm kiss on the skin of her collarbone. "But that has compensations. Lets me concentrate on getting the most out of every… single…moment."

"I noticed." When had her voice taken on that particular low purr? *You can't be distracted like this,* some cold part of her brain said. *You're drunk on him. Sober up. There are things to do.*

She couldn't stop touching him.

His lips moved across her throat, up to the column of her neck.

"I have to…get…the package," she murmured.

"Yes, you do."

"Things to do."

"Important things."

Her fingers curled in the waistband of his pants.

"I just got those on," he murmured against her skin. His hands were wandering, too, down her back, down the smooth curve of her hips. Inward.

"Stop." She tugged at his pants, pulling him harder against her when he tried to move back for better access. "I have to go downstairs."

"Like that? They'll be thrilled."

"Dressed. I have to get dressed." She finally found some strength to put behind that statement. "Ben, no. I have to do this."

He stopped playing, and the smile slowly died. "Do you?" He searched her face intently. "Are you sure?"

"I'm sure that I can't live like this. And neither can you, or Jazz, or for that matter, Simms and Borden. If Simms is right, I could be the only one left standing if I don't act. So yes. I'm sure." She read the fear in him. "I'll be all right."

"Simms sold out about twenty of his friends, so far as I could tell. Forgive me for not trusting him with your life."

She stopped him with a kiss, a long one. "I have to go."

She dressed quickly, just underwear, jeans and T-shirt, feet in a pair of flat shoes. Her hair still looked loose and tumbled, and she could smell McCarthy all over her skin.

She reset the alarm on the way out—native paranoia— and took the stairs to stretch the soreness out of her leg muscles. Marsh glanced up as she came out the fire door, took in the way she looked, and wisely said nothing beyond a polite, "Good morning, Ms. Garza." She signed the clipboard and picked up the package. It was, as Gregory had predicted, heavy; not something one could slip easily into a purse. She'd need a duffel bag, or a backpack.

She was thinking about it on the way back up the stairs, but the extra weight in her arms made her slower. She stopped to readjust the weight on the third floor landing, and as she did, she heard the ground floor door open, and hard-soled shoes coming up. Men's shoes, from the sound of it. Two or three pairs of them.

"—both there. Be ready. She's a tough little bitch, and McCarthy's a stone-cold killer. He'll fight to protect her. I don't want any shooting if we can help it."

"If it comes to that—"

"If it comes to that, kill McCarthy, but *don't* kill her. We need her. Understand?"

Voices carried. Lucia ran almost soundlessly up another flight, eased open the fire door and sprinted for the elevator. There was an intercom button next to the Up and Down;

she slapped her palm on it, juggling the package clumsily. "Security! Security, pick up!"

"Security, yes ma'am."

"Get up to the sixth floor. There are three men on their way to my apartment and—"

"Ms. Garza? This is Marsh, ma'am. Those men are police officers. They came in just after you picked up the package—they had a warrant. Nothing I could do."

"Shit," she whispered, and slapped the call button for the elevator. "Marsh, listen to me. Those men are *not* police officers."

"I checked their badges—"

"Marsh!" She cut him off coldly, furiously. "I need you to go along with me here. Please. You have information that they're imposters, and you're just doing your job when you *lock the damn fire door on the sixth floor!*"

"Ma'am…" He debated for a second, then another. "I suppose they could have been fake credentials. We have to take all reasonable precautions."

They'd be to the fourth floor by now. Maybe the fifth, if they were in a hurry. "Marsh? Are you locking them out?"

No answer.

The elevator arrived. She lunged into it and hit the sixth floor button convulsively, willing it to go faster.

The intercom inside of the elevator came alive. "Ms. Garza?"

"Yes, Marsh!" Dammit, she hadn't even brought her gun. Hadn't come prepared at all for trouble. *This is what happi-*

ness brings you. Disaster. She had let herself be comforted, and that was death to caution.

"We appear to have had a circuit fault on the sixth floor fire door. It's locked down. The cops are making their way up to seven."

"And that one will be locked when they get there?"

"Probably. Fault in the system, ma'am. But I can't promise you more than ten minutes, max. That's the most I can do."

"That's good enough." The doors opened on the sixth floor. "Thank you."

She made it to her apartment, unlocked the door, and caught McCarthy in the act of putting on his shirt. He looked up, startled, and she saw him take in the expression on her face.

He reached for his shoulder holster and strapped it on. "Trouble?"

"Ken Stewart's coming with some kind of warrant. No idea what it is, but it doesn't matter. Eidolan's nervous. He's here to slow us down," she said. "Take this." She handed him the package and grabbed the first thing she could find in the closet—a black canvas backpack, sturdy enough. The alarm started a shrill warning beep by the time she shoved the EMP device inside and zipped the bag.

"You going to shut the alarm off?"

"No. The more confusion, the better." She grabbed her gun, holster and purse, and moved past him to the closet at the back. "Come on." She shouldered the backpack.

"Where?"

"Back door."

It wasn't, exactly, but what building engineers didn't know wouldn't kill them. Though it might give them a good fit of pique… She shoved aside the coats in the closet and pressed hard on the wall behind, which swung open with a sharp pop of magnets coming loose.

It had been opened before. She saw sets of tracks in the pale dust. Gregory Ivanovich. He'd known that she would have built in an escape hatch. And he'd used it against her.

"What the hell…?" McCarthy marveled.

"Shut it behind you." She ducked into the crawl space. Short and dusty, it led into wiring tunnels, which dumped into a service shaft for the air handlers, with a long straight ladder down a central column. She started downward.

Somewhere above, in her apartment, she heard the alarm start to wail. Good. That meant confusion, more cops, possibly even a fire truck or two. The building's clientele this rich, and most of them important. The rich also came with an automatic upgrade of press coverage. With any luck, it would turn into a zoo outside.

She didn't trust luck. She jumped the last five rungs of the ladder, landed flat-footed in a crouch and had her gun in a two-handed grip as she advanced to the door.

No sound beyond. She eased it open a fraction of an inch, but the basement hallway was empty.

"Right." She shut the door and turned to look at McCarthy. "We need to make it to the Hummer. They'll be waiting somewhere along the line. They may even have the garage exits blocked off."

"They could have towed the truck," he reminded her.

"No, I don't think so. Not many towing services could handle it, and they'd have a hard time getting a flatbed truck down where we parked it, or getting the Hummer out if they did. Low ceilings. They'll just guard it. Less trouble."

He nodded. "I'm right behind you."

"I know."

"Try not to shoot anybody."

"Funny," she said grimly, "that's what they said. They want me alive."

That sparked something in his eyes that was hot and hungry. "I take it back," he said. "Shoot somebody. Preferably that rat bastard Stewart, if you see him."

She took a deep breath and swung open the door, then ran, light-footed, to the end of the hall. The parking lot beyond seemed deserted. No sign of surveillance or ambush. The Hummer loomed huge and black at the far corner, apart from the smaller cars and trucks.

She started to move forward, but McCarthy caught her arm and shook his head. He mimed splitting up, him to the right, her to the left. She shook her own head and fished the keys out of her pocket.

"Together," she whispered, making barely a sound. He stared at her face, and nodded.

"Together." It wasn't more than a movement of his lips, but it was a promise.

They broke from cover and ran for it.

Nobody stopped them. She hit the alarm remote control and unlocked the doors, threw herself into the driver's side and put the backpack on the floorboard as Ben climbed in the passenger door. The interior looked cool, dark and un-touched.

"Too easy," he said, and immediately began to look for trouble out the windows.

Nothing moved.

"Maybe the alarms upstairs distracted them," she said, and hit the ignition. The SUV started up with a rumble, and she backed it fast out of the space, not particularly worried about crumpled fenders or damaged quarter panels.

"They'll have us blocked in," McCarthy warned. His gun was out.

She nodded and gave him a lupine grin. "Let me worry about that. The army doesn't use these monsters just be-cause of their pretty paint jobs."

"Manny's going to kill you."

"Better him than Ken Stewart, wouldn't you say? And if you're going to shoot, roll down the window."

He shook his head and watched the parking garage whip by as she accelerated the Hummer up the curving ramp to-ward escape. "Wild woman."

Bet your ass, she thought, and pressed the accelerator to the floor when she saw daylight, and two police cars block-ing it. She honked, a loud blare, though they could hardly have missed a huge, black SUV barreling upward, engine roaring. Sure enough, the cops had prudently decided to leave empty cars in her path.

The Hummer hardly even shuddered at the impact. It slewed out into traffic as she whipped the wheel, burned rubber, and it stayed upright only because of the wide wheel base as she steered it down Vine Street.

"You realize that I'll be going to back to prison," McCarthy said, almost casually. "Doing crash tests with squad cars, that's some kind of crime. I know—I used to be a detective."

"Shut up. You're a hostage."

"I'm a what?"

"Hostage. You can truthfully say that I abducted you. I'm driving, after all."

"You know, my life with you might be short, but damn, it's going to be memorable."

She dug one-handed in her purse, came up with her cell phone and flipped it open. Voice-activated a call to Jazz, because she needed most of her attention for keeping the Hummer on the road and watching for any police cars moving to intercept. She had to get this thing off main streets fast, before air surveillance could get to them. Preferably, they needed to change cars. The closest chance would be six blocks away, in a parking garage behind a bank building.

"Yeah?" Jazz sounded sleepy.

"Three detectives showed up at my place this morning, with friends in patrol cars," Lucia said. She hit the speakerphone button and dropped the phone to the seat. "I can't come back to Manny's. We need to move, *now,* or we won't get another chance."

"Damn!" Jazz was wide awake now. "Don't you go without me."

"I may not have a choice. Jazz, I don't think it's safe for you to leave the bunker."

"Have I ever done what's safe? I'll get Manny in motion on the computer stuff. *Wait for me.*"

She hung up. Lucia shook her head and whipped the Hummer into a hard right turn, slowed her speed and then made an immediate left into the parking garage.

"What are we doing?"

"Switching cars."

Ben sighed. "Car theft. I'm almost *sure* that's a crime."

"It's my own car. I have three of them, parked in central locations around the city, all accessible from mass transportation."

"Look," he said slowly, "don't take this the wrong way, but who hides cars all over the city and has a secret escape hatch in her apartment, just in case?"

She took the ramp up. Second level. The Hummer barely made it—this was an old structure with low ceilings. "I'm a professional, Ben. And that's really all you need to know until I can get you into a warm bed, serve you some wine and tell you the story of my life."

"Promise?"

"Yes," she said softly. "I promise."

She pulled the Hummer into two spaces—it wouldn't fit in just one—next to a dull green minivan. "Out. Grab whatever you think we'll need from the back. Flak vests, definitely. Rocket launchers optional."

She took her purse and the backpack holding the EMP.

She had the minivan started when McCarthy slid inside. He had a Kevlar vest. "FBI issue," he noted.

"Without the FBI printing. Yes. I think Manny has some friends in federal procurement. Did you get one for me?"

"Basic black," he said. "Goes with everything. Jazz is meeting us?"

"Says she is."

"I got extra."

"Of everything?"

"Pretty much."

They hit sunlight, and she steered the minivan toward the freeway.

"I forgot to ask," he said. "Where is Eidolon's great big headquarters of evil, anyway?"

"Las Vegas," she said.

He smiled.

"Yes," she agreed. "After we save the world, we can take in a show."

"We take Simms, we could gamble." Ben glanced out the window, checking for tails. "What about a Vegas wedding?"

"That can't be a proposal."

"Why not?"

"Let's see—I hardly know you, we're on our way to a suicidally crazy mission, and I'm pregnant from immaculate conception. You'd be insane to propose to me now."

"Haven't you noticed that I'm not necessarily sane?"

She stopped for a light, the last one, and looked over at him for a long few seconds.

"I have," she admitted. "It's one of your better qualities."

"Vegas wedding," he said, and leaned his head back against the plush upholstery as she accelerated the van through the green light and made the on ramp. "I'm going to sleep now."

It was going to be a twenty-hour drive, at least. Lucia settled in, and wondered how Jazz was expecting to meet her.

She just knew, though, that somehow, Jazz would.

Jazz showed up at a diner outside of Fremont Junction in Utah, and immediately took a turn behind the wheel. "Simms," she said, which eliminated the need for any other explanations. Lucia, who'd already switched off with McCarthy once, gladly gave up driving and stretched out on the bench seat behind. McCarthy stayed in the passenger seat, talking in low tones with Jazz, and Lucia slipped off into a deep, exhausted sleep for a few hours, until the van stopped for gas again in Cedar City. She was driving once more when they crossed a narrow strip of Arizona desert, black and hypnotic at night, and then into Nevada.

The sun rose as they approached Las Vegas, and all three of them were wide awake for it.

"Straight there," Jazz said, as she stripped off her flannel shirt and pulled a bulletproof vest over her long-sleeved T-shirt. She snugged it tight, then donned the flannel shirt again. "No stops, right? Simms said it himself. The more we keep in motion, the harder it is for them to predict where we're going to be."

"I hope he's right," Lucia said grimly. "This isn't home turf for either of us."

"We'll be okay." Jazz grinned at her, the devil in her eyes. "We're the scary ones, remember?"

"Boy," McCarthy said without looking up as he cinched his own vest tight, "you're really not wrong on that one."

They cruised down the strip, because it was there and besides, it was on the way, and Jazz made verbal note of all the things she wanted to do later, when things were over. It was nervous talk. No matter how it came out, Lucia doubted they'd be hanging around to catch Cirque du Soleil.

Jazz got on the phone. "Manny? Your guy ready to rock?"

"Two guys," he said on speakerphone. "On your word. Jazz? Got a call from Agent Rawlins. They're letting Susannah Davis go today."

"What? They were supposed to keep her in protective custody!"

"She stopped cooperating. He said either we pick her up, or they show her the door and she can call a cab. What do you want me to do?"

Jazz chewed her lip and raised her eyebrows. Lucia said, "Can Pansy pick her up? Bring her to the bunker until we get back?"

Manny didn't like it; that much was obvious from his tone. "Yeah. Okay. Not for more than a day, though. She *doesn't* stay here."

"Fine. Thank you, Manny. Go with Pansy, okay?"

"Of course. Hey, I got the Hummer back. Cops are looking for you, but I guess you already knew that. Thanks for the damage."

"Yeah, sorry."

"I just ordered a red one. And it cost me ten grand to get the upgrades transferred over. You're paying for it."

He hung up.

Jazz sighed. "Unbelievable. You've seen the office, right? Ten grand to him is what he finds vacuuming the carpet."

"He's getting a red one? I didn't think it could possibly stick out any more."

"Well, let's face it, we don't love the damn thing for its ability to blend in…."

They both fell silent as Lucia made the last turn, and Jazz silently checked addresses. She pointed to a ten-story building at the end of the street. It wasn't pretty, wasn't ugly, wasn't much of anything. A nondescript structure, a victim of industrial-park architectural school. Glass and granite, concrete and steel. It looked strong, but not imposing.

"Parking," Lucia said. "On the street?"

"We all going to have our vests covered?" asked Jazz.

For answer, McCarthy put his shirt on over his and buttoned it. It looked tight, but would pass a quick visual inspection. Lucia had a problem for a second, because she didn't want the sweat-and-blister-inducing Kevlar against her bare skin, but by the time she'd pulled into a space, Jazz had found an extra T-shirt in her duffel bag. Lucia donned it, then the heavy armor. McCarthy tightened the straps for her, although she didn't need the help, and Jazz handed her a blue-and-white-checked outer shirt. She buttoned it as far as her collarbone and picked up the backpack.

"Ready," she said.

Jazz slid back the door under the blazing morning sun.

"I hope to hell it's Casual Friday in there." She opened the phone and speed-dialed Manny. "We're going."

Ben, as they'd worked out on the drive, took up a post sitting in the lobby. He didn't look out of place, especially when he sat down with a copy of *Business Week* and relaxed with a foam cup next to him.

It was surprisingly easy infiltrating the headquarters of Eidolon. Part of that was due to corporate mentality—there was security, and it involved key cards, but loitering at the elevators, talking idly until a group of workers showed up, netted a ride upstairs. Jazz and Lucia just drafted on the first one's key card through the big glass doors into the work area.

Jazz knew the floor plans backward and forward, evidently. She unhesitatingly turned left, then right at a junction, then left.

They ended up at the bathrooms. Lucia blinked, startled, but Jazz just lifted a shoulder. "Look, I've been on the road for what feels like a week, and if we're going to do this, the last thing I need is a full bladder, if you know what I mean."

Lucia choked down a laugh and followed her.

Business done, they took a quick stroll around the slowly filling work cubicles. It was a busy place—apparently, evil's stock was up this week—and every person they saw might know them, or at least their photographs. But this floor seemed to hold worker bees, not executives, and be devoted to systems and finance.

There was an empty cubicle against the far wall. The

server room—which they couldn't possibly get into—was on the other side. Lucia set the heavy backpack down with a breathless sigh of relief. "You're sure there isn't shielding on the room?" she asked.

"Not in the plans," Jazz said.

"We can't get this wrong."

"The server room's locked off, with special access. Our chances of getting in there—"

"Go pull the fire alarm."

"What?"

"Go pull the fire alarm. All electronic doors have to unlock in the event of a fire alarm. It's code."

Jazz stared at her for a few seconds, then took out her cell phone and speed-dialed Manny once more. "Get ready. Two minutes." She hung up without waiting for his reply. "Right. Give me your stuff."

Lucia handed over her purse and phone.

"I'll evacuate with the herd. You find me," Jazz said.

"Okay."

Jazz grabbed her by the hand. "L. Don't disappoint me and get killed, okay?"

Lucia, for answer, pulled her into a quick hug, kissed her on the cheek and said, "Go."

Then she grabbed the backpack, shouldered it and watched Jazz head for the fire alarm. She pulled it casually and kept walking.

Alarms and overhead strobes erupted. A computerized voice came on the intercoms, over groans and shouts, and instructed everyone to head for their designated evacuation routes. Lucia stayed where she was, fiddling with her back-pack, as people passed her cube. When she didn't hear any more footsteps, she ducked out and down the hall.

The server room doors, labeled with warnings for halon gas systems, plus Restricted Access, Security Area signs, were unlocked. Heart pounding, she stepped inside, blinked at the huge array of servers. Ranks of boxes; blinking red and green lights. The air was cool and dry, the floor a raised, nonstatic surface, springy under her feet.

She spotted a surveillance camera in the corner. They'd have seen her by now. She had very little time.

She slipped the backpack off her shoulder.

During the endless drive, when McCarthy had been at the wheel, she'd unpacked the EMP generator. It came in two pieces—the guts of the unit and a huge, heavy battery. She knelt and took the two parts, mated them together with a snap and flipped the toggle switch.

Lights came on.

"Gregory, if you've screwed me, I swear to God..."

She reached for the activate button, and froze when something cold touched the back of her head.

"This," a male voice said, "is the barrel of a Beretta, and you're going to want to take your hand off the bomb."

Fear and fury raced through her, powerful enough to make her sway, but she slowly raised both hands in the air.

"On both knees," he said, and kicked at her right foot, which was still on the ground. She shifted and obeyed. "Hands behind your head."

The voice sounded familiar, but congested, as if the

speaker had a bad cold. She wanted to turn around, but the gun pressed to her head convinced her that curiosity was a bad idea.

"You expecting McCarthy to charge up here to the rescue? That son of a bitch is in custody downstairs. So's your friend Jazz. So you just be a good girl and take these—" a gleaming pair of steel handcuffs jangled in front of her face "—and put them on your right wrist first."

She knew the voice now; she'd finally placed it. Detective Stewart. He really didn't sound well. "You don't have jurisdiction here."

"*This* has jurisdiction pretty much anywhere, bitch." He pressed with the gun barrel, hard enough to bruise. She winced and involuntarily moved her head forward; the gun followed. She took the handcuffs and snapped one on her right wrist, then—unasked—put her wrists behind her. He snapped them shut.

"Ready?" a voice called from the doorway.

"Yeah, she's restrained. Come on in."

The gun finally withdrew, letting her breathe a little, and she couldn't resist twisting to look over her shoulder as the door opened.

Ken Stewart looked terrible—really terrible. His pallor had taken on a corpselike appearance, and his breathing seemed labored. His eyes were bloodshot and red-rimmed. He stepped back, giving the newcomers a respectful distance. There were three of them, all with executive polish. The one in front was middle-aged, with dark hair and dark eyes and a foxlike face that looked clever and cold. A slight asymmetry to his face made the right eye look smaller.

He was rich, well-groomed, with an aura of absolute power.

"You're Lucia Garza," he said, and stepped forward. "Stand up. Turn around."

"Careful," Stewart said. "I said she was restrained, not safe."

The man nodded. Lucia got up and turned to face them. "I don't think we've been introduced," she said.

"Not formally, no, but I've been screwing with your life for quite some time now," the man said coolly. "My name is Gil Kavanaugh. I run Eidolon Corporation."

The man—no, the *psychic*—Simms had handpicked as his successor. The man who was the brains behind this side of the chess game, as Simms was behind the Cross Society. He seemed young for it, but she supposed that monomania was possible at any age.

He looked her in the eyes and said, "I'm not responsible for what was done to you. That was the Cross Society, playing God. If I'd had my way, Ben McCarthy would never have lived to get out of prison, and you wouldn't have ended up on a table with your legs apart, getting raped by doctors. Have they told you why it was so important?"

She felt a cold wave wash over her, and then hot prickles, as if her whole body had experienced numbness and rebirth. Her mind felt extraordinarily clear. "You saw the pictures."

He smiled. "I see everything." He tapped his forehead. "I'm tuned to your channel, you see. Yours, your friends'—

at the moment, you really do matter quite a lot. Pity about McCarthy, though. You never should have fallen in love with him. I warned you it would be a mistake—all right, I was somewhat oblique about it, but you're a bright woman. I admit, I didn't expect McCarthy to hold out like he did—I mean, what straight man just out of prison would? Look at you. Simms must have been *pissed,* after all the trouble he went to." Kavanaugh tilted his head slightly. "Are you sure you don't want to know about the child?"

The fire alarms cut out suddenly, leaving a taut silence and a continuing ringing in her ears.

"Last chance," he said. "It's a limited time offer."

"No," she said. "I don't want to know what you see."

Kavanaugh sighed and shook his head. "Right," he said. "Let's get her upstairs—"

It was all falling apart. He wouldn't balk at putting bullets in their heads and burying them out in the desert. And she loathed that salacious gleam in his eyes when he'd talked about the pictures. About being in her head.

She avoided Stewart's grabbing hand, let her knees collapse, and fell sideways. Her elbow smacked down hard on the EMP device, on the green button.

"No!" Kavanaugh screamed, but it was too late. There wasn't a buildup and there wasn't a warning. It fired.

There was a smell of frying circuitry, cracks and pops, and every electronic circuit within a thousand feet went dead.

Including the lights.

Lucia rolled, banged into Stewart and sent him stum-

bling; he fired blind. By the muzzle flash, she got a snap-
shot of where everyone was standing, and she kicked both
feet up, catching Stewart hard in the groin and lifting him
literally off the ground. He hit the wall and screamed in
high-pitched agony. She slithered backward in that direction and felt his gun on the floor, grabbed it in her cuffed
hands and twisted on her knees.

Another muzzle flash, and something like a sledgeham-
mer struck her in the chest. A hit, low and on the right. The
afterimage showed her that the two men with Kavanaugh
had their guns out. Kavanaugh, preternaturally quick, was
already through the door.

She braced herself for the pain, cocked her elbows, and
fired without letting herself think. The recoil slammed up
through her arms, hard enough to make her cry out, but she
didn't let it stop her. Two shots, directed to the positions
where she'd seen the two men. She heard one hit the floor.
The other staggered, then went down.

She struggled to her feet, sweating and light-headed. It
was unnaturally silent, with not even the air vents working in the room.

She hit the glass doors with her shoulder, praying that the
locks hadn't been reset, and saw Kavanaugh rounding the
corner up ahead. He'd be getting help, and she was handicapped, gun held behind her back. With Jazz and Ben out
of action, she didn't have a hope in hell….

And then Kavanaugh backed up, looking as if he'd seen
a ghost.

And maybe he had.

Max Simms came into view. He was armed with what looked like one of Jazz's guns, and in that moment, Lucia wondered if they'd all been taken for a ride by the frail-old-man act, because the expression in his eyes…she'd never seen anything like it. Power. Terrible power.

"Endgame," Simms said. "Your move, Gil."

Chapter 17

"You can't be here," Kavanaugh said. He backed up, collided with a padded cubicle wall decorated with crayon drawings and clipped-out Dilbert cartoons. "You *can't* be here. You're dead."

"Do I look dead?" Simms asked mildly.

"I saw you die."

"What, the vision you saw of your man coming up behind me and putting a bullet in my brain?" Simms smiled. "In some reality that happened. Not this one. You should learn to parse time lines better, Gil."

Kavanaugh glanced desperately around, but he was trapped. Lucia, to his right, had her gun on him; Simms had him from the front. A blank wall to his left. A cubicle wall at his back.

"An endgame," Simms continued, "is nothing but the last moves of a foregone conclusion. You were always going to lose, Gil. It was just a matter of sacrificing enough pawns to draw you out."

"Like her?" Kavanaugh's eyes cut to Lucia. "Two for one, is that it?"

"Oh, they're not my pawns," Simms replied. "We may very well be theirs. Didn't you understand that when you failed to keep McCarthy in prison by stealing Jazz's files on the case? Or by trying to have him killed inside? *This had to happen.* Inevitability at work, and neither you nor I have anything to do with it."

"You're insane," Kavanaugh said flatly.

"You've made a fortune out of the disasters of others," Simms said. "So have I. Maybe that does make us insane. It definitely makes us culpable."

"Then kill me."

Simms smiled. "Now that *is* inevitable."

Lucia, intent on holding aim in an achingly difficult position behind her back, heard the elevator doors rumble open, and shifted her attention that direction.

Uniformed guards. "Simms!" she yelled, and darted out of the line of fire. Kavanaugh was already moving. When she looked back, Simms was gone, Kavanaugh was heading for safety, and she was on her own. Again.

She dodged through the cube farm, hoping she wouldn't reach a dead end, and somehow found the stairs. She elbowed the handle down and tried to decide which direction would be best. Down was obvious, and that was why she hesitated.

"Lucia!" Jazz's voice echoed in the stairwell. "Get your ass up here!"

She breathed a sigh of relief, wished she could wipe her sweaty hair out of her face, and took the stairs up at a run.

Jazz and Ben met her on the seventh floor landing, and Jazz had the handcuff keys out. She spun Lucia around and worked the lock, and Lucia, panting, said, "What the hell happened?"

"Complicated," Jazz said briefly.

"Jazz got the handcuff key and Taser out of your purse, opened her cuffs and took out the guards," Ben said.

"Okay, not so complicated." The handcuffs clicked free. "Simms is here."

"Yes. I saw him."

"EMP go off?"

"Their servers are completely dark. If Manny has managed to take down the backups—"

"He will." Jazz looked vivid with the excitement of the chase, green eyes gleaming. "All of them. Cross Society servers, too."

"What?"

"I talked Borden into it," she said. "We tracked the system through Gabriel, Pike & Laskins, and found their server nodes. Manny's working on it. By the time this is over, both sides should be down for the count."

"Except for the psychics."

"Yeah, well. Beyond going on a killing spree—which I'm not in favor of for once—I don't see a way around that."

"Maybe it doesn't matter," Ben said. Lucia pulled out her gun and checked the clip. "Simms said that their psychics are specific in their predictions. Maybe they can still help people. It's when it gets to be a strategy that things go to hell."

"You know what? Not my problem." Jazz looked at each of them in turn. "You good to go?"

"Yes. Where?" Lucia asked.

"Roof. Kavanaugh's got a nifty black helicopter."

They took the stairs at a run.

Kavanaugh was already on board, and the rotors were turning, when they banged through the exit. Lucia's feet slid on gravel as she stopped. Kavanaugh was facing them, and his eyes widened. He said something into a headphone.

"Uh-oh," Jazz said. "That's not good."

Max Simms was in the helicopter, too. Handcuffed.

"Oh, *dammit*!" Lucia took aim, but the chopper was moving and the shot was risky; with Simms in the aircraft any shot she could make would be potentially lethal. She let her gun fall back to her side.

Simms was watching her with those wide, cold blue eyes. Smiling in that creepy, secretive way. Lucia felt McCarthy's hand on her shoulder, urging her back to the cover of the concrete wall. "Guards could be coming!" he yelled over the chop of the rotors. The helicopter was ten feet up, and rising. "This is done—we can't do anything. Let's go!"

There was a flutter of color on the gravel, something red, half buried under a handful of rocks. Lucia ran for it, grabbed it, and made it back to the safety of the wall as the helicopter gracefully spun in the air, preparing to head out. It exploded.

The concussion hit with a wave of pressure that triggered Lucia to involuntarily cover her head and close her eyes, and then the unbelievably loud roar of the explosion rolled over them.

She forced her eyes open and saw the blackened shell of the helicopter heading back to the roof at terminal velocity.

"Run!" she screamed, and pushed the other two ahead of her.

They made it to the back of the roof just as the wreck crashed in a fireball, sending blazing fragments spinning. Rotors broke loose and pinwheeled wildly. Lucia went flat, taking Ben and Jazz with her, while metal hissed overhead. Some of it embedded itself in the low wall at the edge of the roof, as if a nail bomb had gone off.

She felt heat on her back, then slaps. She was on fire. She rolled and stripped off the blue-and-white-checked shirt. Jazz was slowly getting to her feet, staring at the inferno that was melting the tar around it in into a hissing pool.

"Holy Christ," she said. "Two psychics, and they didn't see that coming?" She holstered her gun and held out a hand to Lucia, but Ben was ahead of her, a strong presence lifting her upright.

He had a long bloody cut on one cheek that would need stitches. Other than that, none of them was harmed.

Lucia tried to get her head together. "We need to retrieve the EMP and get the hell out," she said. "Now."

Jazz nodded. "And how do we do that without running into their guys coming up?"

McCarthy, for answer, unbuttoned his flannel shirt to show the vest underneath. He had his old badge on a chain, and he pulled it out so it showed on top of the black ballistic nylon. "Show your Kevlar," he said. "Get out your guns and follow me."

They hit the stairs, and were two flights down before they heard the sound of running feet headed up. The fire alarms were pulsing again. The building was a kicked ants' nest, people flooding in from every floor, confused and afraid.

"Make way!" McCarthy yelled. "Move right! Move right! FBI! FBI!"

And, miraculously, it worked. In the confusion, nobody had time to question; even uniformed guards pressed to the side as they plunged down another flight, then another and another.

They burst through the stair doors onto the server floor and headed for the room at a dead run. It didn't matter now who saw them; everyone was running, clutching purses and briefcases and laptops. Yelling questions and panicked instructions.

When they opened the server room door, Ken Stewart was standing there, swaying, with the EMP. It was dead, of course. But it was physical proof of what had just happened, and it had Lucia's fingerprints on it.

Their guns leveled on him. "Drop it," McCarthy said. "I mean it, Ken."

"You're going to jail." He looked feverish, spots of color

high in a chalk-pale face. He coughed, and there was blood
on his lips. He wiped it off on his sleeve. "I'm dying, but
I'll still see you in hell."

He could barely breathe, Lucia saw. He'd looked sick before, every time she'd seen him—progressively worse, in
fact. Coughing. Taking pills.

Taking *antibiotics*.

"Oh, my God," she said. "Anthrax. It was *you*."

Stewart dropped the EMP. It hit the floor with a heavy
boom, and McCarthy edged forward to pick it up. "Watch
him," he warned, and holstered his gun. Jazz and Lucia kept
their aim steady, but Stewart just stared down at McCarthy
with furious, glittering eyes. "Why? Why try to kill her?"
Ben asked.

"Because it got to you."

McCarthy's back was to them, but Lucia saw rigidity in
his shoulders, down his spine.

"Where'd you get it? The anthrax?"

Stewart grinned, showing bloody teeth. "Amazing what
you can find, working anticrime task force. Bullshit red-
neck biochemists all over the place these days. Think they're
saving the world from whatever it is they hate. You were
right, Garza. I'd been to that lab before. Bought myself a
nice little present."

"You stupid, twisted bastard," McCarthy said. "How long
have you worked for Eidolon?"

"Since they told me you shot three people in the head. I
trusted you, man. I *liked* you."

"I liked you, too," he said, and backed up. "But you got

played, Ken. Just like I did. Only you got played a hell of a lot worse."

"And he's about to get played one more time," Lucia said. "Surveillance was digital, and it's as trashed as everything else. All that's left is physical evidence." She tossed Stewart his gun, careful to keep her hand wrapped in the sleeve of her shirt. Even sick as he was, he caught it out of the air, steadied it and instantly focused it on her.

And fired.

Click.

"Thank you," she said. "I removed the rounds, obviously, before I returned it to you. And by the way, those two men on the floor? They're on your service weapon. Just like the three bodies in Kansas City were on Ben's. I hope you have better luck explaining it."

McCarthy had bagged the EMP, and now zipped the backpack shut with a decisive jerk. Stewart was staring uncomprehendingly at the gun in his grasp. He coughed again, and more blood spattered his hand as he tried to cover his mouth.

"Oh, man," McCarthy said, watching him. "I hate you, Ken, but I don't hate you that much. Get some help."

He shouldered the backpack.

They joined the rush downstairs.

Lucia sold the van for cash at a sleazy-looking, no-questions-asked lot on the outskirts of town, and used the money to buy them plane tickets. They shipped the guns and bulletproof vests to a dead drop that Manny had set up in Kansas;

they could retrieve them later. The journey back to Kansas City was short and uneventful, and Lucia managed to sleep most of the way.

Before they landed, she pulled out the red envelope she'd retrieved from the roof and read the words that Max Simms had left them as a legacy.

EVERYTHING YOU DO MATTERS. PROTECT YOUR CHILD.

And, scrawled apparently in haste, P.S.—TRUST BORDEN.

She showed it to Jazz, and saw some inner tension finally relax. That had been hard on her, not trusting Borden.

Manny picked them up at the airport in his new red Hummer. It was so outrageously attention-seeking that Lucia had to laugh, wearily, at the sight of it. She curled unconsciously into McCarthy's warmth on the way to the warehouse, and the weight of his arm around her shoulders felt like the best safety she had ever known.

"We need to get you to a doctor," McCarthy said softly, just for her ears. "Have you checked out."

"I'm fine."

"I mean—"

"I know what you mean. I'll go and let them do the poking and prodding, but everything's okay."

Talking in code. That would have to stop soon; they'd have to tell everybody the news of her pregnancy. Probably not the details, but the fact, at least. *Uncle Manny. Aunt Jazz.* The kid would, at least, have a colorful childhood.

They were pulling into the armored ground-floor

garage when Manny suddenly said, "What do you want to do about the guest?"

"Guest?" Jazz looked blank for a second, then chagrined. "Oh, shit, I forgot. Susannah, right? She's still here?"

"She's upstairs. What do you want to do with her?"

Jazz sighed long-sufferingly. "I guess I'll take her for the night. Tomorrow we can figure out a long-term solution. New identity, new life—"

"Let's just get through the rest of the day without anybody else dropping dead," Lucia said.

"Sounds like a good plan."

They trooped wearily up the stairs, pausing for the obligatory code entries, and as he opened the top door, Manny said, "Pansy, we're—"

And Susannah Davis shot him.

The sound of the hot crack echoed off of concrete and steel. Manny staggered back into Jazz, who caught him reflexively, yelling something Lucia couldn't catch because she was already moving past Jazz and Manny, cutting behind a concrete pillar.

Susannah Davis had a gun, and she had Pansy as a shield. She was holding Pansy's silky black hair in one hand, pulling her onto her tiptoes to keep her in place. Pansy appeared terrified, eyes round in horror. Susannah jerked her backward, moving fast, trying to keep the killing angle.

Lucia instinctively went for her gun.

Empty holster. They'd shipped their guns back. *Damnation*. There would be a small arsenal in the Hummer, but there wasn't time to fetch it. Manny had been hit in the stomach, and he needed a doctor *now.* He was propped up against Jazz in the doorway, holding his hands over the wound, staring at Pansy and Susannah. God, there was a lot of blood.

"Don't you dare," he whispered. "Don't you dare hurt her."

"I don't want her," Susannah said. "Callender. Garza. Out here, now. I'll let her go if you step out."

Lucia exchanged a quick look with Jazz. There was desperation in Jazz's eyes. *Think of something. Anything.*

McCarthy was even more helpless, trapped behind Jazz on the stairwell. Unarmed.

Lucia didn't see any way out of it.

"Seriously," Susannah said. "I'll blow her head off. I swear." She sounded so very different from the beaten woman Lucia had rescued in the parking garage, and the scared one who'd talked about her abusive husband. Even from the manipulative fragile one who'd talked about the SubTropolis conspiracy.

Games, and games, and games. She'd even confessed to something, though Lucia hadn't realized it at the time. Omar. *I let him in,* she'd said, talking about Leonard. And she undoubtedly had. They'd been in it together, from the beginning. Playing the abused and abusive spouse, maneuvering to get things right where they wanted them. Omar had been a complication. Maybe Leonard had killed him, and maybe it had been Susannah, after all. *No defensive wounds.* Omar would have let her close enough.

Then she'd killed her own partner in crime to get a better chance at them.

Which she finally had.

It wasn't about Lucia herself. Susannah had had plenty of chances to kill her, but she'd never had a clear run at Jazz. Until now.

"Stay!" Lucia snapped, when Jazz started to move Manny away from her lap. "Jazz, don't you move!" Because Jazz was the target. "Susannah, listen to me. You got paid to kill Jazz, am I right? You and Leonard? But things went wrong. You had to improvise. You've been out of touch. It's over. There's nobody left to pay you off. Quit while you're ahead. Don't make us kill you."

"You're not going to kill me." She stretched Pansy higher with a tug of her hair. "At least, not before this one bleeds."

"There's no way out of this for you."

"Trust me. There is." Susannah looked utterly cool and calm about it, and very, very serious, and Manny was bleeding internally, and they *didn't have time*. "I'm going to start shooting Pansy now. Take off an ear, some fingers—"

Manny made a tortured sound and tried to move. Jazz held on to him, grim-faced. As angry as Lucia had ever seen her.

Lucia risked another look around the pillar. The situation was still the same, except that there was a flicker of movement somewhere in the back.

Borden.

He looked pale and scared half to death, but he was moving. He had his hands clasped in front of him, and for a second Lucia didn't remember why. And then she did, with a vengeance.

Careful, oh God, careful…

Jesus, his hands—he was still handcuffed. Surely Manny had let him loose…or Jazz, before she left…. No, maybe Manny had followed orders a little too well, after all.

"Susannah," Lucia said again. "Susannah, don't hurt her. Listen, tell me what you want, okay? How much is it going to take to buy you off on this? A million dollars? I can get it for you."

"My reputation's worth more than a million," Susannah spat. "And I don't believe I'm not getting paid, so you can shove your bribery. Stand up, Jazz. Let me see you or I swear to God, I'll put bullets into Manny's little girlfriend until you do."

Borden was two steps away, right behind her.

"No?" Susannah asked. "Fine. Manny first." And she switched the gun from Pansy's head to aim at Manny's defenseless body again.

Borden looped his handcuff chain across her throat and yanked. She let go of Pansy and the gun to instinctively grab for the chokehold, and Borden yanked up and back, pulling her into him.

Lucia charged forward, shoved Pansy out of the way to safety, and got there just as Susannah's right hand fumbled for something in her left sleeve.

Lucia grabbed hold of Susannah's arm as the knife plunged toward Borden's groin. She twisted Susannah's wrist, and smashed the heel of her right hand up into the woman's nose. Borden, shocked, staggered backward.

Susannah flexed her knees and slipped out of the noose of his handcuffs.

The knife was still in her hand, and from the way she held it, she knew how to use it.

"Back!" Lucia yelled at Borden, and he retreated. He hustled Pansy to the doorway, where she collapsed to her knees beside Manny, holding him.

Jazz came running toward Susannah, and so did McCarthy.

But Jazz got there first.

Susannah was unprepared, even though she was as quick and dirty a fighter as Lucia had ever seen. Jazz slammed her forehead into Susannah's bloody nose, grabbed her knife hand and almost effortlessly flipped her around. It was like dancing; Susannah began the turn off balance, ended on one foot, kicking for Jazz's face. Jazz floated backward, grabbed her leg and torqued it sideways. They both went down. Susannah twisted and yelled, and the knife flashed—

And Jazz jerked out of the way at the last possible second, a move Lucia would never have attempted. She didn't have the strength or the speed….

Susannah missed, couldn't check her own momentum, and a flick of Jazz's wrist buried the blade in Susannah's side, hilt-deep.

"Oh, *shit*." Susannah yelped, surprised, and pulled it out.

A jet of bright arterial blood arced as high as a fountain.

"Shit," she repeated, and laughed. "That just *sucks*. Somebody call me an ambulance." She jammed fingers into the wound, suddenly clammy and gray-faced. Wobbling.

Lucia picked up the fallen gun, watching her. Jazz deliberately turned her back to go for the phone.

Susannah flipped the knife, and prepared to throw it at Jazz's exposed back.

Lucia fired.

Jazz didn't even turn around as she dialed 911.

Epilogue

It was, the doctors informed them at the hospital, a serious but not life-threatening wound. Some bowel resection, and he'd be uncomfortable for a while, but Manny was going to live.

And so would Susannah Davis, who'd been absolutely livid that Lucia had wounded, not killed her. The FBI had been happy to take her back, after all; Agent Rawlins had even seemed smug about it. Lucia had suspicions that they'd been used, again.

She intended it to be the very last time.

Their offices had been open again for six weeks when she went to the doctor for an examination. McCarthy went with her. There was an ultrasound, and for the first time, she saw the tiny gestational sac, with a flickering heartbeat of life.

She couldn't reconcile that miracle with the cold invasiveness of what had been done to her, but she couldn't not love her child, in that moment.

"Beautiful," she whispered, and caressed her still-flat stomach. "Oh, God, Ben. So beautiful."

He touched the screen, tracing the outline of what would become their baby. He didn't speak, but she could see the love in his face. In that moment, he was luminous.

And when he got her home, McCarthy made slow love to her in ways that told her without words how deep the emotions went in him. To the bone. To the soul.

The next day, Pansy came into her office with an opened FedEx envelope. She was trying to be offhand, but it was obviously a struggle. Lucia, in the middle of a client meeting, immediately asked for a recess and stepped outside, shutting the door behind her. Jazz, sensing trouble, was already there.

"What?" Lucia asked. Pansy mutely tilted the envelope so that they could see inside.

A red envelope.

"The good news is, there's no powder," Pansy said. "The bad news is, it ain't Valentine's Day."

Lucia sucked in a deep breath and took the envelope out. It had JAZZ CALLENDER AND LUCIA GARZA block printed on it. The FedEx label came from a firm she'd never heard of: Black & Foxworth, Attorneys At Law.

"No," Jazz said. Simple and definite.

"No," Pansy confirmed, with a decisive shake of her head. "Not that I get a vote, but…no."

They both looked at Lucia, whose vote did count. She looked at it. Turned it over and studied the invitingly open flap, the cream-colored sheet of paper showing like a tease.

"Shredder," she said.

Pansy dragged the device out from behind her desk.

Lucia dropped the envelope in the teeth of the machine, and it chewed it into ribbons in five seconds flat.

"We make our own choices," Lucia said. "Deal?"

"Deal," Jazz said, and they shook on it.

They were walking away when Pansy said, "Um…I think there was a check in there."

And Lucia began to laugh, and Jazz joined in, and just for a moment, there was brightness all around them.

"Well," Jazz gasped, "that was a hell of a choice."

"Shut up, Jazz."

"Ooh, touchy. Love you, too."

"Go earn us some money."

"Somebody's got to, if you're going to shred all our income…." Jazz grinned and went back to her office.

Lucia sat down at her desk, smiled and resumed work.

* * * * *

WHAT'S THE PRICE OF A DEAL WITH THE DEVIL?

Jazz Callender's whole life just got turned upside
down. Her friend Ben's been convicted of a
crime he didn't commit and Jazz is determined
to clear his name, even if it means enlisting
the help of dark forces.

As she's thrust into a world of psychic powers and
dangerous magic, Jazz isn't just bargaining for her
friend's freedom. She's bargaining for her soul too.
And how high a price is she willing to pay?

M302_DB

DON'T LOOK AT THEM
DON'T SPEAK OF THEM
NEVER ENTER THEIR WORLD

Those are the rules that Ethan Chase lives by
when it comes to the dark fairies that
robbed him of his sister.

But now the deadly fey are at his school, colliding
with his real life, Ethan will sacrifice everything to
keep his mortal friends safe, even if it means
becoming entangled in the world he's spent
his whole life trying to deny.

His destiny and birthright are calling.

And now there's no escape.

www.miraink.co.uk

M297_TLP

HUNTED, KILLED— TRIUMPHANT?

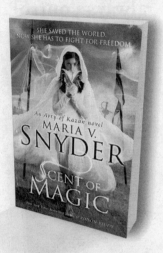

As the last Healer of the Fifteen Realms, Avry of Kazan is in a unique position: in the minds of friends and foes alike, she no longer exists.

With her one-of-a-kind powers, Avry must now face an oncoming war alone and infiltrate deadly King Tohon's army to stop his most horrible creations yet: a league of walking dead soldiers— human and animal alike, and beyond any known power to defeat.

Unless Avry figures out how to do the impossible…**again**.

www.mirabooks.co.uk

There's a darkness within me, something I can't always control.

In 1897 London, sixteen-year-old Finley Jayne has no one…except the 'thing' inside her—a frighteningly abnormal strength, a violent power, a darker side urging her to danger…

Only Griffin King sees her magic secret as something special. The richest young duke in England, an orphan, a misfit—*like her*—Griffin wants to add Finley to his little company of strays. But first she must be willing to put her life in his hands.

Book 1 of The Steampunk Chronicles

www.miraink.co.uk

In a future world, vampires reign. Humans are blood cattle...

In a future world, vampires reign.
Humans are blood cattle.
And one girl will search for the key
to save humanity.

Allison Sekemoto survives in the Fringe, the
outermost circle of a vampire city. Until one night
she is attacked—and given the ultimate choice.
Die...or become one of the monsters.

www.miraink.co.uk

Join us at facebook.com/miraink

Read Me. Love Me. Share Me.

Did you love this book? Want to read other amazing teen books for free online and have your voice heard as a reviewer, trend-spotter and all-round expert?

Then join us at **facebook.com/MIRAink** and chat with authors, watch trailers, WIN books, share reviews and help us to create the kind of books that you'll want to carry on reading forever!

Romance. Horror. Paranormal. Dystopia. Fantasy.

Whatever you're in the mood for, we've got it covered.

Don't miss a single word

 twitter.com/MIRAink

let's be friends

 facebook.com/MIRAink

Scan me with your smart phone

 to go straight to our facebook page